Hamilton walked to the hospital's parking lot. His mind searched for the reason why he was going out of his way to help her. He was drawn to her which supplanted his need to get to know her better. He remembered her scent, the delicate floral fragrance that emitted from her. Even today, he could still smell traces of the fragrance she wore. When he first met her at the church, he wanted to comment on the scent, but thought better. And the way her pale pink suit hugged her curves. Umph, was all he could muster at the crime of a woman being shaped like Shari. He had watched her stroll down that aisle, her head held high, her shoulder-length mahogany hair flailing behind her. Yes, he thought, she was like no other. And it had been a long time since a woman had that effect on him — too long. He thought of his last relationship.

Hamilton had met Janice at a party given by his boyhood friend and fraternity brother, Matthew. He hadn't expected to meet anyone, he just wanted to hang a little, have a few beers, spend some time with his boy, and possibly play a few hands of Bid Whist. When he had entered Matthew's home, he spotted Janice sitting next to Kara, Matthew's girlfriend. Janice's green eyes never left his face as he made his way across to them. Even when he bent to kiss Kara on the cheek, the woman sitting next to her never looked away.

Kara introduced them, got up, and pushed Hamilton to sit next to Janice. When he protested lightly, saying something about getting a beer, Janice jumped up and went in search for one. And though Hamilton wasn't in the mood to chat, he ended up spending most of the night engaged in one exhausting conversation after another with Janice.

At the nights end, Hamilton asked for Janice's number. He didn't know why he did it. Maybe it was the polite thing to do or maybe it was those 4 plus beers he had ingested that spoke for him. Either way, they began to date, but as he got to know Janice, he didn't like what he saw. She was always trying to find ways to get over to his place, reasons to spend the night. It took him nearly a month to even sleep with her, and that was after her accusation that he either didn't find her appealing or that he was gay.

BY DESIGN

BARBARA KEATON

Genesis Press Inc.

Indigo Love Stories

An imprint Genesis Press Publishing

Indigo Love Stories
c/o Genesis Press, Inc.
1213 Hwy 45 N, 2nd Floor
Columbus, MS 39705

ISBN 1-58571-088-1
Manufactured in the United States of America

First Edition

Visit us at www.genesis-press.com
or call at 1-888-Indigo-1

DEDICATION

This book is dedicated to my mom, Aurelia Keaton, and her sisters, my girls, Lorene Robinson, Mary Harris, the late Willie Geneva Hill, Audrey Miller-Bibbins and Carrie Oliver. Much of who I am, and hope to be, I owe to each and everyone of you!

ACKNOWLEDGMENTS

As always, I must thank my Lord, God, and his son, Jesus Christ for all the blessings bestowed upon me—I am truly grateful. To my family and friends, for their undying and continued love and support. To the many readers, especially the book clubs (Sister Circle Book Club in Dallas, I luvs ya!) — this is all for naught without you. And a special thank you to Angelique Justin for helping to pull this out of me! Thank you! Thank you! Thank you!

CHAPTER 1

Shari Thomas stood at the base of the numerous marble steps, closed her eyes and inhaled deeply. She loved the way the warm June breeze filled her lungs. She opened her eyes, then rubbed her hands briskly together, a wiry smile spread across her face as she looked up at the massive steeple of St. Simon the Apostle Catholic Church—the church she had attended mass as well as its attached grammar school. Shari glanced at her watch and laughed. She was on time, had to be for the christening of her best friend's first child.

The smell of incense swept into her nostrils as Shari opened the large wooden doors to the church. She paused at the small marble bowl, dipped her two fingers into the holy water, crossed her self and continued down the long aisle. Shari focused her smoky brown eyes on the large painting ahead, situated at the end of the sanctuary. A portrait of a black Jesus, draped in a white robe, his arms out stretched, with the hands of God behind him, welcomed her. As she continued down the aisle, she thought of the countless days spent in this pristine house of worship. She had planned to marry Bruce in this very church—had envisioned herself walking down the aisle dressed in white. Shari shrugged. She wasn't sure that that dream would ever become a reality; especially since she had no real prospects in her life.

the christening. She knew just about every one in attendance. Shari smiled and nodded as she stopped several times to chat with each one.

She paused when her gaze rested on a broad smile that met her.

Umph, she thought, as she absorbed the warm chocolate face which stared intently at her. He reminded her of a dark angel—warm, protective and inviting. And those eyes. They were the color of light-brown sugar, a stark, but beautiful contrast to his dark smooth complexion. She nodded her head slightly in his direction as she continued toward the front of the church. She felt his eyes on her back and forced herself not to turn around, instead she focused her attention on her best friend, Deborah Anderson-Wilson as she met her half way.

"Hey, you made it," Deb pulled Shari into an embrace, then pulled back.

"Now, Deb," Shari said. She looked at the woman who was actually more like a sister to her than a friend. She noticed the brightness in her brown eyes, the comforting glow of her oval shaped warm brown face. She hugged her again. "You know I wouldn't miss this for the world. How could I miss my goddaughters christening?" Shari smiled, then turned to see the chocolate angel still watching her. "Where is my baby?" She looked back at Deb, then slipped off her olive green overcoat to reveal a pale pink bolero jacket with a matching skirt that rested inches above her knees, her eyes drifted back toward the dark stranger.

"Darrin has her." Deb pointed to her husband at the front of the church, then turned her attention to Shari's distraction. "Cute, isn't he?"

Shari's head snapped around. "Who?"

Deb chuckled. "Hamilton."

"Hamilton?" Shari responded, a slow smile crossed her face.

"Yeah," Deb took Shari by the elbow. "Hamilton Edmunds, Junior. He's Darrin's cousin. On his father's side. Hamilton's mother and Darrin's father are sister and brother."

"Oh," was Shari's only reply as she wondered why she hadn't met him before. She steeled herself against taking another glance at the handsome dark man who sat a few feet from her. She turned her attention to the front of the church. When her eyes rested upon Darrin, Shari walked past Deb and stood next to him as he stood next to Father John, the parish priest, and his best friend, Mike. Darrin grinned upon see at Shari, embraced her, then kissed her on the cheek.

"Deb was so worried you wouldn't make it back from Paris in time for the baptism," Darrin said. "But I know you. I knew nothing would keep you from this day." He handed his daughter over to Shari. Shari snuggled little Daneda Shari Wilson against her bosom. The chubby 4-month-old cooed warmly as Shari rested her eyes upon the baby's warm cocoa face. She saw that the baby had her fathers deep, dark eyes and his warm complection, but Daneda had Deb's small, flat nose and squared chin.

How could I miss this, Shari thought as Father John signaled to the participants to join him so he could begin the Roman Catholic sacrament of baptism. She followed the priest and the others to the altar where the baptism bowl rested upon a large grey and white marble stand. She smiled warmly as the baby cooed and gurgled while the priest began the ceremony with the anointing of oils.

Shari looked at Deb, then Darrin who stood immediately to the right of her. Darrin's best friend, Mike, was to her left. Her face flushed as she thought of the love they shared—the warm bundle in her arms a testament. Inwardly, she sighed. Designing and sewing had always been her first love, and as she reflected, her only love. As a head buyer for Macy's Department Store, Shari was able to indulge in her love by selecting the latest in haute couture for women across the nation. Those very designs would later serve as a catalyst for her own designs. Yet, lately, she had begun to question her reasons for working at Macy's, which had her out of town on business at least two days out of the week, with nearly two months spent abroad. Her messy break up with her long-time beau, Bruce, had her examine her true feelings for not fully loving him. He had accused her, on more than one occasion, of choosing her career over him. At the time, she thought that she could have them both. Had she been wrong? She wondered.

Shari glanced up into the eyes of the large mosaic of Jesus, then back into the face of Daneda. Daneda's birth had made her think of what she truly wanted in her life: a family of her own. Shari prayed silently for peace and direction.

The sound of baby Daneda's gurgling brought Shari back to the present. She smiled at her goddaughter, dressed in the beautiful satin christening gown she had personally designed and sewn with her own hands.

The entire bodice was intricately covered in lace, with countless, small mother of pearl ornate intertwined throughout and a matching white satin bow at the base of round the lace collar. Shari had to admire her creation—for it was truly a labor of love. This was what she truly wanted to do. This was her calling—designing. Not shopping for others, but creating a unique style—a style a woman, or a man for that matter, could call their own. Sort of like a signature. It was a dream that Shari couldn't seem to shake. A love that wouldn't let go, wouldn't allow her to fully turn her back on. Something would always bring her back, make her take fabric and create a wonder of art. A blouse, with billowing sleeves. A short boule jacket of worsted wool. A long, white flowing gown of satin, small crystal beads sew throughout the bodice and down the train. She smiled, lost in the thoughts of her next creation.

"Will you promise to stand by Daneda Shari Wilson, guiding her on a Christian path of love and spirituality?" The priest asked. Shari blinked, then nodded her head. The priest looked at her. Shari quickly found her voice and responded with a firm "yes" before she handed Daneda over to the priest. Shari marveled at how well Daneda reacted as the priest poured holy water over her face. The baby was unfazed, for her rapt attention was focused on the purple cord that dangled from the priest's garment just above her head.

As quickly as Daneda's attention had been grasped it quickly turned, for once the purple cord had been drawn from her grasp, Daneda began to cry. Shari looked at her, noting the slight uncertainty which had crept into the baby's dark eyes. Shari took the baby's hand in hers. She rubbed her small fat fingers in her own. Daneda quieted as her eyes never left Shari's. Shari fought back tears, as a silent bond of love and trust established itself between her goddaughter and herself. This was what she wanted. *Why can't I have it all?* she wondered.

Once the baptism was over, Shari took Daneda back into her arms.

"Girl, I am so glad to see you," Deb squealed as she tied, then re-tied Daneda's lace bonnet. "And look at you!" She stepped back to eye Shari's attire. "You're looking good, my sister. Real good."

Shari twirled around, her eyes caught a glimpse of Hamilton as he stood next to Darrin. She knew the pale pink suit hugged her in all the right places without overstating her shape.

"Girl, you ain't doing too bad yourself. That dress is you," Shari complimented. She nodded her approval of Deb's simple Salmon colored, sleeveless sheath, the hem rested several inches above her knees, her feet were adorned in salmon colored, cloth high-heeled slings. Shari thought the shoes were just the right touch to set off the simplicity of her attire.

Shari shifted baby Daneda from her hip to cradle her in her arms. "Hey, baby. Is this my baby?" Shari sang as she placed a kiss on the baby's chubby cheek and was quickly rewarded with a toothless grin.

The trio headed down the long aisle toward the exit, Deb's arm around Shari's shoulder. "I tried to call you in Paris," Deb began. "I wanted to make sure you were going to be here. There wasn't going to be a baptism without you. You know that, don't you?"

"Girl, I know. It's bad enough that I missed her grand entrance." Shari sighed, then frowned. She and Deb had always been close. As roommates in college, then sharing a house after graduation, Shari considered Deb the sister she never had. It hurt her that she had been in Italy for the preview of fall fashions when Deb's daughter had been born. Shari was supposed to be at the birth. Yet, all the while she was in Italy, and for the first time since she had become head buyer, Shari had been unfazed by the designs that had floated by her. Daneda's birth had forced her to realize that she wanted a family of her own. In the all her years of being the constant voice of reason, the one who insisted that you only live by loving, it took the end of her long-term relationship with Bruce for her to realize that she had never truly been in love. *Shoot*, she thought, she hadn't a clue as to how love was supposed to feel. The thought both enthralled and frightened her. She thought about Deb and how she hooked the couple up. She had to smile. Shari had meddled—had gone to great lengths to bring Deb and Darrin together. She had provided Darrin with plenty of personal information as a means to woo Deb. Just the thought of it all brought a wicked smile to her face, for it was one of her most successful plans to date.

"Excuse me," Deb interrupted. "Let me go get Darrin, so we can get to the repast."

Shari watched as Deb approached her husband, her hand rested on his broad shoulder as she stood in front of him. As they whispered among themselves, their bodies close, Shari wondered if the kind of love she was searching for was the kind she witnessed in Deb and Darrin. She could only wish.

"Hi, I'm Hamilton. And you must be Shari."

Shari looked up into Hamilton's eyes. They were the color of light-brown sugar. She also noted the deep cadence of his voice. She smiled as he extended his right hand. Shari shifted Daneda from one hip to the other. She took his offered hand in hers and saw that his larger one covered her entire hand up to her wrist.

"I've heard a lot about you."

"You did?" Shari's arched eyebrows rose, her slender mouth a slight pout. "Good things I hope," she replied as she let her eyes take in the large, muscular frame. She knew he was at least six-foot-four, with a fifty-inch chest. As she continued her visual assessment of what she considered the most handsome, bald man she had ever seen. She noted his fragrance, a hint of patchouli mixed with a deep woodsy scent, and allowed it to seep into the deep recesses of her mind.

"Nothing but." Hamilton stepped closer, his eyes rested upon Shari's face, then to Daneda, who's chubby hands clung to Shari's jacket. "Mind if I hold her?"

"You know how to hold a baby?" Shari quizzed flirtatiously.

"I've got ten nieces and nephews," Hamilton chuckled. He put his hands out to the baby and smiled as the child reached for him. Shari marveled at how well the baby took to Hamilton, then remembered that Hamilton was no stranger to Daneda—he was her father's cousin and had probably spent a lot of time at the Wilson home. So, why hadn't she met him before now? She wondered.

"Looks natural."

"How about you?"

"What about me?" Shari looked at Hamilton. His round face was framed by a neatly cut mustache and goatee, followed by the most regal nose she had ever seen on a man. Broad and long, his nose made her think of a black Seminole Indian, like the one described in Beverly Jenkins' romantic historical, Topaz. His even smile and intense gaze created a warmth that swept across her entire body, leaving a heady sensation behind.

"Any children?"

"No. None. And You?"

"I told you. I've got ten nieces and nephews." He tilted his head slightly to the left. "No children. But I would love to have at least three."

Shari wondered how an innocent hello could quickly turn into a conversation about children. She looked away to where Deb and Darrin stood.

"Now, have you ever seen two people more in love?" Hamilton asked. Shari nodded and thought of their courtship. Darrin had continually shown Deb how much he loved her. As a witness to their love, Shari knew in her heart that there was more to dating thing than what she had experienced thus far. Truth be told, Shari wanted what Deb had found: a solid, passionate relationship built on mutual trust, love and respect.

"Are you going to the house for the repast?"

"Yeah. You?" She felt implored to ask, because for some inexplicable reason she wanted to see Hamilton again.

Hamilton nodded, then smiled at her. She noticed the deep dimples, which she felt added to his allure.

"Then I'll see you there," Shari smiled demurely, took Daneda from Hamilton, then stepped closer toward the exit. She began to talk to Daneda again—the perfect excuse to try an erase the strange sensation Hamilton's closeness stirred within her.

As Shari continued her word play with her goddaughter, Deb

came to stand next to her. "Where's Denise?" She inquired as she blessed her goddaughter with holy water, followed by blessing herself.

"She and Jon were suppose to be here. I guess they're on their way. Nowadays, they seem to be arriving later and later," Deb replied.

"They're next."

Deb snickered. "Maybe they're off trying." She nudged Shari. "Denise has been trying to get pregnant. Buying ovulation kits and all that. Girl, she said that she calls Jon at work when the kit says she's ripe." Deb laughed. "No wonder poor Jon is always tired."

"I didn't know that."

"Yeah," Deb looked past Shari towards the entrance. "I tried to get Darrin to wait a while, to see if they'd show, but you know Darrin, he wasn't trying to hear any of that. He said that as long as you and Mike were here, he didn't feel the need to wait." Deb kissed the side of her daughters face.

"So, how is Darrin liking fatherhood?"

"Aww, girl—this child has her Daddy wrapped around her little finger."

Shari watched Deb's eyes twinkle at the mention of Darrin's name. The love in them was unmistakable.

"See you at the house," Hamilton appeared at Shari's side. He nodded at her as his arm brushed lightly against Shari's, then continued out of the church. She watched his broad back fill the door, loved the way his shoulders were square and erect. And that cologne, she mused silently, as remnants of the fragrance remained long after he was out of her sight.

"Well," Deb grinned. "I see you've finally met Hamilton. You know he's single?"

Shari faced Deb. "I didn't ask you all that."

"F-Y-I," Deb replied.

Shari shook her head at the clever expression on her best friend's face. She changed the subject. "Oh, my mom and dad sent Daneda a gift. It's in the car." She started for the door.

"Hamilton will be at the house, Shari."

Shari rolled her eyes. "I'll give you the gift at the house, Miss Know-it-all." Yet, she had to admit to herself that all she wanted was one more look at the handsome Hamilton. Shari shrugged her shoulders and turned in time to see Denise cross herself with holy water, then quickly genuflect before she ran into the main sanctuary of the church. Shari stretched out her free hand to support Denise as she tripped over her own feet.

"It's as if this place is always tripping me up." She hugged Shari, then Deb, referring to when she and Jon were married in the very church they stood.

Denise and Jon's wedding had been just as comical as the way the two had met: in a grocery store with carts bumping one into the other, and canned goods rolling haphazardly down the aisle. Their wedding had started two and a half hours late, with Denise getting the train of her dress caught in the limousine door, leaving behind a noticeable oil stain on the tail. To add to the scene, the singer lost her voice in the middle of Ribbons in The Sky, Jon fell off the alter upon Denise's entrance, and they ended the ceremony with both Denise and Jon nearly fell over the runner, head first. All aside, the ceremony had been beautiful, and Shari felt that Denise and Jon were a perfect match.

"We're about to go to the house for the repast," Deb said. She took a look at her watch.

"I missed the baptism?" Denise's eyes were wide as Shari and Deb both nodded. "I am soo sorry. Traffic was a monster out there. Some idiot ended up on the El tracks," Denise offered.

"How bad?" Shari asked.

"Bad enough that they shut down the El and the Dan Ryan."

"Well, at least you made it in time to head over for some food," Deb replied. "Wait. Where's Jon?"

"Parking the car. He'll be in, in a minute," Denise rushed on. "It's good to see you both. Umm, Miss Shari, just where have you been? I've really missed you." Denise pouted.

"I miss you too. I just got in from Paris."

"Go 'head Sistah!" Denise sang. "My girl! You meet any fine men?"

"All of the men in Paris are fine," Shari chuckled, then thought, well not all of them. She was tired of the countless trips to Europe. At first it had been exciting, just what she needed to get over her failed relationship with Bruce, and she had been courted by more than her share of European men who found her sepia complexion intriguing. But now that she had accomplished her goal of becoming head buyer she knew it was time to branch out. Time to open her own design company.

In all her years as a buyer, she had seen the clothes designed by the famous fashion houses. And though their designs were quite exquisite, they catered to the masses—Caucasian women, not African American women. She longed to design a line of clothing for African Americans. This was her dream.

"Hey, gimme my baby." Denise held out her arms. Shari handed Daneda over. She thought about what Deb had said about Denise trying to get pregnant. Shari looked at Denise and tried to imagine her pregnant. Cute, was the only word she thought would describe a pregnant Denise, her slender, cocoa face full, her hour-glass figure round with child. She looked at her closer and thought that Denise's face did seem rounder. She could be pregnant now, Shari mused to herself.

The group exited the church. Denise walked pensively behind her as she cooed and snuggled a gurgling Daneda. Shari thought of the dark angel who awaited her arrival at the repast. She inhaled deeply as she thought of his eyes and the way her head had swam when he was close to her. She dismissed the feeling and chalked it up to just being nervous. *But I'm not the nervous type,* she thought, curious about the strange new emotions.

CHAPTER 2

Shari stepped into the red-brick bungalow Deb and Darrin called home. Her eyes scanned the faces. She searched for Hamilton—wanted one more look at the man whose mere presence raised goose bumps across her back.

Shari joined Deb and Denise in the kitchen, Shari quickly donned an apron and began placing various food items on platters. The trio worked side by side and began to laugh and reminisce about their college days when the three of them shared an apartment.

"I'm so glad to have my sisters here with me," Deb said. "We don't get together enough, especially with Shari gone all the time."

"The traveling is about to change." Shari paused, her hand covered with crumbs from the bread she was arranging on a platter. "As a matter of fact I'm thinking about quitting."

Deb and Denise stopped, then looked at each other, their mouths open.

"What?" Shari responded to their silent question. "Haven't y'all ever heard of someone quitting a job?"

"This isn't like you, Shari. What gives?" Denise asked, her high-pitched voice dragged out the last syllable as she swept her shoulder length, honey blonde micro-braids from her face and looked Shari in the eye.

"I've been doing a lot of thinking lately. I want to start my own line of clothing. I want to design full time."

"It's about time," Deb breathed out. She continued to scoop potato salad into a ceramic bowl. "I wondered when you'd get tired of working for other folks with all the talent you have." Deb looked up to Shari, then to Denise. "Take that christening gown. Denise, have you ever seen anything like it? The detail was just beautiful."

"Truly beautiful," replied Denise as she removed several platters from cabinets. "And don't forget about my wedding gown and the suit I wore to my honeymoon."

Deb interrupted. "Which didn't stay on for very long."

The trio laughed, then fell silent. Shari was the first to speak.

"Well, to me its about time. I've written a business plan and will begin shopping it to a couple of banks."

"Have you thought about taking in private investors?" Deb asked.

"Yeah, I thought about that too, but the thing is how private are they going to be. I don't need a whole lot of people telling me how to run the business."

"No. Silent, private investors."

"That's an idea. Like venture capitalists?"

"Right. They loan you the money, set a rate, and sit back. As long as you pay them back as agreed, they're no problems."

"I'll have to consider that. Got anyone in mind?" Shari asked as she arranged slices of bread on a platter.

"Darrin and I."

Shari stopped, then wiped the crumbs from her hands. "You would do that?" Her face softened.

"In a heart beat."

Denise spoke up. "Jon and I, too. Don't forget about us."

Shari shook her head to keep from crying. "I don't know what to say."

"Say nothing," Deb came to stand next to Shari, her arm draped across her shoulder. "Just tell us how much and we'll have the papers

14

drawn up for the loan." Denise joined them.

Shari smiled. "Will do."

"Great, now if we can just get you a husband and have you some babies ..." Deb looked at Shari. "Oh, and did I mention that Hamilton is single?"

"Don't start." Shari let out with exasperation. "No meddling."

"You know one good turn does deserve another."

Shari placed her hands on her ample hips and shook her index finger at Deb. "Now look. Don't be trying to fix me up and all that jazz. Besides, I'm on hiatus. I'm giving myself a break. And with my staring my own business I won't have time for dalliances."

Deb snorted. "Wow! Big word. So you say, but that's quite a catch out there."

"Who's a catch?" Denise asked.

"Hamilton!" Deb breathed out.

"Oh, Darrin's cousin. Girl, that man's a real cutie. If I wasn't married..."

The trio laughed again.

"Well, enough of Hamilton for now," Deb winked at Shari. "Tell us more about your plans."

Shari went on to outline her plans to design a line of casual and formal wear marketed specifically for African-Americans, with special attention to men. Deb responded to each idea of Shari's with a question; ask. She had thought about private investors in addition to possibly a small business loan from a bank. Shari hadn't thought about private investors and as she listened to Deb fire off more questions, Shari had to stop her.

"Let me get a pen," Shari said as she searched Deb's kitchen drawers for a pen and an old envelope.

"Did Darrin teach you this?" Denise asked. Shari had thought the same thing. Since marrying Darrin, she knew that Deb had become a partner in his computer business, but she didn't realize that Deb had learned so much about the intracacies of running one's own business.

"Thanks for the information. I'll incorporate some of this into my business plan."

"Have you shared your idea with the parents?" Deb raised her right eyebrow.

Shari looked from Deb to Denise, then shook her head. The creased worry lines stretched across both of her friends foreheads. As an only child, Shari's parents, Linda and Leonard Thomas, had invested their whole lives into her. They had sent her to the best schools and had enrolled her in Jack and Jill. Simply put, Shari's mother could be best described as snobbish, for her mother had always talked about how she should marry a doctor or a lawyer, "folks who were doing things." As for her father, he seemed to go along with her mother's program. When Shari prepared for college, he had insisted that she major in "something that will get her a job." And for a while, during college, Shari had gone along with her parents wishes and chose Economics versus Fashion Design as her major. She had never told her parents that she was a double major, Economics and Fashion Design.

"I'm not ready to share with them just yet. I want to work the kinks out. Get started. Then I'll tell them."

"How are you going to keep something like that from them?"

Shari rolled her eyes. "I don't know. I'll think of something. Besides, I'm a grown woman—I'm too old to let them run my life."

Deb and Denise chuckled at the same time. Denise spoke first. "Yeah, tell that to Linda. She doesn't seem to have loosened up much. She still has her baby on a short leash."

Shari started to protest, then thought better. In many ways Denise's words rang true. She lived on the second floor of a two-flat building owned by her mother's best friend; she had purposely let her mother and father continue to think she and Bruce were still an item; and, for many years after graduation from college, she had purposely allowed them to believe she was a business manager versus a buyer at Macy's. Shari sighed.

"Well, we are here if you need us. And you know Darrin and I will invest if you need us to."

"Jon and I, too!" Denise added.

"Okay, ladies, the natives are getting restless." Darrin stepped into the kitchen interrupting their conversation. "I know yall catching up, but do you think we can get some food before next week?"

Darrin ducked as Deb tossed a dish towel at his head. "We're done. The food is on its way. Is Daneda asleep?"

"Down for the count. Hamilton rocked her to lullaby land."

"Good." Deb smiled a knowing smile at Shari. "Okay, ladies lets feed the masses."

Shari followed Deb, then Denise out of the kitchen. They laid trays, platters and bowls of food on the large dining table. She spotted Hamilton as he headed in her direction. She rushed back into the kitchen.

When Shari returned to the dining room, she noticed that Hamilton was standing nearby with his hands outstretched, the outline of the veins of his large hands visible. "Anything else needs to be brought out?"

"No, this is it." She handed him a platter of assorted meats.

The twenty-plus family and friends gathered around the table as Father John requested all to take hands and bow their heads to give thanks. Shari bowed her head, then closed her eyes. Feeling a hand enclose hers, she opened her eyes slowly, taking in the same hand she saw moments ago. She let her eyes trail up his arm to his smiling face.

She quickly bowed her head again.

After the meal, Shari helped clean up, dismissing Hamilton's insistence that he wash the dishes.

"That's nice of you, but that won't be necessary. They have a dish washer. I'm just going to pile them in there."

"Sure you don't need any help piling in the dishes?" Hamilton beamed, his smile stretched across his handsome face. "I'm good at household chores. I'm even house broken."

Shari laughed at his joke, but still dismissed him by pushing him out of the kitchen. It wasn't that she didn't want him to help, there were a lot of dishes, what she didn't want was the certain headiness she got every time he was near her.

After cleaning the kitchen, with Denise's help, Shari began to feign tiredness. She knew she didn't want to sit near Hamilton another minute, less she loose her mind. Sitting next to him during the meal, intermittently glancing in his intense light eyes, the electricity that shot through her when their hands had grasped the same glass, was more than she could handle for one day. Shari looked at her watch, then went to search for Deb. When she didn't find her on the main floor, she asked Darrin. He told her where she could find Deb.

Ascending the stairs, Shari found Deb breast feeding Daneda. She watched silently as Deb hummed to her nursing child, rocking steadily to and fro in a white rocking chair. Shari could see her goddaughter staring up at her mother. Shari's eyes misted at the loving sight.

"Shari," Deb called out. "Come on in."

"Sorry, didn't mean to interrupt."

"Not a problem. What's up?"

Shari looked around the baby's room, taking in the stark white crib, with a deep yellow blanket and matching bumper pads. A matching dressing table sat at the foot of the crib and a play-pen was situated in one corner. Her eyes settled on the white walls with a pale yellow boarder at the top. Decals of baby chicks and rabbits were stenciled on the walls, the ceiling painted full of stars and a full moon. The baby's room spoke of pure serenity.

Shari sat on the floor nearby. "Girl, you know I would love to stay, but I'm beat. You won't be mad if I duck out on you, would you?"

"Is Hamilton still here?"

"Yeah. Why?" Shari huffed.

"Just wondering. Don't get so testy." Deb laughed. "I guess God mommy can leave," Deb spoke to Daneda. "But only if she promises to have lunch with me real soon."

"Promise. I'll call you day after tomorrow, after I catch up on some much need rest."

"You'd better. I really miss my sister-girl-friend."

"So do I," Shari rose, then leaned over to hug Deb, followed by a kiss to baby Daneda's cheek.

"Besides, Darrin is always asking about his accomplice."

The two laughed, both thinking of how Shari's interference had been the catalyst for Deb giving her all to Darrin.

Shari hugged Deb again, then left the room. She crept down the stairs, stopping in mid stride when she heard Darrin and Hamilton talking.

"Next Saturday, right?" Shari overheard Darrin ask Hamilton.

"Sure thing. Think you can hang?"

"Hang?" Darrin replied. "Brother, I'm gonna step all over them young bloods. Who's the quarterback?"

"None other," Hamilton replied with a hint of pride in his deep voice. "Be there at 7 a.m. We start our first game at 8."

Shari began again, then halted at hearing her name.

"So, why haven't I met her before, Darrin?"

"Who? Shari?"

"No, the Queen of England. Yes, Shari. Man's she's gorgeous. And those eyes."

Darrin chuckled. "She's always traveling. Besides, you weren't much for dating when I first wanted to introduce you to her."

She heard Hamilton sigh. "I know. But you've got to put in a good word for a brother."

Darrin chuckled. "Consider it done. Besides, I owe her one anyway."

"What?"

"Never mind, its a long story. But I want you to know that Shari is special to us—she's like family. So, if you aren't serious, then don't even step to her. Got it?"

"Got it," Shari heard Hamilton agree, then switch subjects. "Hey, show me that new program you created."

Shari waited until their voices faded before she continued down the stairway. She sought out Denise and her husband, Jon, said her goodbyes, then stepped out of the house, getting into her midnight black Alero to head toward her apartment located in the heart of Bronzeville. Shari drove slowly on the Dan Ryan Expressway, opting to roll along in the far right lane, versus the left she normally used. Normally, she was a demon for speed, but on this day, Shari wasn't in the mood. Her mind was being occupied by thoughts of her starting her own business and her break-up with Bruce. They had met the same night Deb had met Darrin—only she and Bruce's relationship didn't end like Deb's had. Shari had cared deeply for Bruce and when he proposed she had been excited. But she didn't love him, yet thought that with time she could grow to love him. Six months before the wedding, Bruce came to Shari and broke off the engagement, saying that he knew she did not love him. In the beginning she was angry with him for ruining what she felt was her one opportunity, then slowly she came to the realization that Bruce had done her a tremendous favor. And she had yet to thank him for it.

Back to the present, Shari inhaled deeply at the sudden smell of Hamilton's cologne seep from her senses. She looked around her car. Hamilton wasn't there, so why was his scent floating among her?

She shook her head, replacing the scent and the subsequent image of Hamilton with ones of making her life-long dream of becoming a designer a reality. Okay, she mused, she mentioned her dream to Deb and Denise. They're all for it. Next, she reasoned, came the countless items that would have to be accomplished for her to start her own clothing line. She had saved over twenty-thousand dollars herself, but she knew she needed more, much more. Deb's idea of private investors made sense, and both Deb and Denise had offered to invest in her company. But she didn't think that between the two of them, that they had the more than quarter of a million dollars she estimated she would need to start her own business.

Then there were her parents. Shari's thoughts ran and tumbled. Eventually she would have to tell her mother and father. And to be truthful, she wasn't looking forward to it, for Shari knew that quitting a job and starting her own company just didn't make the least bit of sense to her mother; and it stood to reason that her father would agree with his wife. But to Shari, what her parents didn't understand was her fierce love of creating, of dreaming up patterns and styles. It's her first love. Sure, she liked buying clothes, and got a kick out of seeing women walking down the streets of Chicago in attire she had personally selected for Macy's, but that's where her feelings ended.

Passion. The word jumped into her mind without warning. *Passion.* The image of the large poster that adored the wall of her design studio situated in the basement of the two-flat building she lived in appeared in her mind. The Essence of Passion was her life's mantra and she knew that if she lived her life without passion, then her life really had no meaning. "Yes," Shari stated loudly. "I'm going to do it! I'll take Deb and Denise up on their offer."

A smile crept across Shari's face. She was going to start her business, this day, by completing several designs she had started six months prior and add them to an investor's portfolio Deb had suggested she create. She fished the envelope from her purse, her eyes darting from the notes she had taken, then back to the road in front of her. She knew it was going to take her at least one year, if not more than eighteen months to get the business up and running. In addition, she mused, there was the endless documents and finances needed to last her at least two years. She tucked the envelope back in her purse.

Shari became giddy, her heart lifted slightly as thoughts of seeing her dream creations on men and women of color danced in her head.

Her mind now renewed, Shari began to search under the passenger seat of the car for her CD case. She just had to hear some Minnie Riperton. And she didn't care which song, though she had a fierce preference for "Here We Go." She leaned her body slightly to the right, while trying to keep an eye on the cars in front of her. From the corner of her eye, she could see the strap of the CD case peeking out from under the seat. She stretched her slender fingers toward the strap. If she could just hook her finger around it.

Suddenly, Shari's head hit the side of the steering wheel, as the impact from the vehicle behind her lunged her body forward, sending her car careening up the grassy embankment. A sharp pain traveled from her feet to the top of her head, as Shari felt the car come to a snapping halt. She blinked several times, her eyes attempting to focus on the chain link fence in front of her. She touched her forehead lightly. Where's that case? She thought as her eyes fluttered and her head began to throb. Shari's eyes closed as her head slumped backward.

Hamilton hummed along to the tune playing on the Urban Contemporary station, V103. He smiled as he thought of Shari, then removed the phone number Darrin had given him.

Hamilton laughed. "Can't escape that fast, Miss Shari Thomas."

Hamilton slowed his Ford Expedition as the traffic ahead came to a stand still. He could see over the various vehicles and watched as a black car flew up the grassy embankment. He watched as a car pulled over onto the shoulder. A man and woman stepped out and ran to the vehicle. He continued to watch as the woman opened the door, her hand gestures wild and animated, her mouth moving rapidly. "*Wow*," Hamilton thought as he continued watching the scene. His eyes widened when the man joined the woman and pulled the vehicle's occupant from the wreck. "That's Shari!"

Racing the accelerator, Hamilton pulled onto the shoulder. Upon reaching the scene, he jumped from his vehicle and raced to where Shari lay on the grass. He knelt beside her.

"Shari! Talk to me!" Hamilton took her hand in his. He looked into the faces of the couple. "Call 911." He turned his attention back to Shari. "Shari," he called her name. "Shari, open your eyes."

Slowly her eyes opened. Shari blinked, slowly turning her head to the left, then gasped softly. *Truly I haven't died and gone to heaven*, she thought, for the eyes staring into her were familiar, the lightness of them intense, magnetic. And that scent. What an angel, she thought as her head spun and her eyes struggled to focus as she attempted to take in the rest of the strangers features.

"Shari? Are you okay?!" she heard the voice repeat the question. *How does he know my name*, she wondered, then felt her body being lifted. She heard someone mention the word gasoline and sparks. She began to see double all around her, yet the strangers light eyes remained unmoved. Shari's hands crept up her rescuer's arms, then around his neck. She smiled. Her last thought was of the feel of a smooth, wide neck as her eyes shut once again.

CHAPTER 3

Hamilton paced the narrow corridor of the emergency room at the University of Chicago Hospitals. He rubbed his hands over his bald head. He couldn't believe he was standing in an emergency room. He had left Deb and Darrin's shortly after Shari had, and had been thinking of her when the accident occurred. His heart had skipped a beat as he watched the stealth movements of the car. Literally, the car went airborne before landing.

When he jumped out of his SUV, his first thought was making sure Shari was alive. His heart had begun to race faster when he smelled gasoline. Carrying her away from the scene, he had looked down into her face and found her to be the most stunningly beautiful woman he had even seen. He had never seen such perfection up close. Her sepia skin was baby smooth, not a blemish to be had.

Setting her on the grass, Hamilton watched over Shari with rapt amazement as her eyes fluttered behind her lids several times. He smoothed the furrow that had grown between her arched brows. For 10 minutes, though it seemed an eternity to Hamilton, he had tried to comfort her, had stroked her face in an attempt to soothe her. Once Illinois' finest arrived, the Illinois State Troopers, followed by an ambulance, he was asked if he knew her.

Opting to leave his red Ford Expedition on the expressway, Hamilton watched the paramedics as they took her pulse and blood pressure, then placed a large white plastic brace around her slender neck. Before leaving, Hamilton rushed to her car and retrieved her

purse, taking her keys out of the ignition. Upon returning, the paramedics asked him her name and address. He shook his head.

"I just met her a few hours ago. All I know is Shari Thomas," he
replied, then watched as the two paramedics exchanged odd looks. He
began to go through her purse in search of her wallet. He felt like he
was invading the most secretive part of her life. Yet, as an editor for a
newspaper he knew that it was the secrets people held close that made
for the most interesting plots. And a person's wallet could tell a lot
about its owner.

Hamilton had found and opened Shari's wallet. He flipped
through several credit cards—Marshal Field's, American Express
Platinum, Carson's—before coming to a picture. He paused, then
smiled at the picture of his baby cousin, Daneda. He flipped past
another plastic holder until he found her drivers license. He studied
the slightly narrowed eyes on the picture—the DMV never did justice
to a person—then read her information. Shari J. Thomas, 3500 S.
Martin Luther King, Jr. Drive. She lived in his backyard, just blocks
from him.

When the paramedics signaled to him they were taking Shari to
the hospital, Hamilton jumped into the back of the ambulance.

Shari was still unconscious when they arrived, a noticeable bruise
and lump had formed on her forehead. The paramedics said she
would have a nasty headache, but at that moment she was experiencing mild shock. Nothing life threatening.

"Mr. Edmunds," a nurse appeared at the door. "Your girlfriend is
awake."

"Umm, she's not my girlfriend."

The nurse turned her head to the right. "Okay," she smacked in
between chews of gum. "Well, the woman you came in here with is
conscious and asking for you."

Hamilton followed the nurse into the triage treatment area. He scanned the various faces of the patients lying on hospital beds. He heard moans coming from behind one curtain and prayed it wasn't coming from Shari.

The nurse led him to a partially open curtain. Hamilton poked his head around the curtain and smiled at Shari, her intense smoky brown eyes drew him to her like a magnet. He saw that they held a fire, a smoldering flame which flickered when she set them upon his face. *Damn, she's fine*, he thought as he nodded his head at the nurse, walked over to the chair near the bed, and then sat down. For several awkward moments the two stared. Hamilton cleared his throat.

"How's the head?" he looked at the bandage across Shari's forehead.

"Hard as a rock," Shari mumbled. "I hear you rode in the ambulance with me. How did that happen?"

"I was traveling a few cars behind you."

"Following me home?"

"No, not my style. I didn't know it was you until a man and woman pulled you from your car. They left when the ambulance arrived. No one got their names."

Shari nodded. "I owe you."

"No you don't. But, what happened?" Hamilton pulled the chair closer to the bed.

"One minute I was reaching for my CD case and the next I'm here. I think I pressed down on the brakes, versus the accelerator. The cops were here. It was a hit and run, but the culprit left behind a calling card. The front licence plate was at the scene."

"I guess that's a good thing. Whoever it was will be charged with several violations. Striking from behind is against Illinois state law. And so is leaving the scene of an accident."

"I didn't know that."

"Yeah. State statute," Hamilton replied, his eyes settled upon Shari's face. He felt he could sit all day and just stare at her. *What am I thinking*, he berated himself, *get a grip*. He changed the subject. "So, how long are they going to keep you?"

Shari attempted to sit up, but her head spun wildly. "They said they're going to keep me overnight for observation. I have a slight concussion."

"Sorry to hear that, but I guess its best."

Shari watched the concern on Hamilton's face, the intensity of his eyes. She averted her stare, focusing on his white shirt and blue tie, with specks of red and green, which was loosened at the neck.

"You're not getting dizzy are you?"

"A little. Why?"

"You've got that same look on your face you had when I first approached you, then later just before you passed out."

"I hope I passed out pretty like. You know?" Shari snickered at the bewildered expression on his face. "You know? Straight into your arms, not with my legs going east and west."

Hamilton laughed. "Oh, no, it was pretty."

Shari shivered. Her eyes absorbed the man who had come to her rescue. His arms straining the fabric of his shirt, seemed large and absolute, and beckoned her to touch them just one more time. When she had regained consciousness, her first memory was not of the accident, but of the feel of his arms, the smell of his masculine scent mingling with his cologne. Shari felt her face flush.

"You sure you're okay?" Hamilton stood quickly, then gestured toward the nurses station. "You're getting that look again. Do I need to call the doctor, or something?"

"No, I'm okay. I'll be even better when they let me go home."

Hamilton remembered that her car was probably still on the expressway, along with his. He watched as Shari looked into his eyes. He shifted his weight from one foot to the other. Just as he was about to repeat his question, the pair was interrupted.

"Shari! My God, girl, what happened?" Deb spoke rapidly as she stepped around the curtain to the side of the bed. She hugged Shari.

"I was looking for a CD when I guess my foot pressed down on the brakes instead of the accelerator. Someone hit me from behind."

"Shari, you have to be more careful," Deb chided, then looked across the bed at Hamilton. "How did you get here?" Deb raised her eyebrow.

Hamilton smiled. "I was traveling a few cars behind."

"He is being modest, Deb." Shari interrupted.

A sheepish expression crossed Hamilton's face. "Well, it wasn't nothing."

"Nothing?! Deb, he carried me from the accident. He thought the car was going to explode."

Shari watched as Deb stifled a laugh. "Well, now, isn't that something. I'm glad to see that you're not seriously hurt. Hamilton, thank you for taking care of my girl."

The sheepish expression returned to Hamilton's face. "Now that I see you're alright, I need to be going. My truck is still on the Dan Ryan. They'll being towing before nightfall."

"Oh, I forgot about my car. What am I going to do?"

Deb looked at Hamilton, then back to Shari. "Well, Darrin and Daneda are in the waiting room. Tell us where it is, and we'll make sure its taken care of."

"Thanks for everything, Hamilton," Shari looked into Hamilton's face. "I really appreciate it. I don't know how to make it up to you." Shari ended noting the various expressions roam across his face. She could sense from his expression that he was thinking of ways for her to pay him back.

"We'll come up with something," he smiled at her, the dimples of his cheeks deepened. "I'll check on you later. I hope your headache gets better, Shari. Take care." Hamilton nodded then disappeared.

Deb peered around the curtain and watched Hamilton walk away. "Gives a whole new meaning to a knight in shining armor."

"Tell me about it." Shari shook her head. This wasn't real, she thought, this just couldn't be happening. Hours ago, she was sitting next to him, exchanging glances, admiring his form, then bam! She's in the hospital with a concussion, Hamilton to her rescue.

For over two hours, Shari and Deb talked, while waiting for Shari to be moved to a room for the night. Even Darrin poked his head around the curtain, commenting on the coincidence of Shari's savior for the day being his cousin Hamilton.

Once in her room, Shari began to drift, groggy from the day's activities and the heavy medication the nurse had given her for her headache. As Shari closed her eyes, sleep making its way, she thought of Hamilton and his expressive light brown eyes and the way his scent and very presence caused an involuntary shiver to ride along her entire body. Truly, she thought, she couldn't be falling so fast for a man she didn't even know, much less had laid eyes on before this day. As she drifted off, images of Hamilton, walking toward her, his head held high, his arms out stretched, danced in and out of her dreams.

Hamilton arrived at his home, an old Victorian grey stone built in the early 1900s, and plopped down on the couch in his den. He rubbed the faint stubble on his face, thought it was time to shave, then grabbed the television remote, surfing through several channels before stopping on ESPN2. His eyelids felt heavy, almost like lead, as they struggled to stay open, a vain attempt to watch a classic football game between the Pittsburgh Steelers and the Cleveland Browns.

He pulled animatedly at his eyelids—more out of habit than not wanting to go to sleep. After 20 minutes of struggling to stay awake, Hamilton thought better and headed up the stairs to his bedroom. He picked up the phone resting on the night stand next to his bed and heard the familiar tone signaling he had messages. He dialed the number to voice mail and laid his long, broad frame out on his bed. He listened to message after message, mentally discarding one after another. Hamilton was about to hang up on the messages when he heard a familiar female voice.

"Hey Hamilton, its Deb. I thought you would like to know that Shari's been moved to room 415 and will be released tomorrow after 2. See ya soon. Love ya."

Hamilton smiled. He knew just what she was doing and he liked it. He looked at the clock, it read 8 p.m. If he hurried, he could catch his mother at their family-owned flower shop and have flowers delivered. He dialed the digits immediately.

"Edmonds' House of Flowers," he heard his mother cheerfully answer.

"Hey mom," Hamilton said.

"Hi, baby. How's my boy doing this evening?" Hamilton's mother responded, her light voice floated across the phone line.

Hamilton couldn't help but blush. At 39, his mother still called him her baby. He didn't mind, for he knew he was a momma's boy—was Ella Edmunds baby, her only son—and he was proud of it. He wasn't tied to her apron strings, or anything remotely close to that, but he and his mother had been close, even more so after his father's untimely death from a stroke six months prior. Hamilton thought of how far his mother had come in running the family business, for before his father died, she had stayed home and raised her family—Hamilton and his four sisters.

"I'm okay. I need a favor."

"What is it, baby?"

"Is it too late to have flowers delivered?"

"Have we found a nice lady?"

Hamilton didn't want to say too much. After his father died, Hamilton's mother had been after him to settle down and give her another daughter, not like she didn't have four of her own, and some more grandchildren—she had 10 total. Yet, he had felt something as he held Shari in his arms, then later as he looked into her smoky brown eyes. He wasn't sure, but there was something about her, her stare, in the way she looked him in his eyes, which made him hope. He didn't want to get beside him self, but he wanted to get to know Shari Thomas, and he didn't want to be just her friend.

"Well, a friend of Darrin and Deb's isn't feeling well and she's in the hospital. But she's going to be released tomorrow. Can we send them?"

"Speaking of Darrin. How was the baptism?"

"It was a baptism. The priest poured water over the child, crossed her, then blessed her."

"Smart aleck," Hamilton's mother responded, laughing. "Anyway, considering the time, you're going to have to deliver the flowers yourself tomorrow. I'll make up an arrangement of daffodils and lilies, and maybe a few carnations or roses. Then you come by here first thing in the morning and take them to the hospital. I guarantee it'll leave a lasting impression."

BARBARA KEATON

Hamilton rolled his eyes heavenward. He loved his mother and knew just what she was attempting to do. He had to admire her, though. He thought of the love she and his father had shared. They could sit together, silently, seeming as if their thoughts were intertwined. For all of the forty-five years they had been married, his father had sent his mother flowers every day with a card that simply stated "I love you".

A single tear escaped the corner of Hamilton's eye. He thought of the love and passion they had, how his father had been a pivotal force in all of their lives. If he lived another 20 years, Hamilton mused, he would be lucky to find what his parents had.

"Okay. I'll be by in the morning to get the flowers," he agreed. "What are your still doing at the shop?" Hamilton slipped off his black cap-toe, wing tips, letting them fall to the floor with a loud thud.

"Baby, pick up your shoes," his mother said. Hamilton laughed. His mother continued, "I had 4 orders for funeral sprays today. And six wedding arrangements. I just finished the last spray." He heard his mother sigh before continuing. "It's funny, before your father died, he always joked that if he didn't see another flower it'd be too soon. But, he loved the texture and scent of them. Could work wonders with them." The pair laughed at the irony, each with their own thoughts of the man whom they shared a great love for.

"Who's there with you?" he asked.

"I'm okay. I'll be leaving the minute I finish with the arrangement for your friend."

"No, mom, I'll get something else. I want you to go home."

"Now, ain't this something," Ella laughed. "I use to have to get at you to leave the office early, now look who's giving orders."

"Mom, I just don't want you down there by yourself."

33

"Junie just left," Ella replied, speaking of her 14-year-old grandson. "I'll be leaving shortly."

"Did you drive?" Hamilton asked. His question went unanswered, because he knew his mother didn't want to tell him the truth. She didn't like to drive and only did so when no one was available to take her where she wanted to go. Hamilton assumed one of his sisters had dropped her off and he knew she was going to walk the five blocks to the house.

Hamilton's father had always driven his mother around. He had once asked his father why his mother didn't drive and was told that the time they spent alone in the car, no matter how short, was quality time, especially with 5 pairs of nosey eyes constantly on them. "Mom, sit tight. I'll be there in 20 minutes."

Hamilton hung up the phone, looked at his shoes in the middle of floor, decided to forego them, then stepped into his walk-in closet. Changing from the dress slacks and shirt, he put on a pair of black jeans, a black t-shirt and a pair of black Nike's. He grabbed the keys to his Expedition. Images of Shari's smiling eyes and arduous stare became locked firmly in his mind as headed out. For some inexplicable reason, he knew that he would never be free from the effect this woman's whole being had on him and he wasn't sure if even wanted to be.

CHAPTER 4

"Yes, mother, I'm fine," Shari breathed into the phone as she listened to her mother's deep, resounding voice questioning her. "Mom, all I have is a slight concussion. They're releasing me today." Shari rolled her eyes upward. Shari's mother had always been protective over her one and only child, and Shari's father, Leonard, was no better. She was beginning to regret having called them, but she knew if she hadn't she'd never hear the end of it.

"Shari, your father wants to talk to you. Hold on."

Shari knew her father would parrot her mother and she braced herself for the onslaught.

"Hey, Princess," Shari heard her father say calmly. "I hear my princess has a bump on her head." Shari's father chuckled.

Shari's eyes widened. Her father was never that calm, but more importantly, he hadn't called her princess since she was a teenager.

"I'm okay, daddy. I wasn't paying attention and mashed down on the brake instead of the accelerator. Darrin said the axel is broken, there's major rear end damage, and some other stuff I can't remember, but I'll be fine. Like I told mom, they're releasing me today."

"Well, your mother has booked us on the next thing smoking. So, we will see you soon."

Shari sighed. "That's not necessary, Dad. I wish you guys would stay put. Besides, Deb and Denise are here. And Mrs. Ponticello is here. So, you see there's no need in coming from New Mexico just for a bump on the head."

"I know, Princess, but try and tell that to your mother. She has us packed and ready to go." Shari's father laughed. "Wait. Hold on a sec." Shari heard her mother's voice in the background. "I'm back. Our flight leaves here at 3:30."

"How are you guys going to get from the airport?"

"You know your mother. We'll rent a car. So, take care and we'll see you later."

Shari's father hung up before she could convince them otherwise. Great, she thought, that's all I need, my mother and father hovering over me like a child. But for as long as she could remember, her mother had always fussed over her, with her father solidly supporting it. Yet, something was different. He father's tone didn't possess its normal passiveness. His voice seemed deeper than she remembered, and calmer. He seemed clam, almost aloof over her situation.

Shari slowly swung her feet around to dangle over the side of the bed. She stretched out her right foot in an attempt to feel the cold linoleum floor. She wanted to stand up, move around. She was tired of lying in the bed. On a normal Sunday, she would be up milling about her apartment, cleaning and listening to gospel music. Lying in bed past 7 a.m. was not something she did.

With one foot solidly on the floor, Shari attempted to have the other foot follow. Instantly, her head began to swim, her vision clouding over. She shut her eyes, willing her head to stop, to still itself, but her head was ruling her body and had plans of its own. Shari felt herself beginning to float, spiral downward, and she braced herself for the fall.

"Whoa, Shari," Hamilton's deep voice broke in. "I don't think you're suppose to be up yet. They haven't released you." Hamilton grabbed Shari around her waist, picked her up and placed her gently onto the bed, pulling the single white sheet over her shoulders. He had spied a toned thigh just as she began to sway, the hospital gown rising dangerously up. If he was to remain a gentleman, he knew he needed to cover up her entire body. Yet, even that didn't do any good, for under the flimsy sheet and blanket, he could make out Shari's vicious curves. He shook his head, loosening the erotic image which seared into his memory.

"Umm, that's twice," Shari whispered, her eyes shut tight as she slowly regained her senses. "What are you doing here?" She asked, not daring to open her eyes—she didn't have to. The arresting cologne, followed by the deep, melodic voice was now ingrained in her very pores. She knew she would know his voice anywhere. And those strong arms—the feel of them wrapped around her body left indelible prints. No, she wouldn't be able to forget this one so easily.

"Well, I thought I'd bring you these." Hamilton stood by the bed, waiting for Shari to open her eyes. He watched in rapt amusement as her eyes fluttered, then opened, resting upon his face, then to the large floral arrangement he had set on the floor near the door.

"Those are so beautiful," Shari responded and held out her arms. Hamilton walked to the door, retrieved the flowers, then handed them to Shari. She bought the flowers closer, with Hamilton's hand supporting the base of the vase, and inhaled the sweet fragrance. "I love Lilies. How did you know?"

As soon as the words were out, Shari laughed. This was all too familiar. Hadn't she supplied Darrin with the same type of information when he was pursuing Deb?

"I didn't. My mother created this arrangement. Lilies are a favorite of hers."

"Oh," Shari replied. "Your mother?" She motioned for Hamilton to place the flowers on the table by her bed.

"Yeah, she makes floral arrangements for all types of events.

Weddings, funerals, sick folks. After my father died, she took over the business. I had no clue she had such an eye for it."

"Sorry to hear about your father." Shari looked at Hamilton. She wanted to say more, reach out and touch him, but she didn't know him—didn't know if he even wanted to be reached out to. Besides, as she watched him, she noticed that his expression never altered. She thought he hid his emotions well and decided to move the subject back to his mother. "How long has your mom been creating arrangements?"

"About six months, now."

Shari looked at the arrangement. "Your mom has a real creative flair. This is really something else. Please thank her for me." She looked at Hamilton, his eyes bored into hers. She took the presented opportunity to again fully absorb the man who had rescued her the day before. His smooth opaque skin owned a proud jaw, his chin jutted forward slightly. His lids drooped, almost shielding his deep set, light eyes, with specks of pale green in them. Shari liked the way his head was shaped, perfectly round and bald. His body was shielded in a black, short-sleeved t-shirt, and black, form-fitting jeans. The muscles of his arms stretched the fabric of the shirt, while his chest proudly proclaimed its massive stature. She could see the outline of well-formed pectorals, with wisps of dark hair peeking from the collar. Shari liked what she saw. Yes she did.

"Well, I hear you're going home," a nurse entered the room, breaking the long silence Shari and Hamilton were sharing.

"I thought I wasn't being released until after 2?"

"No, you can go home now."

"But, I'm still experiencing a little dizziness."

The nurse rounded the bed, stuck a thermometer in Shari's mouth, then secured a blood pressure cuff around her arm and commenced to take her pulse. "That's to be expected. You've got a nasty bump. But we'll get you out of bed and see how you feel." The nurse wrote down Shari's vitals then looked up at Hamilton standing near-by. "If this strong, handsome man will assist me, I think we can get you up and walking around."

Hamilton nodded his head as the nurse pulled back the covers. He quickly closed his eyes, hoping the nurse would hurry. His eyes opened slowly upon hearing the nurse clear her throat. "Sir, take her by the hand."

He reached out for Shari's hand, taking it firmly in his, and gently assisted in pulling her from the bed. Her body rested closely to his as her feet came to rest on the floor. He looked over her face, before letting his gaze sweep across her shoulder-length mahogany brown hair tosseled about her head. He smiled down at her, his 6-foot-four frame shielding her own smaller one, which he guessed she had to be close to 5'3. He felt her hands travel slowly up his arms, her weight shifting, allowing him to hold her.

"Shari, you have to open your eyes. Give them time to focus. Once you do that, everything will right itself." The nurse instructed.

Shari did as she was told, looking up into Hamilton's face, as he took a small step, guiding her with his strong body. Shari moved with him, her legs working in sync with her mind. She stopped, then dropped her arms reluctantly from Hamilton's. She was slightly dizzy, but felt better.

"See. Now, I'll help you dress, that is if you don't want your boyfriend here to do it."

Shari's spoke quickly. "He's not my boyfriend."

She could see the shocked expression on the nurse's face. She quickly dismissed it and requested her clothes.

"Do you have a ride?" Hamilton asked.

"No, I don't, but I'll call Deb. She was coming to get me. She's under the impression that I would be released after 2 o'clock."

"Don't worry her. I have my truck here, so I'll take you home."

"That won't be necessary," Shari replied, shooing him away.

"Yes it will," Hamilton replied. "You get dressed and I'll go and pull the truck around." He moved toward the door, then faced the nurse. "Will you be bringing her down?" The nurse nodded. "Good, I'll be waiting. I'm driving a red Expedition."

Hamilton quickly moved toward the door. Shari watched as his wide back fill the doorway, then disappeared.

"Girl, umph," the nurse began. "If that tall, chocolate drink of water isn't your boyfriend, then I'll take him."

Shari grinned. "No, he isn't my boyfriend, but I sure need to correct that, now don't I?" The pair laughed.

"Let's not keep that tall, dark drink of water waiting." The nurse giggled. "I'll get your clothes."

Hamilton walked to the hospital's parking lot. His mind searched for the reason why he was going out of his way to help her. He was drawn to her which supplanted his need to get to know her better. He remembered her scent, the delicate floral fragrance that emitted from her. Even today, he could still smell traces of the fragrance she wore. When he first met her at the church, he wanted to comment on the scent, but thought better. And the way her pale pink suit hugged her curves. *Umph*, was all he could muster at the crime of a woman being shaped like Shari. He had watched her stroll down that aisle, her head held high, her shoulder-length mahogany hair flailing behind her. Yes, he thought, she was like no other. And it had been a long time since a woman had that effect on him—too long. He thought of his last relationship.

Hamilton had met Janice at a party given by his boyhood friend and fraternity brother, Matthew. He hadn't expected to meet anyone, he just wanted to hang a little, have a few beers, spend some time with his boy, and possibly play a few hands of Bid Whist. When he had entered Matthew's home, he spotted Janice sitting next to Kara, Matthew's girlfriend. Janice's green eyes never left his face as he made his way across to them. Even when he bent to kiss Kara on the cheek, the woman sitting next to her never looked away.

Kara introduced them, got up, and pushed Hamilton to sit next to Janice. When he protested lightly, saying something about getting a beer, Janice jumped up and went in search for one. And though Hamilton wasn't in the mood to chat, he ended up spending most of the night engaged in one exhausting conversation after another with Janice.

At the nights end, Hamilton asked for Janice's number. He didn't know why he did it. Maybe it was the polite thing to do or maybe it was those 4 plus beers he had ingested that spoke for him. Either way, they began to date, but as he got to know Janice, he didn't like what he saw. She was always trying to find ways to get over to his place, reasons to spend the night. It took him nearly a month to even sleep with her, and that was after her accusation that he either didn't find her appealing or that he was gay.

He knew the minute they had finished making love that he had made a mistake. After that, Janice had begun to call him no less than three times a day. Once in the morning, once again around lunch, then late at night. She was smothering him. Besides, he had thought, she was too content with life. He had dreams and ambitions that he

41

wanted to realize, and when he told her of his aspirations, she had laughed in his face.

"You're going to quit your job at the Times to do what?" she had asked, amusement written all over her face. "You're a fool if you walk away from a nearly six-figure job to write full time. You're a bigger fool than I thought."

With that, Hamilton knew that Janice wasn't the woman for him—knew her days were numbered. He felt that if a person couldn't see beyond their own narrow scape of the world, they most certainly didn't see yours. And one thing Hamilton didn't invest in was negativity. He didn't subscribe to it and wouldn't have anyone in his life who did. What he wanted was a woman who was unafraid to live, to experience life to the fullest. He wanted a woman who was passionate. *Passion. Yes, passion*, he thought as he climbed into his Expedition, is what I'm looking for.

He started up the vehicle and drove to the front of the hospital. He spotted Shari sitting in a wheel chair, her eyes shielded behind a pair of dark sun glasses, her shapely legs crossed one over the other. He liked the pale pink suit and matching shoes, thought it brought out the warm reds of her complexion.

Hamilton parked, jumped out of the vehicle, then raced around to open the passenger door. He stepped quickly toward Shari, his gait lighter than he had known. Without warning, he bent slightly, then scooped Shari up into his arms and placed her gently into the seat. He reached across her and buckled her seat belt, then slid behind the wheel.

"I need your address," Hamilton smiled. "Otherwise, I'll have to take you home with me."

Shari smirked, glad her eyes were shielded from his penetrating stare. Because most certainly had they not been, Mister Hamilton

Edmunds would have been able to clearly read the sensual thoughts that raced through her mind.

Hamilton pulled away from the hospital. En route, Shari's cell phone rang in her purse.

"Hello," she answered.

"Hey girl. Where are you?" Deb asked.

"I've been released." Shari replied.

"I thought you wanted me to pick you up?"

Shari chuckled as she looked over at Hamilton. "No, that won't be necessary, Deb. Hamilton is taking me home." Shari smiled. "Plus Mom and Dad are on their way from New Mexico."

"Oh no." Deb responded. "Now, that should be fun."

"Yeah, don't I know it," Shari replied sarcastically. "Girl, they're a mess. But mom just has to see for herself that I'm okay."

"How long are they going to stay?"

"I don't know, but the good Lord knows that for my sanity to remain in tact, I'm praying it won't be any longer than two days."

"Well, if you need anything, just call."

"Sure will. I may need you to run a little interference. You game?"

"Sure. Let me know. Now, get off the phone and pay that man next to you some attention. Bye."

Deb disconnected before Shari could respond.

"Your parents are coming to Chicago?" Hamilton quizzed. "Are you their baby?"

"I'm their only. And Lord knows they try and treat me like one, even though I haven't lived at home for nearly 20 years. What about you? Do you have any brothers or sisters?"

"I've got four sisters, no brothers."

"Wow, that must have been something, growing up in a house full of women. Where do you fit in?"

"I'm the second to the youngest. But it was fun. I don't play with jacks and the only dolls I play with are real ones." He glanced over at her, his right eye brow raised. "But they did teach me to jump double dutch."

Shari snickered. "Double dutch?!"

"Better than most females."

Shari laughed out loud. "Not better than me, I bet."

"How much?"

"How much, what?"

"How much are you willing to loose? I'm still pretty good at beating the pavement." He glanced over at Shari, a look of disbelief spread across her face. "You're on! I've never met a man who could jump double-dutch, much less one who'd admit he could."

"Shari, I'm not like most men." His tone turned serious, his stare intensified. He wanted her to know that she would probably never meet another man like himself. Sure that sounded a little arrogant, but according to his baby sister, Helen, most men were insecure and afraid to show emotion. For Hamilton, he was quite sure of himself, and owned a strong sense of self-love, which had been encouraged and supported by his family. "Anyway, what shall we bet?"

"How about dinner?" Shari replied.

"You got it. But under one condition."

"What's that?" Shari asked, amusement rang in her voice.

"Can you cook?"

"Like I sew—very well." She replied with mock attitude.

"We'll see." his deep voice sang. "So, you agree that the looser has to prepare a home-cooked meal. None of that fast food or microwaved stuff. I want a serious meal."

"Micro-waved?" Shari playfully slapped Hamilton on the arm. "The only thing I use my microwave for is to heat up left overs. But seeing as how you're going to loose, heating up my own leftovers will be quite unnecessary."

Hamilton laughed, the deep sound of it filled the small space between them. Shari watched his eyes crinkle, the laugh lines pronounced. "You're on, girl. I'm gonna jump you into the ground. And you will never outlive it."

The light banter ended and Shari became solemn once she realized the ride was over as they pulled up in front of the two-flat she lived in.

"Sit tight," Hamilton ordered, stepped out of the vehicle, came around to the passenger side, then opened the door and effortlessly picked Shari up out of the passenger seat.

"You don't have to do this, I can walk."

"I know I don't have to do this, but allow me to. Will you?" He looked into her face, waiting for her protest to pass. When it did, he stepped up to the door of the two-flat. "Where are your keys?"

Shari was so enthralled by Hamilton that she had forgotten to fish her keys out of her purse. She fumbled around in one pocket, then another. "They were here yesterday."

"Look in the side pocket," he said.

Shari did as Hamilton suggested and upon finding the keys, placed them in the lock.

"Where to?" Hamilton asked. Shari pointed upward. "Second floor it is." He descended the stairs, taking them two at a time. Shari was impressed with his strength.

"What's going on here?" Shari's landlady appeared at the foot of the stairs.

"Oh, hi Mrs. Ponticello. Nothing's going on. I'm just getting out of the hospital and this gentleman here is helping me."

Shari looked over Hamilton's broad shoulder to see Mrs.

Ponticello looking pensively up at them.

"The hospital?" Mrs. Ponticello's steel gray eyes were large. "What in God's name happened, honey?"

"I was in a car accident," Shari began. "I suffered a mild concussion. But nothing to be worried about. I'll be home for a few days, then I'll be good as new. Mom and Dad will be here later."

"Child, why didn't you call me?"

"I didn't want you to worry."

"Next time call. Hear me?" Shari nodded. "How long will your parents be here?"

"A couple of days." Shari rolled her eyes, then muttered under her breath, "I hope." She looked at Hamilton. She smirked as he smiled at her expression.

"I'll be up in a minute," Mrs. Ponticello announced then disappeared into her apartment.

"She and my mother went to college together," Shari began in response to the curious expression on Hamilton's face. "They've been friends for over 40 years. Lucia Ponticello is the only reason why my mother doesn't come here more often."

Hamilton nodded his head, then paused at the top of the landing. Shari was loving the attention, the concern he was showing. A girl could get use to this, she thought as she reluctantly opened the door to her apartment. She felt him stiffen, then take a step back.

"Whoa! That's a mighty big dog."

"Oh, that's just Rocket. Had her since she was a pup. She won't bite."

Hamilton looked at Shari, his eyebrows raised. "The dog has teeth, doesn't she?"

At his words, the dog reared on its hind legs and began to lick Hamilton's hands. "Okay, I guess she's friendly enough. Where's your bedroom?" Hamilton asked as he attempted to shake free of Rocket's lapping.

"Rocket, get down." Shari ordered.

Allowing them to pass, Rocket followed as Hamilton carried Shari in the direction she pointed to. He could hear the tip-tapping of Rocket's paws on the hardwood floor behind him. His eyes swept to his left, taking in the large living room, its walls painted antique white and fastidiously arranged with a sage colored couch and matching love seat, accentuated with an abstract print chair and ottoman. He turned his attention toward the long hall way, and began walking down it, Shari's frame light in his arms.

Hamilton noticed the various pictures, which covered both sides of the hallway. One in particular caught his eye. One of Shari and a caramel colored brother, hugged in an intimate embrace. Shari felt Hamilton stiffen again, then followed his gazed, coming to rest upon the picture she and Bruce had taken in Rio de Janeiro a year before their breakup. She wanted to kick herself. She had been meaning to take the picture down, but the beautiful mountain scenery behind them was soothing.

Hamilton stopped at the door leading into Shari's bedroom. He laughed as the dog raced around them, then jumped on the bed, barking loudly. "Guess someone's glad you're home."

"Yeah, I missed her too. She's good company."

The two fell silent as Hamilton cradled Shari in his arms, his eyes swept across her face, taking in her beauty. "I guess I should put you down now." Shari nodded as he placed her slowly on the floor, his hands secured about her waist. He held her, not really wanting to let go. He bent his head, removed her sun glasses, and watched as her face came closer to his own, her hands held tightly onto his biceps. He closed his eyes, letting his lips touch hers. The fire in them told of something—a searing emotion that would surely burn out of control if not quenched just right. He heard a slight moan escape from her, signaling him further. He parted her lips with his tongue, letting it play with hers. Shari trailed her small hands up to rest at the base of his neck, slightly pulling him closer. The hunger of her mouth reached down into the very depths of his whole being.

Never had he experienced this type of flame, and the longer they kissed, the more intense it became. Hamilton didn't want to stop. He wanted more, much more.

He broke their tryst. "I'd better be leaving now." His words came out in a haunting breath.

Shari cleared her throat, then shielded her eyes, lowering them, her long lashes nearly touching the top of her cheeks. "Umm, yes. Ahh, thank you Hamilton." She motioned toward the door.

"No, I'll see myself out. I'll call you later to check on you."

"Oh, well, umm...thank you again, Hamilton."

"My pleasure," he responded, then left.

Shari stood still, listening to his footsteps on the hardwood floor, followed by the sound of the door opening then closing. She pressed her hand to her tingling lips. If one could fall in love from a kiss, she would be head over heels in love with Hamilton at that very moment. How had she gone from just meeting him to sharing such an intimate act with him? She'd known him nearly 24 hours and here she was kissing him, wantonly at that. She shook her head and thought this was something from a romance novel.

"Some man, ugh Rocket?" Shari spoke to the dog, still sitting atop the bed. She laughed when Rocket made a loud whining sound in response to her question. Shari made her way over to her poster bed, pushing Rocket to one side, then laid down. Rocket's large head came to rest on her stomach. She spied the digital clock atop her maple chiffarobe, then rolled over on her side, Rocket's head coming to rest on her hip. She yawned, then shut her eyes. Visions of she and Hamilton standing, locked in a sweet embrace lulled her to sleep. Her last thought was of him picking her up and lying her on her bed just before . . .

CHAPTER 5

Shari rolled over on her side, adjusting her eyes to the brightness of the room. She felt as if she had been asleep for eight hours, then realized she had only been asleep for a little over three hours. Her ears perked up as she strained to tune into the voices coming up the stairs. *Oh my God, mother's here.*

"Shari Marie Thomas!" She heard her mother use her full, given name. "Baby, are you okay?" Her mother appeared in the doorway, with Rocket standing by her side.

Traitor, Shari thought looking at her dog next to her mother. "Mom, I told you over the phone that I was fine. You and daddy didn't have to come," Shari snapped and was stunned at the tone she had used. In all of her

32-years, she had never spoken to her mother that way. She watched the shocked expression, followed by dismissal cross her mother's face.

"It must be that bump on your head. Anyway, your father and I are here now. Everything's going to be alright."

"Where's Daddy?"

"Bringing up the luggage. We'll stay in the guest room. If you haven't eaten yet, I'm going to make some soup. That is, if you have more in your refrigerator than you did the last time we were here."

Shari sank down under her bed covers and listened as her mother droned on, her voice rising and falling depending on which part of the three-bedroom apartment she was in.

For over an hour, Shari listened to her mothers voice as she picked through her refrigerator, her cupboards, then pantry.

"Leonard," Shari heard her mother call out. "I've made a grocery list. This child doesn't have a thing in here to eat. Let's go. And that dog needs a bath."

Shari laughed as she heard Rocket's paws hit the floor, running to her favorite hiding place—a closet in the basement. Rocket hated baths and Shari knew she would remain there for several hours until she felt the coast was clear.

She smiled at the thought of how Rocket came to live with she and Deb when they shared a house. Deb had found the German Shepherd as a puppy wandering down the street they lived on. After having taken the animal in, Deb and Shari had placed fliers all over the neighbor about the dog. When no one claimed her, they decided to keep the animal, naming her Rocket for the way she tore through the house when it was feeding time. After Deb got married and moved, Shari kept Rocket with her.

Those were happier times, Shari sighed as she listened to her parents footsteps, then the subsequent closing of her front door. She let out a long sigh. Picking up the phone beside her bed, she dialed Deb's phone number.

"*Help*," Shari cried into the phone. "Mom's been here exactly one hour and already she's rearranged my kitchen. You know my closets are next."

Deb laughed. "That's your momma. How about I come over and bring Miss Daneda? Maybe that will distract her."

"Sounds good, but what about the other five days?"

"Sister, you on your own. I've always loved your mom, but I can only take her in small doses."

"So, you know how I feel? Thirty-two and she still treats me as if

I'm five. I've got to get her over this and onto the fact that I'm a grown woman."

"Are you going to tell them?"

"About my plans to start my own business? *Please!* No way. They're not ready."

"Can't put off the inevitable, Shari. Okay, hanging up. I'll be there in an hour."

"They'll be back by then. See you later."

Shari hung up, climbed out of bed, and padded barefoot to the kitchen. She did and she didn't want to see the way her mother had come in and commandeered her space. She turned when she heard Mrs. Ponticello behind her.

"She means well, Linda does."

"I know, but will it ever stop?" Shari asked, then began to rearrange her cupboards the way she had them. Finishing, she moved to the pantry, and upon observing that it wasn't as bad as she had imagined, moved onto her sparse refrigerator. She laughed, remembering the last time her mother grocery shopped for her. She had had enough food to feed three homeless shelters and stock a church pantry.

"Before your mother returns, you want to tell me about that handsome young man who carried you up here?"

Shari tried to hide her wide grin by turning her back to her landlady. Yes, she agreed, he was handsome, with his searing eyes and smooth chocolate skin. "Oh, he's Darrin's cousin. Met him at little Daneda's baptism."

"Met him at the church. That's a good sign. Are you two going to see each other again?"

Shari went on to tell her landlady all about Hamilton, including how it came to be that he brought her home from the hospital. In the end, she knew she wanted to see him again, wanted to at least figure out why she got that heady, swimming feeling each time he was near her.

"Maybe."

"Maybe? You young people sure are different. In my day suitors . . ."

Shari laughed. "Suitors? Sounds like folks trying to get hitched."

"Well, that's what dating is for. For you to find a suitable mate, marry and have children." Mrs. Ponticello frowned at Shari. She just didn't understand young folks way of thinking. "Anyway, in my day suitors made sure you knew that their full intentions were to get married. There were no guessing games like you young folks play today."

"Now you sound like mom. What makes you guys think I want to get married?"

"It's time. You can't live here forever," Mrs. Ponticello smiled. "Even though I love having you here."

Shari stepped to her landlady, took her by the hand, and kissed her on the cheek, noting the smooth texture of the woman's olive complexion. "And I love living here. Just don't be so quick to kick me out." Shari ended with a chuckle.

All conversation ceased as the voice of her mother became clearer as she neared the kitchen.

"If that's what you want to do, Leonard," Shari overheard her mother say to her father.

"Want to do what, Mom?"

Linda came up short upon seeing Shari standing in the kitchen. Shari watched as her mother's eyes swept over to the open pantry. "Leonard, put those on the counter." She pointed.

"Mom?" Shari repeated, as she watched her father place several plastic bags filled with groceries on the counter. Her eyes gazed upon her mother's face—the face so like her own. "Do what?"

"Oh, nothing. Leonard and I was just discussing some stuff. Nothing you need to concern yourself with."

Shari huffed. "So in other words, none of my business." Shari narrowed her eyes, then walked out of the kitchen and headed to her bedroom to lay down.

After an hour of listening to her parents voices, Shari heard the doorbell ring. Jumping out of bed, she rushed to the intercom.

"Saved by the bell," Shari beamed as Deb came into view.

"Hey, what's a sister for?" She hugged Shari, then placed a sleeping Daneda in her arms. Deb stepped over the threshold. "Where's Rocket? The parents?"

"Rocket's in the basement. Mom said something about a bath."

"That'll do it." The pair laughed at Deb's words.

"As for the parents. They're in the kitchen. Mom's making her famous chicken noodle soup. She thinks I don't eat enough."

Without exchanging glances or another word, Shari followed Deb into the kitchen.

"Momma Thomas," Deb called out, then stepped into outstretched arms.

"Deborah," Linda cooed. "You're looking good. Where's the baby and that handsome husband of yours?"

Shari stepped into the kitchen, handed over her goddaughter and watched as her mother snuggled the baby in her arms. "Ohhh, she is so precious. You are truly blessed. See, Shari, this is what its all about. When you and Bruce decide the wedding is on again, I'll be looking forward to being a Nanna shortly thereafter."

Shari rolled her eyes, then sat on the stool next to the kitchen island. She hadn't told her parents that she and Bruce were finished. In their minds, she and Bruce were just taking a break. She knew her mother would scream if she knew that she had no plans on marrying Bruce. And she also knew that her mother thought that with Bruce being a doctor, a surgeon no less, was the perfect man for her only child. Shari looked over at her father sitting on a stool nearby. His face expressionless.

For over an hour Shari and Deb, with Mrs. Ponticello close by, sat and listened to her mother espouse on the benefits of marriage, as she prepared supper. She ended by reminding Shari that she didn't have much time, at which point her father rose and announced he was going to watch some television and to call him once supper was ready.

Shari watched her father's retreat. How odd, she thought, her father normally would chime in, co-signing everything her mother had to say.

At the end of their meal, Deb and Daneda left, followed by Mrs. Ponticello. Shari dreaded being alone with her mother. She loved her mother—deeply—but she had long grown tired of her mother's lectures. Shari decided to forego any additional conversation and announced she was heading to bed. Shortly thereafter, she heard a knock on her bedroom door. "Come in."

"Hey, Princess."

Shari scooted over on the large bay window. "Hey yourself. You know you guys didn't have to come all the way to Chicago. I'm fine." She touched the bandage on her forehead.

"Well, I can see that," Shari's father sat next to her. "But we wouldn't have been satisfied unless we saw it for ourselves." He took her hand in his. "We do worry, though I know you're a grown woman."

Shari hugged her father. It was the first time she had heard her father state the obvious.

"Hey, you've got quite a set up downstairs."

Shari's eyebrows rose. "You saw my studio?"

Her father nodded. "Lucia showed me. I'm truly impressed. I didn't know you were that talented. Think you can make a suit for me?"

Shari couldn't believe what she was hearing. In college, her father had been just as adamant as her mother when it came to her wanting to major in Fashion Design. He had flatly refused to pay her college tuition if she chose what he felt was a waste of her time. At the time, "Sure, dad," was her only reply.

"Well, get some sleep. Your mother and I are going to be here for only a couple of days."

"I thought you guys were staying the entire week."

Shari's father smiled. "No, that's what your mother thinks. We're leaving day after tomorrow. Nite, princess."

"Nite, daddy."

Shari was perplexed at her father's actions. For as long as she could remember, Leonard Thomas went along to get along; now, she was seeing a side of him she didn't know existed. She shook her head, then smiled as the little voice inside her told her it was safe to share her plans with her father.

Shari was deep in thought when the phone beside her bed rang. She looked at the caller-id and grinned.

"Hello."

"How's the head?" Hamilton asked.

"I'm fine. It's fine. What are you up to?"

"Nothing. Sitting here doing a little work and thinking about you."

"Me?" Shari's heart raced.

"Yeah, I wanted to make sure you were alright, that your head was no longer swimming."

"I'm okay. I have a slight headache, but not like I did the first day."

"That's good to hear. Did your parents arrive?"

"Yeah, they're here."

"Sounds good," he replied then grew silent. He wanted to ask her out, see if she wanted to spend some time with him. He changed his mind. "Well, I won't keep you. Just checking on you. I'll call you later."

"Sounds good, Hamilton. Thanks for checking up on me."

"Not a problem. Good night, Shari."

"Nite, Hamilton." Shari held the phone long after Hamilton's call had disconnected. He had called her. She didn't have to wonder how he got her phone number. Shari closed her eyes and pictured Hamilton standing in front of her, their lips touching lightly just before he left. A chill raced down her arms and she began to feel giddy. Her thoughts were interrupted by a soft knock on her door.

"Come in," Shari called out.

"Just wanted to say goodnight." Shari's mother peered around the door. "How are you feeling?"

"I'm okay. No headache."

"Good," her mother stood near the door, her eyes meeting her daughters. She only wanted the best for her only child— the child she had prayed for after five straight years of miscarriage after miscarriage. When Shari had been born, Linda had promised that she would always take care of her—that her daughter would want for nothing. She often wondered why Shari couldn't see that. Linda opened her mouth, then quickly closed it, deciding against saying more. "Well, sleep tight. I'll see you in the morning. Breakfast is at 7:30."

Shari groaned. Breakfast for the Thomas Family, small as they were, was nothing short of a Cecil B. DeMille production. And Shari was sure that her mother would prepare more than enough. Shari decided against protesting. "Okay. See you in the morning. Nite, mom."

With the door closed and her mother gone, Shari slipped back into her day dream of Hamilton. She pictured him sitting in the church, watching her as she strolled down the church's aisle, his light eyes and chocolate face an intense contrast to the other.

Shari shut her eyes and let sleep overcome her. Her last thoughts were of Hamilton as he carried her in his large arms.

CHAPTER 6

Circular clothing racks surrounded Shari as she made her way down the highly polished, marble-tiled aisle. She straightened blouses on their respective hangers and removed items that didn't belong in the Misses Collection, the department she was head buyer for. After several days at home, with her mother, father and Mrs. Ponticello fussing over her constantly, followed by a week of non-stop meetings out of her office, she was more than happy to be back to work and it showed as she hummed a no-nothing tune, her high-heeled sandals made a clacking noise as she moved.

Shari paused and watched the young sales clerk behind the sales counter. She watched the young girl, whom she guessed was no more than nineteen, and chuckled to herself. It had been years since she was a sales clerk, responsible for assuring the area was neat and presentable, assisting customers with their selections. Sales had put change in her pocket during college and had solidified her love of fashions.

Shari sidestepped customers as they moved from one rack to the next. She winced when she spotted a cherub faced baby lean over in his stroller and grab a silk blouse, placing the sleeve of the teal-colored fabric into his mouth, signs of drool now evident.

"Hey, Puddin'," Shari began, smiling as she squatted in order to be face to face with the rosy-cheeked the baby. "Don't eat the clothes." She laughed, then firmly, but slowly removed the article from the child's mouth, while simultaneously removing the blouse from its rack. Shari stood and smiled as the child's mother apologized repeatedly, the young sales clerk coming to join them. Shari smiled politely. "Not a problem. This is washable silk — no harm done."

Shari handed the blouse to the clerk, both concealing grins, and continued toward the bank of elevators at the rear of the store, which would lead her to the offices located on the twelfth floor.

"Hi, Shari," Toni, the receptionist said, smiling at her. Shari nodded, then returned the greeting.

"Hey Toni. Any messages?" Shari asked.

"Tons." Toni placed the messages into Shari's hand. "Oh, and this package is for you."

Shari looked at the large box and noticed the return address. She smiled broadly, then walked into her office.

"Don't forget the meeting at 3 o'clock." Toni called after her.

Shari nodded, then closed the door. She set the package on her desk, removed her cream crochet sweater coat. She smiled again as she tore open the box. She laughed loudly as she lifted the items from the box. A pair of stark white Nike's, a large, blue water bottle, a box of Advil, and a neatly bounded jump rope. Shari noticed the note at the bottom of the box.

"You will need each and everyone of these items if you think you will win. Call me. 555-5754. Hamilton."

Shari picked up the sleek black phone on the corner of her antique mahogany desk. She dialed the number. As she listened to the exchange ring, she was interrupted by the sound of Toni's voice over the intercom.

"There's a Mr. Edmunds on line one for you."

It had been two weeks since the accident and one week since she had heard from Hamilton. His surprise package had given her reason to call him.

"Thanks, Toni." Shari tapped the flashing button. "Well, Mr.

Edmunds, so nice to hear from you again."

"Hey, Shari. How have you been?" Hamilton asked sheepishly. There was just no excuse for his not calling her before now, and he knew he would only insult her if he gave her some feeble excuse about being busy.

"I'm doing well," Shari replied smoothly, when what she really wanted to do was chew his head off for making her hope. She thought of his full lips and how the sensuous, heady feeling she got when he had pressed them against hers. *Girl, what are you thinking?* She chided herself. She cleared her throat before speaking. "You know I was just about to call you. I got your package."

Hamilton laughed. He had wanted to call her everyday, but talked himself out of it every time he reached for the telephone. He didn't want to seem pushy, like he was desperate. But at the insistence of one of his older sisters, Haley, he decided to contact Shari. "Are you ready, Miss Thomas?"

"Ready to watch you cook for me? You bet I am. When and where?" She was glad Hamilton wasn't sitting across from her, for her mind conjured up an image of the brick-built Hamilton standing in her kitchen with nothing but an apron tied around his waist. She shook her head, loosening the electric-erotic thought.

"I'll let you know, but be forewarned, I'm quite competitive and I normally get what I want."

The double entendre wasn't missed. "Well, Mr. Edmunds, there's a first time for everything. So, I guess you better break out them pots and pans, and put on your best apron, because brother, you are going to be one cooking man!" Shari laughed along with Hamilton. "And I don't like micro waved food."

"Got cha," he replied then changed the subject. "Hey, I'm sorry I haven't called you lately. Umm, how's your head?"

Shari thought of the searing kiss they shared the day he brought her home from the hospital. It remained engraved in her mind and on her lips. She grappled to control her emotions. "It's fine," she replied.

"Okay, so how about letting a brother make it up to you. What are you doing on this beautiful, warm evening?"

"I'm not sure right now. Why?"

"Well, I was wondering if we could go out and grab a bite to eat. Possibly take in a movie."

"Can I get back to you later?" Shari began. "I need to make a few calls." She lied. No sense in letting him think there weren't other men begging to be in her company. Shari smirked. Who was she fooling. She had wanted to call him a thousand times since that kiss.

"Sure," came Hamilton's response, even though he wanted to ask her how long it would take for her to get back to him.

"I'll call you," Shari replied. "Bye Hamilton."

"Later." He held the phone as the line went dead.

Shari looked at her appointment book. The only appointments she had penciled in her book was a home-made oatmeal facial, a bag of microwave popcorn and a movie on HBO. *This is crazy*, Shari murmmured. *Call that man and go out with him.* Fifteen minutes later, Shari picked up the phone and dialed the number on the card which accompanied the gifts he had delivered.

"Hamilton Edmunds."

"It's Shari."

Hamilton stiffled a laugh. He knew the game. "What's up?"

"Umm," Shari began. "What time?"

"What time?" he repeated. He had to make her sweat.

"Yeah, what time are you picking me up?" Shari blurted out, then heard him chuckled.

"I thought you had a few calls to make?"

Why is he making this hard? She frowned. "They are all taken care of." She blew out a breath of frustration. She could see he wasn't going to make this easy. "So, what time should I be ready?"

He tapped his fingers on his desk. He decided that maybe she had had enough. "How's seven-thirty?"

"Seven-thirty is good."

"How about I pick you up at your place?"

"Okay, my place is fine."

"See you at 7:30."

Shari placed the receiver on its base and reeled back in her office chair. She smiled broadly as images of Hamilton ran amok. She wondered if he could be any sexier than she remembered.

Shari became giddy—felt like a school girl asked to the prom by the most popular boy. She gasped and looked down at her attire, though chic in her black slacks and black, sleeveless silk blouse, she felt it wasn't suited for a first date with Hamilton. And then there was her hair, pulled back into a pony tail, held in place with a black scrunch. She looked at the clock, then picked up the phone.

"Frankie," Shari began, speaking to her hair stylist. "Can you hook a sister up today?"

"What's up, today? Deb just called."

"Really. What time is she coming?"

"Said she'll be here by 2:30."

"Well, I don't know about Deb, but I've got a date."

Frankie squealed. "Watch out now!" Shari laughed at her response. "If you're here by three sharp, I can get you in and out of here in an hour."

"Great! I'll be there."

Frankie laughed. "Must be a hot date. You haven't needed an emergency hair-do in a long time. It'll be good having you and Deb here at the same time. It's been a long time."

"Sure has," Shari smiled into the receiver. "I'll see you later."

Shari hung up the receiver, then dove into her work, eating lunch at her desk. At 2:30, she rose from her desk, gathered her things and headed out of the office. She knew it would take her approximately 30 minutes to get to Frankie's. She stopped only long enough to say goodbye to her assistant, then sped out the door to her new car. Her insurance company had totaled her Alero, replacing it with a fully loaded, champagne gold Toyota Avalon.

As Shari cruised south on Michigan Avenue, she was grateful for the light Friday afternoon traffic. Everyone seemed to be heading into the city, not out.

When she arrived at Frankie's, she spotted Deb's forest green Range Rover parked in the lot adjacent to the salon.

"Hey, Sista!" Shari called out as she walked into the salon, her head held high. She stopped in front of Deb, as she sat in Frankie's styling chair, then bent at the waist, and placed a kiss on her best friends cheek while simultaneously wrapping her in an embrace. "Frankie told me you were going to be here. How's my baby and my man?"

Deb returned the loving gestured and laughed. "Watch it. They are both fine. Frankie here says you got a hot date. With who?"

Shari nodded, then sat in the black leather styling chair next to Deb, and watched as Frankie combed through Deb's wet, shoulder length hair. "Yes, I've got a date. And you know who it is?" Shari snickered. "Your cousin. You do remember your cousin, don't you?" She raised her right eyebrow. "I mean, you gave him all the phone numbers I own."

Deb covered her mouth, then laughed again. "Umm-mm, oh yeah, Hamilton. Fine and Sexy Hamilton." Deb looked up at Frankie.

"Girl, that brother is one cutie." She turned her attention back to Shari. "So, where's he taking you?"

"Wait," Shari held up her hand. "Why haven't I met him before. He wasn't at your wedding. Why am I just meeting him?"

"Well, when Darrin and I got married he was out of town or something like that. Then you were dating Bruce. When you two broke up, he was just coming out of a relationship himself. But he's free now. So, where are you guys going?"

Shari shook her head. "He said to dinner and maybe a movie."

"Are you guys just now hooking up?"

"I've been busy."

"Busy? Too busy to hook up with Hamilton? That's crock, Shari." Deb turned her head fully to face Shari. "That's not like you, girl. Not like you at all."

"So," Shari stated, then looked at Frankie, a plead of "help" flashed across her face.

"I'm not in it," Frankie replied, turned Deb's head around, then added conditioner to her wet hair.

Shari shrugged her shoulders. "I mean, he's good looking and all, but a man that damn fine has to have a girlfriend."

"I told you he was single."

"But that doesn't mean he don't have a chick on the side."

"Girl, *pahleezze*," Deb drawled out. "Hamilton's not the type. Besides, that hasn't stopped you before," Deb said, then clarified upon a loud gasp from Shari. "I don't mean that you go after unavailable men. It's just that you've always been much more outgoing than me."

Shari couldn't respond. It was true. Between the two, she had been the one who could walk right up to a brother and introduce herself. She'd never had a problem picking up the phone and making the first call, either. But lately Shari had begun to find the dating scene tiring and her good nature had slowly given way to a solemn one. She thought about Hamilton. If he asked her out, then the possibility of him having a girlfriend was remote. Then again, for the past year she had met more than her share of men with wives or girlfriends—long term ones at that. Those were the ones that made her tired of the dating scene.

"Well he called today and asked me out," she stated, then went on to tell of the items she received in the package Hamilton had sent and what they meant.

"Get out girl!" Deb squealed. "I didn't know that. Darrin never said a thing about it." Deb twisted her mouth upward, then titled her head to one side. "And he claims to be able to jump double dutch? Better than most women?" She looked up at Frankie, her eyebrows raised, amusement mixed with curiosity filled her brown eyes. "That's a little...umm, odd. Wouldn't you say?"

"I thought the same thing, but girl, I have got to see this."

"Okay, so what are you gonna wear tonight? Something hot, I hope?"

The pair looked at each other, then doubled over in laughter. "Girl, don't do it. I'm warning you." Shari waved her manicured hand in the air, then pointed at Deb.

"What?" Deb feigned ignorance, her hand fanned across her chest. "I haven't a clue as to what you are talking about." She ended with a slight chortle. "I would never interfere in your relationship like you did mine." Deb widened her eyes.

"Yes you would. Let me handle this? Okay? No interference."

"If you say so," Deb responded, holding up her hands to show Shari her fingers were crossed. Shari shook her head and knew that revenge was a mother, for she had meddled several times in getting Deb and Darrin together.

After an hour and a half, Shari and Deb emerged from the salon. They chatted for a moment, hugged then went in their respective directions, with Shari promising to call Deb the next day with details of her date with Hamilton.

"Wait." Deb called out from the parking lot. "Are we still on for Sunday?"

"Sure are. What time?"

"How about 10:30. We can make 11 o'clock mass. Darrin will watch Daneda. And we can do a little shopping after church."

"Sounds good to me. I'll talk to ya later."

Shari got into her car and headed home. Once there, she walked Rocket, dragging the dog along hurriedly versus the normal leisure stroll they embarked on every evening when she was in town. After walking Rocket, she showered and dressed. She had at least another half an hour before Hamilton would be ringing her bell. She decided to return a few calls.

The sound of the door chimes interrupted her last call to her parents.

"Mom, give my love to Dad. I'll call you guys on Sunday." She hung up the receiver.

"Who is it?" she spoke into the intercom.

"Hamilton."

Shari depressed the entry button. She inhaled deeply and thought about Deb's statement of Hamilton being single. Still, she mused, it stands to reason that a man that fine couldn't possibly be at home dateless on Friday night. She shook the thoughts from her mind and settled on being just his friend, if that was possible.

"Hi, there," Hamilton stopped short of the top stair. "You look really nice." He laughed when the dog's head appeared around Shari's leg, whining loudly. "Okay, Rocket. You look nice too." The dog barked, then jumped up on Hamilton, her front paws resting on his chest.

"Rocket!" Shari pulled the dog down by its collar. "That's not nice."

Hamilton squatted down and began rubbing the dog behind its ears, followed by her stomach when Rocket rolled over on her back.

"Seems as if she really likes you. She doesn't let everyone rub her like that. You seem to have a way with babies and animals."

Hamilton nodded, then looked up as Shari leaned against the door jam— picture perfect, he thought as his eyes absorbed her. He dared not look too long. "You look nice."

"Thank you Hamilton. You don't look so bad yourself. Come on in." Shari said as she watched him interact with Rocket. As Hamilton rose to stand, she took in his large form from head to toe. Dressed in linen, Hamilton looked as if he stepped out of a magazine, his mustache and goatee trimmed to perfection, his bald head smooth and round. When he passed her, she inhaled deeply—he was wearing the cologne he had when she first met him. It was wrecking havoc on her senses. If there was one thing she loved, it was a good smelling man. Shari was in tuned to fragrances—her senses could call forth an image of a man based solely on the cologne he wore. For Hamilton, the image was of him carrying her in his large arms, holding her close to his broad chest was the image that would come forth.

"You ready to go?" Hamilton asked. Rocket righted herself and came to sit by his feet. "No, Rocket," Hamilton looked down at the animal. "You can't go."

As if understanding, Rocket left Hamilton's side and laid down in front of the door.

"Sure," Shari replied. "Let me grab my purse, keys, and wrap." Shari thought of the last time he was in her apartment. His kiss was still on her lips.

"I won't be but a minute."

He nodded his head and watched as Shari turned and headed toward her bedroom. He shook his head slightly, for the sarong red print skirt and olive silk tank she wore showed enough of her shapely thighs and full breasts to make a priest reconsider his vows. Hamilton sucked in his breath. He had been celibate for almost a year. Following his last date, he felt he had to examine why he was attracting what Matthew, his best friend, had called "chicken heads," for all he seemed to attract were crazy women. Besides, he knew that sex had complicated many relationships, and had ruined many potential friendships. Still he found Shari desirable, the look in her warm eyes belied a fierceness that attracted him and made him want to get to know her better. Much better.

"I'm ready." Shari moved Rocket, then shut and locked the door. Hamilton took her wrap from her and stretched out his hand to her. "Where are we going?"

"I know a nice little soul food restaurant on east 75th Street. Army and Lou's. Have you eaten there before?"

"Yeah. Everybody's been there. Even our late mayor ate there. Hell, you'd have your Negro card revoked if you haven't stepped inside the place at least once in your life."

They laughed as they headed to Hamilton's Expedition. Shari paused. Hamilton stood next to her.

"What's wrong?"

"I'm a little short," Shari said, letting her eyes travel from the bottom of the step leading into the vehicle. "These things should have a step stool." Shari thought of the last time she had to climb up into a SUV while wearing a skirt. That time her skirt had been longer than the short sarong she was wearing.

"Here." Hamilton placed his hands about Shari's waist and lifted her. "How's that?"

"Fine," Shari gasped, Hamilton's face inches from hers. She could make out the tiny pours on his chocolate face. Her waist felt hot and she swore he had seared her where his hands rested. Shari blinked. The heady sensations returned. She averted her eyes, casting them downward, her lashes hiding them. Hamilton's hands slipped away.

"Ready?" Hamilton asked as he slid into the drivers seat, then pulled away from the curb. Shari nodded her head.

"You know, I wasn't sure you'd go out with me." Hamilton glanced at Shari. "I mean, a woman as beautiful as yourself has to have a line of men at her door."

Shari sniffed back a laugh. She wanted to say it was so, but truth be told there wasn't any and hadn't been for some time. She looked up into his face, which drew her like a magnet, and the curiosity of what lay behind his eyes intrigued her. He was waiting for an answer.

"Currently, I am not in a relationship."

The curiosity was quickly replaced with relief. As Shari watched him, she had to admit to herself that she wanted to get to know Hamilton better—see what made Hamilton tick. But she also wanted to tread lightly—for the last thing she wanted was to be unsure, to have her feelings tumble out of control. No. She was never to be out of control. Strung out like some crack addict. But, then again ... She looked into his face, watching his eyes crinkle from the grin he gave her. She shivered as he placed her hand to his full lips, pliantly kissing the back of her hand.

"Glad to hear you say that," he responded turning his head forward, attempting to focus on the flowing traffic, one hand on the steering wheel, the other firmly entwined with Shari's. "I was a little worried there for a moment."

Shari looked at his large hand interlocked with her small hand, her gaze swept over his short nails, then up the thick veins visible under his skin. She didn't bother to remove her hand from his—it all felt too right, as if by design.

CHAPTER 7

Hamilton held the door for Shari to enter the restaurant. Every head turned as the couple approached the waitress standing near the door.

"Hey, handsome," the waitress said, followed by a kiss on his right cheek. "How's things? How's your mom? Your sisters?"

"Hi, Mrs. Washington." He returned the kiss, holding the waitress about her waist. The woman's crystal brown eyes brightened, enhancing her cocoa complexion. "Everyone's fine. How've you been? And Mr. Washington?"

"Good, baby. We're doing good. You know our 40th wedding anniversary is next week?"

"Forty years! How did he put up with you for so long?" Hamilton teased, then ducked as Miss Washington swatted him on his shoulder. "Mind your manners, boy." Her smile broadened. She then looked at Shari standing next to him. "And who's this pretty young lady?"

Hamilton smiled. "Miss Washington, this is Shari."

The waitress pulled Shari into a hug. "Glad to meet you baby. Come on ova here, an' let me seat you at my baby's favorite table."

Shari looked up into Hamilton's face and smiled. He took her hand in his and led her to the waiting booth. He sat across from her.

"Yall, take your time. I'll be back with your drinks."

Hamilton smiled as the older woman walked away. "She use to baby sit me and my sisters," he said. "She's like a second mom. Been working here for forever."

"She seems really nice."

"That she is. Took good care of us when mom and dad went out or took a vacation without us, which was at least once a year. And she was quick with a wooden spoon, too."

Shari watched his eyes twinkle and laughed as he told of one mischief after another embarked upon by he and his sisters.

"Yall eat up, now," Mrs. Washington ordered as she placed steaming plates of smothered pork chops, topped with gravy, greens, candied sweets, okra, corn and hot water corn bread on the table. "And, honey." She patted Shari's hand. "You come back and see me anytime. It's good to see this boy out on a date for once. Ain't been on a date in I don't know how long." Mrs. Washington grinned, then walked away.

Shari laughed at the look of pure embarrassment plastered on Hamilton's face. Unbeknownst to Mrs. Washington, she had inadvertently confirmed Deb's statement. Hamilton was dateless.

As they ate, Hamilton provided Shari with bits and pieces of his life. By the end of dinner, Shari knew each of his sister's names, all beginning with the letter "H," his many nieces and nephews, and his love of writing. He was in the midst of writing his first book—a murder mystery. She had smiled at that one, for when he spoke of his dream he did so with a vigor she hadn't experienced with anyone. She found it both frightening and refreshing.

"How about we skip the movie and go to the opening of this art gallery in Bronzeville? A friend of mine is a photographer and he opened his own studio, which will include stills, sculptures and some oils—work by other artists."

"Who's the photographer?"

"Bryant Johnson. I know you've heard of him, maybe even seen some of his work. He's really talented. His gallery is called Steelelife."

"I've heard the name, but I have yet to see any of his work."

"You game? Or would you like to go to the movies instead?"

"No, I'd love to go to the gallery."

Hamilton placed several bills on the table, waved goodbye to Mrs. Washington, then took Shari's hand in his. He assisted Shari into the Expedition, buckled her seat belt, then climbed behind the drivers wheel. He pulled away from the curb slowly, for if he sped then the evening would end too soon.

They pulled up in the front of the two-story building, located on the historic King Drive boulevard near 47th Street. Hamilton assisted Shari from his vehicle and escorted her into the building.

Shari loved the layout, the large open area, its walls exposed white-washed brick. Her sandals made loud click-clacking sounds as she stepped across the gleaming maple hard wood floors to stand in front of an oil painting. Her eyes couldn't pull away from the vibrant hues used to portray the face of a woman, her head high, as if in a defiant pose. Shari stepped closer and read the title: *Head Held High*. She stepped back, tilting her head slightly to the right. She liked the painting.

"That's one of Tara's," Hamilton stated proudly as he came to stand next to Shari, who looked up into his face, noticing the proud glint in his eye.

"You know her personally?" She asked, attempting to hide the cautious tone in her statement.

"Yup. Tara Banfield. We went to grammar school together. She's quite talented."

"Are you guys friends?"

"Yup."

"Is she going to be here tonight?"

"Naw. She's in New York," Hamilton replied, then looked at Shari out of the corner of his eye, noting the pensive expression on her face.

"She's there with her husband."

"That's nice." Was all Shari could say. When in fact she wanted to scream, because she had never been the jealous type and didn't know what had come over her. If there was a rock nearby, she surely wanted to crawl under it. Her thoughts were interrupted by a voice behind them.

"Hamilton!" a medium built man, the color of cool caramel, his dreadlock's kissing the nape of his neck, stated as he grasped Hamilton's hand, then pulled him into an embrace. "Man, I'm glad you could make it."

"So am I. Bryant, this is Shari. Shari, this is the talented photographer, Bryant Johnson."

"Please to meet you." Bryant took Shari's hand in his. "So, what do you think?"

"This piece is really nice."

"Yeah, I agree. Tara's got a real eye. It's for sale, you know?"

Hamilton grinned at Bryant. "Forever the salesman. How much?"

"Oh, no, Hamilton. I can't afford it." Shari protested.

He looked at her. "I didn't ask you if you could afford it or not." He faced Bryant. "How much?"

"Well, its an original oil on canvass. First in its series. It's going for twenty-five hundred."

"Too rich for my blood," Shari replied. She looked from Hamilton to Bryant, then moved to examine the other various oils, as well as black and white photographs hung upon the exposed brick. As she stood examining another oil by Tara, this one of a woman surrounded by several hues of vibrant reds, she felt someone staring at her. Turning, her eyes became large as she watched Bruce standing across the room. He nodded his head in her direction, a slight smile across his handsome face, just as an attractive woman appeared by his side. She continued to watch him as he took the woman by the hand and led her to the door. It had been over a year since she had last laid eyes on Bruce.

A light tap on her shoulder startled her.

"What's wrong?" Hamilton asked as Shari turned to face him, his hands about her arms.

"Nothing," she smiled, knowing the gesture didn't quite reach her eyes.

"Ready to go?" Hamilton looked over her head in time to see Bruce turn in their direction. He felt Shari stiffen.

"No, not yet. I haven't seen all the works," Shari responded, hoping she convinced Hamilton, for she didn't want to chance running into Bruce and his date outside. The entire scene was surreal, Shari thought as she glanced over her shoulder at the now empty spot that Bruce had just occupied. Turning her attention back to Hamilton, she watched as his hazel eyes darkened.

"I guess not," Hamilton stated, then stepped back when he heard Bryant call his name. "I'll be right back," he excused himself and went over to where Bryant stood at a photograph.

Shari wandered over to another oil painting, its subject mere colors and form. She was thinking of the last time she saw Bruce—the night he had come to her and called off the engagement and the wedding. She shivered, not because she was angry, but because Bruce had had the foresight and the common sense to see what she wouldn't allow herself to see. That she hadn't loved him.

After an hour of looking at all of the artwork on display, Shari and Hamilton left. He paused along the side walk, shifting his body slightly toward her to let a couple pass them. Silently, they walked to his vehicle. Shari noticed the change in his mood.

"My turn," Shari placed her hand on Hamilton's arm. "What's

wrong?"

"Nothing," Hamilton lied. He had seen the look in the man's eyes as he stood across the room looking at Shari. Then there was the stiffness in Shari's shoulders when Hamilton had touched her. Not again, he warred. Not another Nicky.

"Yes it is. Tell me." Her voice was low.

Hamilton didn't like what he was feeling—didn't like the sudden pang of jealously mixed with insecurity. *She isn't Nicky*, he reminded himself. He shrugged his shoulders and decided to change the direction the whole conversation was attempting to go in. He wrapped his arm around Shari's shoulder and pulled her close. "Nothing's wrong." He looked into her eyes, her long eyelashes nearly touched the tops of her brows. "Hey, the night's still young." He looked at his watch. "How about we go to the 63rd Street Beach?"

"Sounds good to me," Shari replied, deciding to let him change the subject. Besides, she had to admit that she wasn't quite ready for the night to end. She was truly enjoying Hamilton's company.

Shari settled her body into the coolness of the leather seats, then looked up and out of the moon roof, shielded in a black tint, the moon and stars followed them as Hamilton drove them to the beach.

"I love this beach. The city has done wonders with it, restoring it and all." Hamilton stated as he maneuvered the vehicle into a parking spot. "Do you remember how it once looked?" Shari nodded. "Then you know this is a miracle in comparison to how it was."

"Yeah. I use to come down here on Sunday's and listen to the Rasta's jam. I love Reggae, so it became a Sunday ritual," Shari said.

"You too?" Hamilton smiled. "So, did I. I wonder why I never saw you?"

Hamilton stepped out of the truck, then proceeded to assist Shari. He stopped short as he lifted her, her lithe body slid down his. He cleared his throat in hopes of clearing his head. This sister was too much.

"Let's go sit on the bench."

Shari took Hamilton's offered hand in hers and headed toward a solitary bench feet from the shore. Shari sat on the seat, while Hamilton sat on the back of the bench. He looked down at her. "I have to admit, I've truly enjoyed this evening." He bit his lower lip. He was beginning to sound like he had never been anywhere, had never had a date. This dating thing, he thought, was too much pressure.

"Well, kind sir," Shari stood. "Same here." She walked toward the shore, her ample hips involuntarily swayed with the rhythmic sound of the waves. She smiled when Hamilton appeared beside her.

"So, Miss Lady, you've let me talk the whole night away, but you've said very little about yourself."

Shari smiled demurely. "What do you want to know?" she asked, her right eyebrow lifted as she glanced up at Hamilton. She liked what she saw.

"Okay, so far all I know is that you live blocks from me and your parents baby you. Other than that ... ."

"Well, I grew up here in Chicago, the only child of Linda and Leonard Thomas. They tried to have other children, but weren't successful, so my father doted on me. I went to catholic schools."

Hamilton interrupted her. "Oh, one of those." He smiled. Shari swatted his arm playfully.

"No! Not one of those. Don't let the rumor about catholic school girls fool you. And I'll admit, I was quite popular, but only because I could sew. My grandmother, Eliza, taught me when I was a young girl, so by the time I got to high school I was designing my own gear. Of course, everyone wanted me to sew for them. I almost didn't make it to prom, 'cause I was late making my own dress."

"Wow, a designer."

Shari went on to tell of her majoring in economics, with fashion design as a second major and her plans to some day branch out on her own.

"A design company?" Hamilton said. "Have you given any thought to a name for your company?"

"Well, yes, but I'm not ready to tell. Not just yet. It's in its infancy stage and I don't want to jinx myself."

Silence fell over them. Each in their own private thoughts. Shari liked what she saw in his eyes as she told him her dream. He seemed to understand as she talked animatedly about being a designer, explaining her love for the business, her eye for fashion. Before, she had been reluctant to tell anyone, for she didn't want the response she got from Bruce when she told him of her idea of quitting her job and starting her own clothing line. He had laughed at her and had even gone so far as to tell her she was crazy for leaving the comfort of her job to "chase some pipe dream."

Bright lights from an on-coming car blinded them. Hamilton grabbed Shari by the waist and moved her behind him. A cracked voice seeped out over a loud speaker. "The beach is closed, Hamilton."

Shari looked up at Hamilton who had a large grin plastered on his face. He took Shari by the hand and led her to the police cruiser. "Hey man, what's up?" Hamilton reached inside the open window and grasped the outstretched hand of the officer.

"Not a whole lot. I saw your truck parked back there and decided to harass you."

Hamilton laughed. "So much for Chicago's finest. Oh, wait. Where are my manners? Shari Thomas, this is Matthew Le' Blanc, my best friend and one of the most corrupt cops on the whole force."

"Well, it takes one to know one," Matthew replied, then looked at Shari. "A pleasure to meet you." Matthew shook Shari's hand. She hadn't realized she was holding her breath until she absently let out a sigh. She was relieved that Hamilton knew the officer. "I hope I didn't scare you, Shari."

"Actually you did."

"Some first impression," Matthew chuckled, then turned his attention to Hamilton. "But hey, you two do know that the beach is closed. Right? I could run you both in for disobeying the law."

"Umph, ain't that nothing," Hamilton laughed. "As a matter of fact, Officer Friendly, we were just about to leave, weren't we, dear?" Shari nodded. "See? And we're off. I'll get back with you later, okay?"

Shari watched as the two clasped hands again. Matthew waved, then drove off.

"Sorry 'bout that. Matthew has his own brand of humor. Sorry he frightened you."

"How did you know?"

"I felt your heart beating against my back," Hamilton smiled. "Girl, it was beating a million miles a minute." He tried to shield his eyes. What he wanted to say was how good her breasts felt pressed against the small of his back. He fought to control his growing hardness.

"Hey, I didn't want to become a statistic."

"Not fair. Not all cops are bad. As a matter of fact, its typically one or two that make the whole force look inept. Matt's a good cop. He volunteers and sincerely cares about his beat. He's one dedicated cop."

"Woa, Cowboy! I didn't mean to ruffle your feathers. It's just that . ."

"You didn't. I just don't want you to believe all the bad you've heard and read. There is always two sides to every story."

"And let me guess, as an editor you ensure that both sides get printed?" Shari replied. Hamilton smiled and nodded his head in response. "How admirable."

"I could take that response two ways, but I'll take it in the vein in which I hope it was given. As a compliment."

They returned to the truck, with Hamilton again picking Shari up and placing her gently in its cab. He walked around the truck and slid behind the drivers seat. He looked at her, his eyes swept across her face. He remained silent. Shari watched him soak her up like a sponge and wondered what he could be thinking. He shook his head slightly, gave a searing "tsk" then started up the truck.

"What does that mean?"

"Girl, you are truly something else."

"I guess that's a compliment?"

"None other."

At Shari's apartment, Hamilton did what he had been doing all night: lifted her out of the truck.

"Mr. Edmunds, this has truly been a wonderful evening." Shari stood at the curb. "Thank you."

Hamilton bowed slightly at the waist. "No, Princess, thank you."

Shari blinked. "Princess?!"

"Yes, Princess," he replied, his smooth dark eyebrows raised.

"My father calls me Princess."

Hamilton came to stand close to Shari. She felt his warm breath float across her face. His eyes were hot and intense. "Well, then I shall make you my queen. I've enjoyed assisting you in and out of this carriage all night. You must allow me to do it again. Soon."

Shari blushed at his words. This brother was on cue. "We will have to see about that." Shari walked toward her door. "Good night."

"Wait!" Hamilton rushed up the walk. "At least let me see you safely to your apartment." Shari shrugged and allowed him to enter behind her. He kept his eyes averted to the carpeted stairs—the sway of her hips were too much to bear.

At the top of the stairway, Shari turned and faced Hamilton. "Goodnight and thanks again."

"The pleasure's been mine," he leaned his tall frame against the door jam, a slight smile spread across his full lips. Shari didn't know what to do. She had wanted to kiss him the whole night and now that the evening had come to an end, she wasn't sure if she should. As if reading her rambling thoughts, Hamilton bent and placed a kiss on Shari's lips. She heard him mumble the word "sweet," as he pulled back, tipped his hand to his forehead and left.

Shari closed the door behind her and stood with her back firmly planted on it. "What in the world am I going to do?" She looked down at Rocket sitting in front of her.

The sound of the ringing phone startled Shari and she, followed closely by Rocket, ran to her bedroom to pick up the extension. "Hello."

"Just wanted to say goodnight."

Shari grinned. "Now, that's sweet. If you're not careful, you won't ever get rid of me."

"That's my plan. Good night, Princess." Hamilton hung up before Shari could respond. When the phone rang again, Shari smiled.

"Yes, Hamilton."

"How'd you know it was me?"

"I'm psychic," Shari laughed.

"Would you like to go to a play on Thursday? The Other Cinderella is playing at the Black Ensemble Theater."

"Sure, what time?"

"The play starts at 8. I'll call you. Soon."

"Sounds good to me. Good nite, Hamilton."

"Goodnight, my queen."

Another brownie point, Shari mused as she hung up the phone, then prepared for bed. Once the lights were out, Shari let thoughts of Hamilton roam shamelessly through her head. Yes, she thought, this one might be a keeper.

CHAPTER 8

The white sand gave way to the pounding of Hamilton's bare feet as he ran along its length, his cleanly shaved head glistened in the sun, his wide chest covered in a fine mist of sweat, white trucks hugged his waist. Shari stretched out her arms to him, calling him to run faster. "Yes, come to me," she stated, her voice low and seductive.

As he neared, Shari absorbed the whole of him, his massive muscular legs, his taunt waist, his flat, cut abdomen. Shari's eyes became mere slits. She was going to have Hamilton here and now. As he stood in front of her, sweat glistening his dark chest, she pulled him to her, placed his arms about her, and captured his lips with hers. They sank slowly to the sand, their bodies meshed into one.

"Shari, I love you," he breathed before covering her face with kisses intended to burn a print into her soul.

"Hamilton," Shari whispered his name. "Make love to me."

The sound of the phone woke Shari out of her deep dream. Groggily she rolled over, not wanting to open her eyes, reached over to the night stand and picked up the receiver. "Hello," she stammered.

"Good morning. Sounds as if I woke you."

Shari sat up, a slow smiled formed on her lips, erotic images of a scantily clad Hamilton danced in her head. "That's okay. I need to get up. How are you this morning?"

"Good," Hamilton responded. "But I'll be even better if you tell me what you doing on this beautiful day?"

Trying to see you, Shari wanted to respond. "Oh, not much. I need to work on a few designs and some other stuff."

"Whoa, that's a lot for one day. Think you can squeeze in some play time?"

Baby, I'd play with you anytime, Shari thought. "Ummm, maybe."

"Aww, come on. Give a brother a break. It's been a long time since I've had such engaging company. Besides, there's the annual Reggae Festival at the South Shore Country Club today and I know you like Reggae music."

Shari laughed. "Oh, you do?"

"Yes, you told me you did. See, I remember. I have a good memory. I'll pack a picnic and we can sit on the grass and listen to some serious Reggae. I won't take no for an answer."

A grin appeared on Shari's face. True, she needed to finish the designs and get started on her plan to open her own business, but how could she turn down an offer to spend some more time with Hamilton. She breathed out. "Alright, since you put it that way. What time should I be ready?"

"The festival starts at noon and if we're going to get a good spot, I say lets get there at 11 o'clock. I'll be by to pick you up at 10:30. Sounds good?"

"Sounds great. Thank you."

"No, Princess, thank you. I'll see you in a couple of hours." Hamilton replied then hung up.

Shari replaced the receiver. So what I just saw him last night, she reasoned, fighting with an inner voice that tried to tell her to take it slow.

She got out of bed, then began to mentally check off the items in her closet, discarding one outfit after another, until she decided on a pair of yellow shorts, a white sleeveless cotton polo and white, low heeled sandals. She looked the clock—she could work on her designs for at least an hour.

Shari showered, then dressed in a pair of sweats, topped with a Negro League jersey proudly displaying the insignia of the Chicago American Giants. She walked down the back stairs of the two-flat to the basement, with Rocket close behind, where she had created her design studio with the blessings of Mrs. Ponticello.

In the basement, her eyes took in the large open room—two mannequins stood waiting near her drafting table, both dressed in unfinished creations. One mannequin was dressed in the beginnings of a woman's two-piece double breasted pant-suit of worsted wool, in a golden color of mustard. Shari ran her hand along the sleeve of the fabric—its softness reminded her of silk. The other mannequin boasted a sleek off the shoulder, formal beaded dress.

Shari blew her breath out of her mouth and walked over to her drafting table in the middle of the room. To its left, against the plain, dark paneled walls, sat two sewing machines—an old, coal black Singer once owned by her Grandmother, Eliza, and the other a small cream colored Singer. Shari preferred the older model, for when she sat down at the old machine memories of her grandmother and how she had patiently taught her to sew stole into her thoughts and carried her back to the easy, stress-free days down in DeWitt, Arkansas.

Eliza Philips Thomas had been a seamstress, sewing clothing for folks all across Arkansas. Her father's mother, Grandma Eliza, had patiently taught Shari how to make patterns from newspaper and how to stitch by hand. Shari smiled at the warm memory of she and her grandmother sewing in the little room at the back of the old, shot gun house, her grandmother bending over her as she placed her hand upon Shari's when she made a mistake. Her grandmother's words came to her as if she were standing beside her, "Passion, baby. Take your time and the passion for what you do will shine forth." Shari smiled, a slight tear rolled down her cheek as she thought of how her beloved grandmother had recently succumbed to Alzheimer's disease. The last time she visited her in New Mexico, she hadn't known who Shari was.

Shari wiped her eyes, then turned to the stereo, placing a tape into the player. The haunting music from the soundtrack of Schindler's List surrounded her as she decided to forego finishing the outfits on the mannequin's. She sat at her drafting table, looked up at the picture of she and her grandmother sitting at the old singer she now owned, then began to sketch. Her hands moved effortlessly across the large piece of paper, her fingers becoming covered with black dust from the charcoal crayon.

After an hour, she stopped, stood and stretched, her eyes finally settling on the picture. It was Hamilton dressed in a five-button blazer and cuffed slacks. Shari studied the drawing, trying to decide if she should share it with him or not.

"He'll think all I have is him on the brain." Shari stated to herself, but couldn't resist the pull of how she had captured the deep intensity of his light eyes—they held her, almost trance like, a slight mischeiviousness to them. Umm, she hummed, letting the drawing conjure up thoughts of the two of them, wrapped in a warm embrace, his eyes bored into hers. She blinked. "Get a grip," she said, then placed the picture to the side. She looked at other sketches she had completed and decided to work on the formal dress she had created for Deb. Deb had asked her to design a dress that she could wear at a black tie affair, which was to be held during the Blacks in Technology convention in one month.

Shari stood, stretched, and walked over to the stereo. She chose some reggae. She swayed her hips from side to side as the heavy base rumbled through the speakers. She shimmed over to the mannequin, picked up a thimble from the table near by, placed it on her right index finger, then threaded a needle with clear thread and removed the unfinished bodice from the mannequin. She began to stitch small iridescent beads along the cream colored bodice of the dress. She was so engrossed in what she was doing, she hadn't heard the phone ringing until Rocket began barking. Shari glanced at the clock, then sighed. She knew she wouldn't be able to finish the bodice today.

"Hello," Shari answered picked up the cordless phone, then turned down the music.

"Hey, soror. How are you?"

"Great, Denise. And you and Jon?"

"Well. We're doing well." Denise paused. Shari could hear the excitement in Denise's voice and wished, as always, that Denise would just spit out whatever it was she had to say. "So what's new? You know I live vicariously through you." Denise chuckled. Shari rolled her eyes upward. She loved her soror—loved her dearly—but this hesitating method of giving or getting information drove Shari crazy.

"Denise," Shari began, looking at the large plaque on the wall, their sororities crest carved across the top of the wood shield. "You've got something to say, so why don't you just spit it out, girl." She chuckled.

"You're just like Deb. You would think that after all these years the two of you would be accustomed to my beating around the bush by now." Denise chuckled. "Okay here it is—Jon and I are going to be parents in October."

"Oh, Denise, that's great," Shari exclaimed, followed by a pang of envy. She had never experienced the complicated emotion. She struggled to contain its raging effects.

"I haven't told Deb yet, so mums the word," Denise said.

"Sure, I'll keep quite. But, why are you just now saying anything?"

"I didn't want anyone to know until I made it to my second trimester."

"I understand. So how's the proud papa to be?" Shari asked, even as that wall of envy refused to tear itself down.

"He's so happy. You'd think he was pregnant the way he's been acting. Eating everything in sight and tired all the time." Denise laughed.

"Oh, Denise that's such great news. I'm too happy for you, girl! How are you feeling?"

"Tired," Denise responded. "But other than that, I'm okay. So far so good." Shari noted the hesitation in Denise's voice.

"What's the matter, Ne-Ne?" Shari asked, using the nickname she and Deb had given her in college. "I can hear it in your voice. Tell me what's wrong."

"I'm afraid. We've been here before."

Shari became still. Did I hear her correctly, she wondered. "What do you mean?" Shari didn't want to guess.

"Last year I had a miscarriage."

"And you told no one?"

"It was just so painful. That's why I didn't want Jon telling anyone until we made it to the second trimester, but he's been telling everyone. The man can't hold water." Denise chuckled. "He seems to feel as if this is it this time, especially since the ultra sound shows that we're having a boy."

"Oh, Denise, you should have said something."

"I know, but it was just too painful. You know what I mean?"

Shari wanted to say she did, but she couldn't. Instead, she just absently nodded her head. "Girl, you know we're here for you. You and Jon and the baby are in my prayers. So, if you need anything, you just call me. Okay?"

"Thanks, Shari, I will. Look, I gotta run. I need to call Deb and then head out to the store before Jon gets back. He has been hounding my every step, trying to make sure I take it easy." Denise snickered, but Shari could hear the tension in her voice. "So, I'll get with you later. How about dinner, here, Sunday after next?"

"Sounds good to me," Shari agreed. "Mention it to Deb. And you take it easy and I'll call you later to check up on you. I love ya, sis."

"I love you too. And why don't you bring Hamilton with you? I've already heard all about him from Deb." Before Shari could find out just what Deb had told her, Denise disconnected the call. Some things never change, Shari laughed as she placed the receiver on its base.

She felt bad for her earlier thoughts of envy. Sure she was happy, ecstatic even, for her two best friends, yet their lives only stood to show her how she had no one special to compliment her life. Shari didn't believe that a man completed a woman. Yet, she had to admit that she wanted what Deb and Denise had. No, she didn't covet their lives, she just wanted someone she could share her life with. A husband. A family of her own—someone to come home to everyday. Shari looked over at the sketch of Hamilton.

Shari began straightening her work area, placing her pencils and fabrics into their respective places. Images of Hamilton filtered in and out of her mind and she wondered if he felt the hot electricity that seemed to seep from them when they were in each other's presence. Sure, Shari had dated, had slept with a few men, but none had caused the hair on her neck to stand at full attention—not even Bruce.

Bruce. Shari couldn't believe that after a year of not running into him, no contact, out of the blue, she would see him again. She had wondered how he was doing, and had thought of contacting him just to tell him she was sorry. She knew that she should have paid attention to the little voice inside her when he proposed. But she hadn't. She frowned as she remembered the pained look in his eyes the evening he came to break off their engagement. It ended with a simple question, did she love him. She couldn't even look him in the eyes. He had turned and walked to away. She wanted to say I love you. She had even opened her mouth to say so, but nothing came out. She hadn't loved him. Not the way a woman is supposed to love the man she intends to spend the rest of her life with.

The strong, sudden feelings she was having over Hamilton confused her. She knew that he was the type of man she could become lost in. If she wasn't careful, he'd permanently sear her heart.

Again, the ringing phone broke her from her thoughts of Hamilton.

"Hello?"

"Hey Princess," Shari's father greeted her.

"Hi, daddy. What do I owe this honor? It's not Sunday. Is mom okay? Grandma?" Shari asked, as she shut off the lights and carried the cordless phone up the stairs with her so she could dress for her next date with Hamilton. She motioned to Rocket, opening the rear door leading to the back yard. Shutting the door she continued up the stairs to her apartment.

"Your mother is fine. Bossy as always. And your grandmother is the same. I just wanted to talk to my baby girl. How's things?"

Shari let out a deep sigh. "Fine. I just finished a few sketches."

"They're good, Princess. Real good. Reminds me of your grandmother."

"Thanks." Shari responded, smiling at the compliment. She set on the edge of her bed and removed her shoes. She figured now was as good a time as any to tell her father about her plans. "Hey, I want to run something past you."

"Sure, go ahead."

"Well, you've seen my work." Shari paused, said a silent prayer then continued. "And I really would like to start my own business. You know, full time." She became silent, steeling herself against the lecture she was sure her father would give her.

"I see. You're just like your grandmother. Did you know that my father worked from sun up to sun down, taking side jobs anywhere he could so that she could start her own business? I watched the sacrifice—the real love my mother had for sewing and how my father supported her one-hundred percent."

Shari remembered her grandmother talking about her grandfather, who had died the year she was born, but she didn't know he worked overtime so that Grandma Eliza could realize her own dreams.

"Princess, do you have a business plan? Start-up money?"

Shari's eyebrows raised. She wasn't sure she had heard her father correctly. He hadn't lectured her or attempt to talk her out of her idea, instead he seemed interested. "Daddy, I'm just about finished with the business plan. Deb gave me some ideas to incorporate into the plan. As for start-up money, I've saved about twenty grand."

"Oh, Princess, you're going to need much more than that. Why don't you send me the plan after you've added Deb's ideas and I'll look it over. I may want to invest."

Shari wanted to jump up and shout out loud. This wasn't like her father. He seemed changed and she wanted to know why.

"Dad?"

"Yes."

"Umm, what gives?"

"What do you mean?"

Shari inhaled deeply. "You know I expected you to tell me how crazy my idea is—to talk me out of it."

Shari's father paused before responding. "Time's precious. You've got to make the best of everyday you're given."

Shari chuckled nervously. Something wasn't quite right. "True that, dad. But something's up — something's happened. Tell me."

"I told your mother she should have told you."

"Told me what, daddy?" Shari asked. She steel herself. "Tell me what?"

Their call was interrupted by the call-waiting signal. "Hold on, Daddy — don't hang up!" Shari switched to the other line.

"Hello?"

"Hi, Shari. It's me, Hamilton."

"Hey, what's up?" Shari rushed.

"You okay?"

"My dad is on the other line."

"Got cha. Well, I'll be there in a half hour. Think you'll be ready?"

"I'll be ready. See you soon." Shari switched back to her father. "Daddy? You still there?"

"I could have called you back."

"No, it was Hamilton. We're going to the reggae fest today at South Shore.""

"Is Hamilton the guy Lucia told us about—the one who brought you home from the hospital?"

"Yes, and Daddy, he's okay."

"I guess he would have to be if you're going out with him again. What happened to Bruce?"

"Dad! Don't change the subject," she hissed into the receiver.

"I won't, but first tell me what happened to Bruce."

Shari shook her head. She knew that Mrs. Ponticello would tell her mother about Hamilton, so now was as good a time as any to tell her father about Bruce. Her mother had really liked Bruce, had wanted her to marry him, saying that as a doctor he was a good catch.

"Daddy, we broke up a little over a year ago."

"Why are you just now saying something?"

Shari shut her eyes and was instantly transported to childhood. She saw herself as a 10-year-old, standing in front of her father being scolded for some misdeed. She shook her head. I'm thirty-two not 10, she reminded herself. "Dad, mom was so hell bent on me marrying Bruce. It was the one thing she felt I did right."

"But you could have said something, Princess. I would have understood."

"Would you have, dad?" Shari implored. "And please don't take this the wrong way, but you always seem to stand by mom no matter what."

"That's what a husband is suppose to do. Stand by his wife. But don't think for one minute that when your mother is wrong I keep quiet. I just don't do it in front of you."

Shari heard him chuckle. "What's so funny?"

"Baby, you are more like your mom than you care to realize."

Shari went to the window and looked down, seeing Rocket sitting in the yard. She padded barefoot to the rear of the apartment, descended the stairs, then opened the door. She listened as her father went on tell her the many attributes she shared with her mother. "You two really need to talk. Anyway, finish telling me about Bruce."

"Not before you tell me what's going on—I've let you stall long enough."

Shari heard her father sigh. "About six months ago my I had a prostrate exam and the cells came back cancerous."

Shari jumped to her feet. "And you're just now telling me?"

"Princess, I'm sorry. I know it wasn't right, but the doctor said that it was in its early stages. So, once the surgery was over and a few sessions of chemotherapy ..."

"Surgery?! Chemotherapy?!" Shari shouted into the phone.

"What in God's name is wrong with you and mom?! How could the two of you keep something like that from me?"

"I'm sorry, princess. I know it wasn't right. You're a grown woman and we haven't treated you as such. The whole episode brought home the true meaning that life is frail."

Shari closed her eyes—her face flushed with anger. She breathed deeply through her nose, exhaling through her mouth. "Is the cancer in remission?"

"Yes. The doctor gave me a clean bill of health the day before we came to Chicago. I wanted to tell you then, but your mother thought it wasn't the right time. Is there ever a right time?

"Dad," Shari sighed. "Make me a promise—never keep anything from me. Promise?"

"Promise. Do you forgive me for not telling you?"

"Sure. I forgive you. I love you, daddy."

"I love you too. Now, back to Bruce."

Shari had to laugh. "Dad, what a segue." She paused, realizing that for the first time in her adult life that she and her father were having a real adult conversation. "Truth is: I realized that I didn't love him."

"Hell, I knew that," her father stated. "I just wondered when you would realize it."

Shari smiled, then chuckled. "What?"

"Girl, I'm still a man. And I have eyes. I knew it before either of you did."

"What about mom?"

"She knew it too, she just didn't want to acknowledge it."

"Just like me," Shari agreed.

"Yup. Just like you. So, how you holding up?"

"I'm fine. Bruce actually saved me when he broke off the engagement." Shari sat back down on the bed.

"Good. Hey, I've taken up enough of your time. You need to be ready when that young man comes calling. And don't forget to send me the business plan."

"I won't. I'll overnight it to you on Monday."

"I'll be looking forward to it. What about your mother?"

"Let me tell her."

"Will do, but do it soon — there's been enough secrets."

"I agree. Thanks, daddy."

"You're welcome. Oh, we're coming to Chicago for the Fourth of July. Got any plans?"

"I don't have any plans. Come on."

"Good. Get off the phone. I love you, Shari."

"I love you, too, Daddy." Shari ended the call and smiled broadly as she thought of the conversation she had with her father. Since his last visit, she had wondered why he seemed so different. Now she knew, even thought she would have never guessed it was his brush with cancer that changed him. She had to admit to herself that she really enjoyed talking to him, enjoyed sharing parts of her life with him. Now if she and her mother could talk like that ...

Shari stood and looked at her reflection in the full-length mirror of her closet. She was every bit of Linda Thomas, from her warm sepia complexion to her smoky brown eyes. But she had insisted that the similarity ended there—she thought her views were closer to her grandmother's. But talking with her father had made her realize how much alike they were. Her father was right, it was time she and her mother talked. They hadn't had a heart to heart talk since she was a teenager. And it was long overdue. She would make the time to discuss her life, her dreams and her break up with Bruce with her mother when she came for the Fourth of July.

Shari put the finishing touches on her make-up, dressed, then sat in her bay window to await Hamilton's arrival.

CHAPTER 9

Hamilton pulled up in front of Shari's two-flat. His mind twirled. He was sure that he was losing it. In all his 39 years, he had never a woman with so much fervor. He liked Shari—liked what he saw, liked the silky softness of her husky voice when she called his name. He had watched her the night before, as she listened to him talk. Hamilton had felt the charged attraction, the searing passion in her eyes as she stared at his lips. He was no fool, his four sisters saw to that, for he knew when a woman wanted him, but Hamilton wasn't interested in a hit-n-run encounter. He wanted substance. He wanted a woman he could grow with. He wanted marriage.

Hamilton's eyebrows rose at that last thought. He had only come close to marriage once, and her infidelity had caused a chasm in his heart so deep that even four years later, he still felt a twinge of pain when he thought of the woman he almost married.

Nicky Marquette was truly a beautiful woman, her deep creamy-tanned complexion, and honey-brown eyes, gave her an exotic look that both men and women seemed to drool over. She was built like a brick house—every curve accentuated the next—she was what many men would consider the perfect package.

Although a little high maintenance, Hamilton had been taken with Nicky the first time he had laid eyes on her at the annual Chicago Black Journalist gala affair. After dating for nearly two years, Hamilton had proposed and she excepted. Yet, a little voice in the back of his mind told him he made a bad decision. And it was that same voice which steered him to her condo and into her bedroom, where he stood in the doorway and watched his honey-eyed wife-to-be on the downstroke with some white guy. The guy turned out to be Nicky's boss.

Hamilton had used all his God-given strength to keep from killing them both. Instead, he politely announced his arrival, calmly packed his personal items and left.

Shari isn't Nicky, the voice stated firmly. But what about that guy last night? Hamilton shook loose the thought, then stepped out of the SUV and rang Shari's bell. After announcing his name, he walked up the stairs and was instantly greeted by his angel and Rocket, who greeted him at the foot of the stairs. Damn. He stared up at her as he walked up the stairs. She looked too good in her white polo and yellow shorts. He knew that he had to behave, for this siren in front of him exuded a sensuality and a passion he knew could singe him, possibly leaving him scarred for the rest of his life.

He shook his head slowly, loosening the erotic thoughts. "You're looking good."

"Thank you. Ready to go?"

"When ever you are," Hamilton replied as he stood over Shari and looked deeply into her eyes. They became less and less visible as his face neared hers. He just had to taste her lips.

He felt her hand stroke the side of his face as his lips met hers. She forced his lips open with her tongue, playing with his, willing it to convey a message of things to come. Hamilton accepted the challenge, meeting her all the way, as he pulled Shari's body close. He could feel the hardness of her nipples against his rib cage. He groaned against her lips, this woman will be the death of me, as he broke the kiss.

"Umm, Miss Thomas, I think we'd better go." Shari nodded her head. He continued to hold her, shifting his waist away from her. He wanted a few minutes—some time to regroup—to calm the unmistakable hardness in his pants. He rested his cheek in her hair, the fragrance swept up into his senses. He had to release her, or he would forget he was a gentleman.

As if reading his mind, Shari slipped from his embrace, excused herself, pulling a reluctant Rocket back into the apartment.

"Okay, I'm good to go," Shari announced, purse in hand as she pulled the door closed. She reached out and took Hamilton's hand in hers, then proceeded down the stairs. He assisted Shari into his Expedition then headed to the South Shore Cultural Center. During the drive, though their conversation was light, Hamilton couldn't help but wonder if his search was finally over. The voice in his heart told him that he needed to make sure that this woman was here to stay.

Shari and Hamilton stepped through the large French double doors reserved as a VIP entrance. As a board member for the South Shore Cultural Center, Hamilton had special privileges, like special entry to the annual festival, which gave them choice seating on the lawn. Shari looked out the doors, the lush green grass called her name, the water was inviting. How romantic, she thought, as they stepped down the marble steps and onto the grass. Hamilton nodded and shook the hands of several people, all board members he said to Shari, as they made their way to an area just feet away from the stage.

Shari took the blanket from Hamilton and spread it out, followed by the basket. She sat down then smiled up at him, noticing a curious look on his face as he stared at her.

"Are you okay?" she asked.

Hamilton nodded. How could he tell her that he wanted to share everything with her, wanted to see her again and again. He changed his thoughts, for there was just no way he could be having such strong feelings so soon for a woman he just met. No, it was too soon he told himself.

"I was just thinking how beautiful you look with the lake behind you. Almost like a picture. A perfect picture."

Shari blushed. "Hamilton, that's sweet. Come on, sit down." She patted the space next to her, then looked at her watch. "The first band is going to be on in an hour. What did you pack?"

He sat next to her and stretched out his long legs. She laughed at his mischievous grin as he opened the picnic basket. "Umm, let's see what we have here," he looked around, his light eyes playfully looked from side to side, then he pulled a bottle of wine from the basket. "We are not suppose to have alcoholic beverages on park property." He quickly stuck the bottle back in the basket. "Ahh." He moaned and Shari giggled as he pulled out several containers. An assortment of fruit was in one container. A creamy sauce in another. Finger sandwiches in yet another. All total, Shari counted seven containers.

"My God, Hamilton, who were you planning on feeding? All of Chicago?"

"I wasn't sure what to get, so I got a little bit of everything." He smiled. Shari loved it all—the way his light eyes lit up when he smiled, the way his full lips stretched across his even teeth when he laughed, the melodic cadence of his deep voice. Oh yeah, she liked this man, something fierce. He was doing and saying the things she admittedly wanted to hear—needed to hear to believe.

Shari's eyes absorbed him, taking in his broad chest, down to his long legs. She loved his legs—the dark, strong, muscular legs which begged to be touched. She hadn't touched him like she wanted, to leisurely stroke him from his bald head to his feet—explore every inch of his masculinity.

He caught her watching him. "Say, girl, what 'cha thinking?" Hamilton pulled Shari closer—hip to hip. "Or dare I ask?" he asked as his warm breath caressed her cheek.

"Honestly?"

"Yes, honestly."

"But I can be arrested." She teased.

"Oh, can you?" He looked into her eyes. "I've got bail," he whispered. "Tell me."

"I was just thinking how nice it would be to . . ." Shari was interrupted.

"Hey Hamilton," a petite, dark chocolate woman appeared. "Haven't seen you in a while." The diminutive woman leaned over, then placed a kiss on his cheek.

"Same here. How've you been, Kara?"

"Good. Can't complain. You gonna introduce me?" Kara asked, smiling. "Or have you taken leave of your senses?" She chuckled.

Shari looked at the woman. She looked familiar, she thought, then dismissed it, replacing it with the thought of how the woman was surely one of his many girlfriends. He's never told me about any of his past relationships, she bantered silently, but then again I didn't ask him either.

"Shari, this is Kara. Matthew's girlfriend."

"Please to meet you," Kara said, taking Shari's hand in hers. "Wait, I know you. You're Denise's soror."

Shari nodded. "I thought you looked familiar," Shari replied, remembering the last time she had seen her. "Have a seat." Shari offered, then glanced at Hamilton, noticing that his expression read a firm 'No'. Kara declined.

"It's been good seeing you again. How's Denise and Deb?"

"They're both doing well. Deb's married with a little girl. As a matter of fact, she married the guy she met at one of Denise's annual backyard parties."

"Get out of here!" Kara squealed. "If I remember correctly, he was a real cutie. That's the last time I saw the three of you. And how's Miss Denise?"

"She got married about four years ago."

"Wow. Please give them both my best."

"Small world," Hamilton interrupted. "Talk about six degrees of separation."

"I know," Kara replied, looking over her shoulder. "Here comes your brother now."

Hamilton rose to meet Matthew, clasped his hand in his before pulling him into an embrace. "What's up, my brother? Good to see you again, Shari." Matthew asked.

"Nothing much. How about you?"

"Doing good. Did Kara tell you?" Matthew walked over to Kara.

Hamilton looked from Matthew to Kara, then back to Matthew. "Tell me what?"

"Baby, show him your hand." Matthew grinned. "Bling-Bling!" He laughed as Kara raised her left hand to show off a 2-carat diamond marquis, surrounded by diamond baguettes proudly displayed on her ring finger. Shari took Kara's hand in hers, admiring what she knew was F-grade clarity, light refracting from the top of the clear, colorless diamond.

"He's been embarrassing me everywhere we've been today," Kara said. "He even showed the ring off to anyone that would dare pay him any mind in the grocery store this morning!"

The couples laughed. "Sure you don't want to join us?" Shari asked, then stated "ouch" loudly. "Something bit me," she replied, rubbing her thigh as Matthew and Kara looked at her suspiciously. She wouldn't tell them that Hamilton had pinched her. He mouthed, "Sorry."

Matthew grinned. "Thanks for the offer, but we've got a better spot." He shook Hamilton's hand. "Shari, it was nice seeing you again. Hope to see you soon."

"Same here," Shari responded.

"I'll be calling you," Matthew said.

Hamilton nodded his head. "I know you will. Later."

They watched Kara and Matthew disappear into the crowd. She thought they made a cute couple.

Hamilton rubbed Shari's thigh. "Sorry about that. But I'm not trying to share today."

Shari smiled. "I was only trying to be polite. But I guess I can try and forgive you." She looked into his eyes.

"What do I need to do?" Hamilton asked, his right eyebrow raised, his deep voice strong and insistent. "Tell me and I'll do whatever it takes."

The earlier erotic image snuck into Shari's mind. She shook her head slightly. "You're forgiven this time." She acquiesced, foregoing the suggestive game their conversation was heading in. Hamilton followed suit and changed the subject.

"How do you known Kara?" Hamilton asked.

"We went to college together. For the life of me and Deb, we could never remember her name. But she was always nice, a real sweet person. We tried to get her to join our sorority, but she never came to any of the informational meetings. The last time I saw her was the night Deb met Darrin. How long has she been with Matthew?"

"About four years. They met at a backyard party."

They looked at each other then laughed.

"I wonder if it was one of Denise's famous yard parties?" Shari asked.

"I went one year," Hamilton replied. "I don't remember seeing you."

"We stopped going after Deb met Darrin. Deb was into Darrin and I was traveling a lot for my job. Hey, you weren't at the wedding."

"No, I was out of town on assignment. My mom and sisters went."

"That explains why we've never met," Shari said. "After they married, and Deb and I sold the house we shared, my job had me all over the world."

Hamilton wanted to ask about her past relationships. He thought of Kara's friend, Janice and was glad that she had enough tact not to mention her, or their ill-fated attempt at dating. Thoughts of Janice led to ones of Nicky and he knew that eventually he'd have to tell Shari about the woman he was once engaged to.

Shari and Hamilton settled back and listened to hours of reggae music, their heads bobbed and swayed to the heavy beat as they sat close, hip to hip. At the end of the concert, Shari folded the blanket while Hamilton placed the now empty containers in the picnic basket. He took Shari's hand as they made their way through the ballroom toward the exit. Hamilton paused.

"Hear that?" He tilted his head to the left. "Come on." Hamilton guided Shari into the middle of a darkened room, then stopped. "Wait right here." He ordered softly. Her eyes adjusted as lights shone dimly from the large overhead crystal chandelier.

"Dance with me." He held his hand out to her. Shari walked over to Hamilton and slid into his arms. She rested her head on his chest as the sounds of "For You," by Pieces of a Dream claimed them, wrap-

105

ping them inside a sensuous embrace.

"Thank you, Princess." Hamilton whispered into her hair. He smiled, as the memory of him watching his parents dance in their living room rushed into his mind. He remembered how his father had held his mother close to him, his mouth near her ear moving. He thought of the look on his mother's face, the dream-like look of love and peace was evident. He pulled back slightly and looked into Shari's eyes. Dare I dream, he asked himself.

"Are you okay?" She asked.

"I'm good."

"So, what are you thanking me for?"

"For going out with me. For letting me hold you in my arms."

Shari didn't know what to say. Once she had prayed for God to send her a man who was self assured and unafraid—one who would make her feel a lot like Hamilton was making her feel. Startled at the long-ago thought, she pulled back and looked up into Hamilton's face. She wanted him in her life—wanted to lay her heart at his feet and in his hands, and hope like hell that he would take it and not hurt her. She had never before cared about being hurt, then again she had never been in love. This was moving too fast, she thought. What did he want from her? She began to stammer, "I...I feel I should say something."

"No, just let me continue to hold you—you feel so good in my arms."

Hamilton pulled her closer. He liked the feel of her in his arms, the way her scent swirled around in his senses, the way she held him back. The emotions were unmistakable. How could he tell her what he felt and not have her run away. Then he remembered, he hadn't told Nicky his feelings, had never shared them with her. He thought, maybe that was why she sought comfort in the arms of another.

Hamilton gently lifted Shari's face upward, the tips of his fingers stroking her soft cheek. He looked deeply into her eyes, trying to see into her heart, into her soul.

"My God, woman," Hamilton groaned. "You are too much. Baby, you're gonna burn me."

"No, dear. I will never hurt you," she whispered. "I could fall in love with you." She quickly returned her head to his chest. *Where did that come from?* She wondered and was relieved when he didn't respond. She'd hoped that he didn't hear her. Besides, she thought, it was too soon to be talking about falling in love and all that emotional stuff.

The soft strings of the song ended. Shari remained in Hamilton's arms. "Shari?"

"Umm," Shari didn't want to talk. The state of euphoria was too new, too fresh for her to be able to move out of the sweetness of his arms, the beat of his heart thumped against her ear pressed against his chest.

"The song has ended. It's time to go." He released her and took her hand in his. As they made their way to the exit, Shari stopped suddenly.

"Hamilton, I forgot the blanket."

"Stay right here. I'll go get it."

Shari smiled, then nodded her head, watching Hamilton's large form disappear through the ballroom and out onto the lawn.

"Hello, Shari. Long time."

Shari spun around and came face to face with Bruce. He hugged her. Shari was stunned

"Cat's got your tongue, or should I say man has it?"

She didn't respond, opting to let her eyes travel along the floor, then the walls; anywhere but upon his face.

"Well, since you've seemed to have lost your voice, I'm doing well and I see you are too." Bruce pointed toward the lawn. "Good looking dude." Shari nodded, still silent. "Okay. Anyway, it's been nice seeing you again, Shari. Take care." He leaned over and kissed her on the cheek, then walked away.

CHAPTER 10

Hamilton's emotions began to spiral. He watched as the man leaned over and kissed Shari on the cheek. He wondered who the guy was. Two days in a row, the stranger appeared and twice Shari seemed disheveled.

"Ready?" Hamilton asked, his voice low and angry.

"Yeah—sure," was all Shari could say, hoping like hell that Hamilton hadn't seen Bruce kiss her. They hadn't discussed their past.

Shari followed Hamilton, noting the straightness in his back, the way his shoulders were squared. Yeah, he saw it.

"Hamilton," Shari called out. He slowly turned. "The night's young. How about we go to that little coffee house on Michigan?" She could see he was wrestling with the idea.

"Can I get a rain check?"

Shari hoped the disappointment wasn't evident. "Sure. Not a problem," she replied as she stepped to the SUV. Hamilton opened the passenger door and lifted Shari, settling her into the seat. Placing the picnic basket in the rear, Hamilton couldn't shake the image of that man kissing Shari and she offered no explanation. Yet, he too, didn't want the night to end. He was enjoying her company, the light banter they had been engaging in. He had to admit, Shari was making him live again—making him feel emotions he hadn't felt in a long time. He changed his mind.

Climbing into the SUV, he faced Shari. "Skip the rain check. I'm game." Still, the little unexplained scene warred within him. He knew he didn't want a repeat of Nicky.

Once seated at the coffee house, Hamilton proceeded to tell Shari all about Janice, in hopes that the story would prompt her to tell him about the man he saw kissing her.

After finishing desert, Hamilton drove Shari home, his feelings now fully out of control. During the thirty minute ride, the moon followed along as Shari sat next to Hamilton quietly, silence their only company.

This isn't going well, Shari exhaled, angry at the way the evening was coming to an end. As Hamilton pulled up to her apartment, Shari turned to him and smiled weakly.

"Hamilton, thank you for inviting me to the fest," Shari said.

"No problem," he said tersely.

The pair remained silent before Shari reluctantly broke it. "Well, I better be going. I've got to get up early tomorrow."

Hamilton cleared his throat. "Yeah, me too. I'll call you, okay?"

"Sure," Shari replied, then leaned over and kissed Hamilton lightly on the lips. Sitting back, she watched his proud features, set like steel. She knew he saw Bruce.

She jumped out of the Expedition, noting the change in him. She chided herself, for she should have told him about Bruce. But how could she? She felt that if she explained her feelings for Bruce, or lack thereof, it would leave her looking shallow and fickle. She didn't want him to think that of her. The thought of losing him frightened her.

"Bye, Hamilton," Shari shut the passenger door quickly, then rushed up to the door. Shutting it, she leaned against it as her feelings spiraled out of control. No! She admonished herself, no man has ever gotten to me and Mr. Hamilton Edmunds will be no exception.

Seeing Mrs. Ponticello appear in the doorway, Shari shrugged her shoulders and went to her.

"How was your date?"

"I ran into Bruce. He kissed me and Hamilton saw it. Does that answer your question?" Shari chuckled half-heartedly at the irony of it all. "After nearly two years, the man shows up out of nowhere. Twice, I may add."

"Where was Hamilton?"

"I'm not sure, but his whole demeanor changed when came back into the ballroom."

Shari went on to tell about seeing Bruce the night before, as well as their second date and how it ended.

"Oh, baby, I'm so sorry," Mrs. Ponticello responded as she embraced Shari. "Did you tell Hamilton about Bruce?"

She shook her head.

Mrs. Ponticello held Shari away from her. "Why not?"

"I didn't want to appear shallow."

"Umm," Mrs. Ponticello sat on the bottom stair and motioned for Shari to join her. "You really like this one, don't you?" Shari nodded. "Dear, you've got to tell him about Bruce, otherwise he's going to think all kinds of things. And you don't want that."

"No, I don't." Shari looked at her landlady.

"Then I suggest you march up those steps and call him."

Shari laid her head on Mrs. Ponticello's shoulder. "I think I will."

"How about 'I know I will?' "

Shari laughed. "I will, the minute I get upstairs." She remained seated.

"What are you waiting for?"

Shari changed the subject. "Are you going out?"

"Just to my Sunday Bridge game. I'll be back shortly. Do you need anything?"

"No, just my sanity back." Shari laughed.

"Make that call," Mrs. Ponticello rose. "See you shortly." Mrs. Ponticello left.

Shari climbed the stairs, recalling how just six hours ago she had descended them with Hamilton. Once inside, she put on her night clothes, then sat in her den, absently switching channels—images of Hamilton clouded her thoughts. She knew she should have told him at the Gallery, she should have explained the whole situation. But she didn't think that Bruce would show up two days in a row. Why didn't Hamilton could ask about Bruce? Maybe he didn't care, Shari shrugged her shoulders. She didn't like that last thought.

After an hour, Shari shut off the television and headed to her room. She looked at the phone beside her bed, then picked it up and dialed Hamilton's phone number. After several rings his voice mail picked up. Shari hung up without leaving a message, shut off the bedside lamp, then rolled over. Before finally falling asleep, Shari decided to let Hamilton be. She wasn't about to put up with any madness. Yet, she had dared to hope—dared to let herself believe the possibility that Hamilton might be the one for her.

"Oh well, Que se Ra se Ra." Shari shrugged. Rocket jumped up on the bed and laid her head next to Shari's. Shari shut her eyes and willed herself to sleep

Hamilton had driven aimlessly around, hoping to clear his thoughts. Yet, he couldn't seem to shake the image of that man kissing Shari. After two hours, Hamilton pulled up in front of his home, shut off the engine, gathered the picnic basket and blanket, then headed into the house. *She seemed so different*, he thought as he stepped into the house. The deafening silence reminded him that he was alone. He couldn't shake the thought of that guy kissing Shari. He knew lovers when he saw them, and he had recognized the connection between Shari and that guy. Nicky opened his eyes. He wanted Shari. Well, she won't do me like Nicky, he thought firmly, then climbed the stairs, leaving the picnic items at the entry way.

Undressed, he slid between the covers, then turned on the stereo in hopes of clearing his head. He closed his eyes and smelled the scent of Shari's perfume as it permeated his senses. He imagined her lying next to him, her shapely body nestled close to his. His member stirred to life, providing a not so gentle reminder that it had been a long time since he had felt the pleasure of a woman in his arms.

No good! He chided, then rolled over on his side.

Hamilton turned off the music, reached out to the lamp beside his bed and doused the light. He blinked in the darkness, yawned, then rubbed the hairs on his naked chest. A searing thought of Shari's small hand stealing across his body made him groan.

"Get a grip, Hamilton." He ordered. His last thought, as he drifted to sleep, was of his need to reel in his run-away emotions. If not, he reasoned, then he'd be in for a heart ache and he knew he couldn't stand another one.

CHAPTER 11

For seven days, Shari and Hamilton avoided each other, calling each other when they knew the other wasn't available.

Shari was never one to chase after a man when he didn't want to be chased. And she most certainly didn't want to be involved with a man who wouldn't speak his mind. *He could have asked*, she reasoned. She blew out an exasperated sigh and returned to the cream colored paper sitting on her desk. It was her resignation letter. She looked at the date at the top of the page — it was dated one month from today. Shari had finished the business plan and mailed it off to her father. Within two days her father had called and for over four hours the two talked about her plan. Their conversation ended with his offer to invest forty thousand dollars into her business. Since then, she had taken Deb up on her offer, insisting that Deb become a silent partner in her business. With that, Shari devoted her early mornings and after work hours creating letter head, business cards and applying for a small business loan from her bank. She had no time for dalliances—especially with Hamilton.

Shari placed the letter in her briefcase and began to examine the various samples strew across her work desk at Macy's. The intercom buzzed.

"Shari," Toni, her assistant said. "Ms. Wilson is on line two."

"Thanks," Shari responded, then picked up the receiver and pressed the flashing light.

"Hey, Sister, how's my baby feeling?" Shari asked. Her goddaughter, Daneda, had caught a slight cold. Deb had canceled their outing.

"She's better. The doctor said she had a mild ear ache."

"That's good. I wish you would have let me come over."

"Like I told you, we all had colds and we didn't want to pass our germs to you."

"Well, I'm glad to hear she's fine," Shari responded, then chuckled softly at the sounds of Daneda gurgling in the background.

Deb laughed. "As you can hear, Miss Thing is great. She lying here playing with her teething ring. So, how's things with you? The last time we spoke we talked about the baby. You didn't mention your date with Hamilton. What gives?"

Shari put Deb on hold, instructed her assistant to hold her calls, then returned to the line. "A lot."

"You want to tell me about it?"

"Yeah, I need to unload."

Shari told Deb about her last two dates with Hamilton and the electric fire between them. She ended with the story of Bruce's reappearance.

"Unbelievable," Deb said. "And you think Hamilton saw him kiss you?"

"Based on how he reacted, yes."

"How long had it been since you'd last seen Bruce?"

"It's been over a year, Deb. Then poof! He appeared out of no where."

"Did you explain it all to Hamilton?"

Shari fell silent. "Shari? Did you?"

"Well, no."

"Why not? What are you afraid of?"

"Nothing. I'm not afraid. Look, I've got a business to start. I don't have time for Hamilton."

Deb sighed loudly. "No, you don't want to make time."

"That's not true. Starting my own business is important to me, Deb. All Hamilton will do is get in the way."

"Are you sure?" Deb asked, then fell silent.

"Sure. Besides, he got all funny acting after seeing Bruce. I don't need the drama."

Shari heard Deb let out a long sigh. "Shari, you're making excuses."

"I am not!" Shari defended. "Getting By Design off and running takes time and my full attention if its going to be successful."

"But what about your heart, Deb—doesn't it need some attention?"

"My heart is fine and so is my head, so lay off, okay. Let's talk about something else." Shari became sullen. The same feelings of envy had returned and on more than one occasion she allowed the internal battle to brew—questioning if she could have a family of her own and run a business. She wanted her business and tried to resolve herself to that single idea. No, she had stated, there just wasn't any room for both.

"Have you spoken to Denise?"

"Don't try to change the subject. Hamilton is a good catch, so don't be too slow in coming around. Personally, I think you can have both."

"So you say."

"No, I know. Look, love isn't easy and relationships do take time, but we make time for the things we truly want to. And you and I both know that relationships don't always show up like a planned visitor on the doorstep. It seizes you, makes you see the possibilities, makes you believe in dreams you've only thought of." Deb paused. "Sister, make time. You cannot control everything."

"I'm not trying to! Can't we change the subject? I don't want to talk about Hamilton Edmunds, Junior!"

Deb laughed. "Yes you are—always have been. But, if you don't want to talk about Hamilton, then let's talk about Bruce."

Shari breathed out through her nose, her mouth twisted in a scowl. "I don't wanna go there, either."

"We have to. You and Bruce were, in my opinion, like oil and water. He always went along just to make you happy. He was no match for the strong, controlling Shari."

"Deb! That's not fair."

"Well, then tell me I'm wrong."

Shari fell silent. Deb continued. "Bruce always went along with *your* program, never upsetting the apple cart. The only time he stood up to you, was when he broke off the engagement. And that's the smartest thing he's ever done."

"Ouch, Deb. Tell me how you really feel?" Shari replied sarcastically, then shook her head.

"Oh, I'm not finished. We all saw it, Shari. We all knew that you didn't love him. You and Bruce deserved much more than either of you got. Then enters Hamilton. A strong—self-assured—clever man. Never had a man like that, have you?"

"No," Shari admitted.

"Now you're ready to run, using the start of this business as an excuse. It's safer than facing your feelings."

"Well, I...umm, I..."

Shari heard Deb's exasperated breath. "Now, who are you about to lie to? Cause I know you aren't trying to lie to me. You are scared out of your mind, because this the first man that has made you stop in your tracks. Yet, you want to use the creation of your business become your legitimate excuse. How convenient."

"No, it isn't!" Shari protested, even though the words were true. She wanted Hamilton, wanted to lay in his arms, share her dreams. He had seemed genuinely interested in her plan.

Deb sighed loudly. "I think it is. Hamilton threatens your ability to control your emotions? To just let go and enjoy him."

"I just don't want to be hurt." Shari's eyes widened and wondered where the statement had come from. She hadn't cared in the past. Why now?

"Who does?" Deb's voice softened. "Okay, you know that Bruce wasn't for you, wasn't from the word 'go'. And you won't find out if Hamilton is the one unless you give him a chance. Will you?"

"I'm not sure."

"I know. Invite him to Sunday brunch at Denise's. But explain to him all about Bruce. Don't let the man wonder, Shari."

"Umm ..." Shari tried to think of an excuse.

"No backing out. Remember, he's Darrin's cousin. I have his number and I'll call him myself."

"Okay, okay," Shari acquiesced. "Don't do that." Shari had to laugh. She didn't want the same type of meddling she had done in Deb and Darrin's affairs. "I'll invite him."

"Good, then I will see you both, together, on Sunday." Shari heard her goddaughter's cry in the background. "You hear the little diva has gotten bored. Gotta run. I love ya, Shari. Do me a favor?"

"Anything for you, Sistah."

"Let Hamilton in. You can have both."

Shari looked around her office. "I'll try."

"Good enough for now. Talk to ya." Deb hung up.

Shari placed the receiver in its cradle, leaned back in her chair, then rubbed her forehead. She picked up the phone receiver, dialed Hamilton's home number, left him a message inviting him to the brunch, then hung up. Next, she told her assistant to put calls through again and went back to working on the Spring display project. Deb had rightfully and correctly put her feelings into perspective, and for once in her life, Shari felt that maybe it was time to let someone else do the driving.

"Hey, baby brother, how are you?" Haley sang as she watched her youngest brother stroll into the house they grew up in. Haley was proud of her brother, of the man he had become. She looked at him, noting that out of all of the siblings, they looked the most alike, almost like twins.

"Good," Hamilton replied, then kissed his sister on the cheek. "What's up with you? Where are the kids?"

"I made them go to the store with momma. You know she's gonna buy a farm and two cows for the barbeque."

Hamilton chuckled. "I know." He smiled, thinking about the numerous family get-together's; yet, out of all of them the Edmunds Annual Family Fourth-of-July Barbeque wasn't to be missed. Ella Edmunds expected and got all her family together, including a few wayward cousins, uncles and aunts. In all, nearly 50 people, which didn't include the large immediate Edmunds tribe, would filter in and out the entire day. Hamilton's mother would start her preparations a full two weeks in advance.

"Are you bringing someone this year?" Haley spied a look at Hamilton.

"Why? You ask me that every year."

"Well, I was hoping that this year would be different."

"I was." Hamilton walked away and headed toward the kitchen. He felt his sister close on his heels.

"Was? Spill it!" Haley sat at the kitchen island. "You haven't brought anyone since that Nicky chile. And that's been what? Four years ago. Okay, so what's her name?"

Hamilton sniffed, his smile slow coming as thoughts of Shari seeped into his head. "Shari. Shari Thomas." Hamilton looked at Haley, then fell silent.

"Shari. Shari Thomas," Haley mocked. "What about her Hamilton?" Haley watched her brother closely. She could always tell when something wasn't quite right, and right now something wasn't right. "What's the matter?" Haley tapped her brother's hand.

"We've been playing phone tag."

"And?"

Hamilton sat across from Haley and looked at the sister who was two years older than he. As kids it was Haley who could cajole and finesse information out of Hamilton. The older they became, the closer they became, so much so, that it was always Haley whom he sought answers of the heart from. He liked her thought process, liked the way she could see both sides without judgement or condemnation.

"Have you ever felt so in touch with a person that it scared you? I mean, you know, right here." He tapped his chest, right over his heart. "That the person is right. You feel it's right, but then something happens and you aren't so sure anymore?"

Haley smiled. "My baby brother is in love. How did you meet her and how long have you known her?"

Hamilton told of how they met, and their subsequent two dates, as well as the mystery man.

"Cousin Darrin did well hiding her, didn't he?" Haley laughed. "First off, the way I see it, you two are afraid, and I don't blame you.

But here's the thing. How much of this fear will the two of you allow to interfere in the inevitable? I know that kind of fear, had it when I married Lance, but its the fear of wanting things to go right, to be perfect. Well, baby brother, nothing and no one is perfect. But more importantly, Shari is not Nicky. As for the man, did she explain?"

Hamilton shook his head.

"Did you ask her?"

"It wasn't any of my business." Hamilton rose from his seat, his back to her.

"You mean to tell me, that you watched some guy kiss your date and you didn't ask her about it?! Why not?"

Hamilton shrugged his shoulders. "Just didn't."

"You know she's going think you don't care."

Hamilton faced his sister as she walked over to him, placed her arm about his waist, and leaned around his large frame to look into his eyes. "You didn't ask because you instantly thought of Nicky. Forget Nicky. It was over before it started."

Hamilton conceded. "You did warn me."

"Yes I did. Now, it's time to move on. She's moved on with her life and so must you. So what you two weren't right for each other? Every blind person in Chicago could see that. Be fair to yourself and Shari—ask her about the guy. You look her in her eyes and ask her. I bet there's more here than you're willing to acknowledge. Besides, its time you let the pain of Nicky go."

"Spoken like a true trooper," Hamilton replied, somewhat smugly. It was easy for her to say. She hadn't witness her husband screwing another woman. He looked at his sister.

"I know what you thinking and you need to scratch that, too" Haley demanded. "And I've been cheated on. Caught my boyfriend kissing my best friend, but that didn't stop me. Just think, had I let it, then I wouldn't have been open enough to let Lance in." Haley rubbed Hamilton's smooth head, and gently brought his cheek to rub against hers. "Call her and invite her to the barbeque. I'll look her over and tell you what I think, but I believe you already know."

"Okay." Hamilton hugged Haley. He picked up the phone resting on the kitchen wall and dialed Shari's number. Her machine came on and he left a message that included the invitation.

"That was weak, but I'll let it go."

"What was weak?!" Hamilton cried.

"Leaving a message. You should talk to her. Face to face, preferably. But I guess that will do for now."

The pair laughed as their mother, with Haley's two boys in tow, appeared in the kitchen loaded with plastic grocery bags. Ella kissed her children on the cheek, then instructed them to go out to the car and retrieve more bags. Hamilton paused at the door, watching his mother move around the kitchen. Had his father been alive, he would be right here, helping with the menu and sitting in the kitchen as she cooked the various entree's. Hamilton knew he was searching for what his parents had, and had hoped that Shari could possibly be the one. He heard Haley call his name, then appeared before him.

"What they had was one of a kind, Hamilton. And if you ask mom, she'll tell you that it wasn't all roses. Make up your own dreams, baby brother. Call her back and talk to her."

Haley went outside, with Hamilton close behind.Hamilton kissed Haley on the cheek, before grabbing several bags. It's time, the voice commanded: It's time.

CHAPTER 12

Hamilton readjusted the glasses he used when sitting in front of the computer. He stared absently at the screen. He glanced up at the clock on the pale cream wall, then back to the words on the screen. He couldn't concentrate. His mind was clouded with thoughts of Shari.

"Hey, Hamilton," his co-worker, John, called out. "You finish with that story? The typesetters are looking for it."

"Yeah, I'm putting the finishing touches on it now," he partially lied. He was having a hard time shaking the feel of Shari's lips upon his, the warmth that emitted from her waist when he had placed her in his SUV. God, he thought, that woman was beautiful. He shook the thoughts loose, least they lead to more erotic ones. He forced himself to finish his work.

"Say John," Hamilton raised his head from the screen, then leaned back in his chair. "The story's on its way. Are we ready to go to bed?"

"Yeah, quit'in time." John appeared at Hamilton's cubicle. "How about a few rounds."

"Sounds good. Let me call my boy, Matthew." Hamilton picked up the phone on his desk. "Matt, my milla. John and I are heading to the Old 50. You wanna meet us there?"

"Sure. What time?"

"In about 30 minutes. Sounds good?"

"Sounds good. Besides, I got a lot to unload. Plus, I want to know all about that fine filly I saw you with. What, twice now in less than a week?" He laughed.

"Yeah? Well, I've invited her to the family barbeque."

"Aww, dog, must be serious. The last woman you took to the family barbeque was Nicky."

"Don't remind me. And this one is a far cry from Nicky."

"We'll see if she passes Helena."

"Don't you know it. Gotta jet. See you in a minute." Hamilton disconnected the call. He thought of his oldest sister Helena. She could be a pill—good or bad depending on who she turned her medicine on. Eight years older than he, Helena hadn't liked Nicky on sight. At first Hamilton thought it was Helena being over protective of her baby brother, for she took her role as the eldest quite serious, but after several conversations with his sister Haley, he knew that Helena had been on point — he just didn't want to acknowledge it.

Thoughts of Shari pushed its way into his mind. He hoped she had gotten his message and wondered why she hadn't returned his call. Hamilton shut down the computer, rose from his chair, then placed papers into his leather satchel. As he made his way to John's cubicle, the sound of his name stopped him.

"Hamilton!" the editorial assistant called out. "Call on line three."

"Got it," Hamilton replied, then made his way back to his cubicle. "Hamilton Edmunds here."

"Hi."

"Hey," he replied, then sat down. "How've you been?"

"Busy. We are in the middle of preparing for the fall fashions and our annual Spring show for next year, so things get a little harried around here. How about you? How've you been?"

"About the same, but I'm not going to complain. Did you get my message?" He let his eyes trail around the various objects on his desk.

The Peter Lisagor award he won last year for his story on the homeless; a picture of he and his family, taken one month before his father died; the large desk calendar with words of inspiration for every month given to him by his sister Helen. All arranged so neat and compact. Just like Shari.

"Yes, I got it," she paused. "I'd love to go, but there's one problem."

"What?"

"My parents are coming to town. They will expect me to hang with them."

"Not a problem. Invite them. There'll be plenty of food."

Shari looked at the clock on her wall. Bring my parents, she said to herself. She thought that introducing parents to your date meant that person was special. But wasn't Hamilton doing the same thing by inviting her to his family barbeque? Shari shrugged her shoulders. She decided to invite her parents to the barbeque. "Okay, what time will you be picking me up?"

Hamilton expelled his breath, not realizing he had been holding it in as he waited for her response. "The Barbeque starts at noon. Say around 11:30 or so. I'll call you."

"Sounds good to me," Shari responded. "Say, did you get my message?"

"Yeah. Ditto. I'll go."

"Okay," Shari replied, wanting to say more, to tell him about Bruce, to bare the feelings she had over him. She changed her mind. "Well, dear, I must take leave. I have a meeting in a few minutes. I'll talk to you later."

"Bet on it."

"Bye," she disconnected the call. Hamilton sat, holding the receiver to his ear, the sultry warmth of her voice reverberated around him. He wanted to call her back, wanted to see her tonight instead of next week. He shook his head.

"Must have been some call, cause you gots that hooked look."

Hamilton placed the receiver in its cradle. "Yeah right. You ready?" He looked at his co-worker and friend, noticing for the first time the dark circles that appeared around his eyes.

"Well, there's been a slight change of plans. The wife expects me home," John shrugged. "Gimme a rain-check. I'll get with you guys another day."

Hamilton nodded and decided against ribbing his friend. He knew what it took to sustain a relationship and sometimes it wasn't easy. "You got it. I'll see you on Monday." Hamilton grasped John's hand, then stood and looked around the large news room. The grey colored cubicles, which sat atop deep charcoal-colored carpet, were situated twelve deep and were evenly lined up along both walls; the chief editor's cubical was at the front, with the assistant editor's cube next to it.

He enjoyed working for the Times, had always wanted to be a journalist, having worked on his high school and college newspapers. Now, he was working on a new dream—his first book, a murder mystery with a fiery vixen at its core. He knew the impetus for the vixen was his former fiancé, Nicky. Well, Nicky's gone, Hamilton consoled, and Shari's here.

Looking at his watch, he knew he was going to be late meeting Matthew. Hamilton headed down the aisle, waved his hand over his head, shouted out a "have a good weekend, yall," then walked out the door.

Hamilton walked into the bar and paused at the entrance to let his eyes adjust to the dimness of the expansive establishment. When he spotted Matthew, he headed in his direction.

"Good looking out," Hamilton tapped the top of the table, then sat down. "I hate sitting at the bar."

A young waitress, dressed in a black mini-skirt and white crop top, and a visible belly ring, approached them. "What can I get you gentlemen?"

Matthew looked at the young woman and smiled. "Baby, what you can get for me would be considered a crime," the friends chuckled. "But lets start with a Lowenbrad.î

"I'll take a Courvoisier. Water on the side."

The waitress scribbled on her pad. Hamilton noticed the long, multi-colored nails and gold rings on each finger. He looked up into her mocha colored face and thought she was pretty, her almond shaped eyes held hazel colored contact lens. He smiled as her eyes met his. "Be right back with yall drinks."

"She's barely 21. They gettin' younger and younger," Matthew said.

"Tell me about it," Hamilton glanced over his shoulder at the waitress, noticing her build. Built like a brick house. He shook his head, then faced Matthew. "So, what's been up?"

"Kara."

"What's wrong?"

Matthew sighed, then looked Hamilton in the eyes. He looked away, rubbing his hands one over the other. Hamilton knew he was nervous, and started to say so, but decided to ride out the nervous gesture.

"Man, I'm scared."

"Aren't we all." Hamilton's words rang true, more for himself than for Matthew. At least Matthew had asked Kara to marry him. Hell, he thought, he hadn't even told Shari he cared.

Matthew snorted. "Damn, skippy! Hamilton, she's everything and more than a man deserves. I mean." He blew his breath out. "Am I good enough for her?"

"Man, you're just second guessing yourself. Why wouldn't you be good enough for her?"

"She's smart. Beautiful. Sexy as hell. And she's . . ."

"Yours, Matthew. She is all yours." Which was more than he could say about Shari. "Look. Your fears are understandable. You know how us brothers are. When it comes to women, we are forever wondering, assuming and guessing the wrong things. We know what they want. Giving it to them seems to be the problem. But, dude." Hamilton tapped the table with his fingers. "If she loves you in the morning, as bad as you look." The pair laughed. "Then she loves her some you. Don't push this one away, Matt. It's okay to love her."

"When'd you get to be so deep?"

"I've got four sisters, remember. Them women are hard on brothers to come correct. And I watched them, closely, and have learned a few things in the process. But I've got to admit, I don't always use what I've learned from them."

"I wish I had your sisters."

Hamilton laughed again. "Take them."

"I will—you know I love them. But I believe if I had sisters, instead of being an only child, I wouldn't have wasted so much time on women who I knew weren't for me."

"I hear you. When I was a teenager, they always preached about how women wanted to be treated, that women don't want their emotions to be toyed with. And to prove the point, they discarded any brother who tried to play games with them. And they didn't look."

"True that—the games *are* tiring. But man, the vulnerable thing is hard. Being open enough to let her see all the sore spots."

"Tell me about it, I haven't gotten to that one yet."

The pair laughed. Matthew looked around the bar, his gaze following two well-built sisters as they came into the establishment. He noted their tight attire, then looked back to Hamilton.

"One day you will," Matthew said. "Maybe that one day is today. With Shari."

Hamilton blinked at the words his best friend had spoken. He knew Matthew was a deep thinking man, lied to no one, often making enemies because of it; but as they grew older, he saw the man his friend had become. It would take a strong sister, one who was comfortable with and loved herself to be with him. That sister was Kara. It was also Shari. Her face invaded his thoughts.

"Really? How did you come up with that?" Hamilton asked.

"I peeped you that night, all hugged up. Then again at the Reggae fest. Didn't want me and Kara to sit down." Matthew laughed. "Your body language said it all. And that little pinch, shoot man, I knew you weren't trying to have me all up in your Kool-aid." Hamilton laughed as he listened to his best friends assessment. "But dude, it was in your eyes. I watched you watch her. Deep man. I can't wait 'til the Barbeque. Besides, I wouldn't miss the Edmunds family barbeque for the world."

"If she can pass that one…" Hamilton let the thought linger. He decided against mentioning the man who kissed Shari.

"That's for sure. Those sisters of yours will be scrutinizing her from head to toe."

Hamilton thought of his four sisters and it was Helena he was most worried about. He didn't want a repeat of four years ago when Helena had dismissed Nicky with a wave of her hand, literally.

"Hey," Matthew began. "Kara and I will be there around 2 o'clock. And for the record, Kara understands about Janice. I told her from jump that you two wouldn't make it."

"Thanks. She was some piece of work."

"I know. Enough of all of this," Matthew said, his eyes meeting Hamilton's. "Do me a favor?" Hamilton returned the stare. "Try and keep this one, okay? I hear she's a good sister." Hamilton nodded his head. The friends laughed, then toasted once the waitress brought their drinks. Matthew's words rang in his head: *keep this one.*

Hamilton sat in his home office, his fingers typing furiously as the words flowed from his mind onto the screen. He was near the end. Twenty more pages and his first literary work would be complete. In a couple of days he'd send it to his editor. He smiled and his motions slowed as he looked at the clock on the computer. His thoughts trailed to Shari. It was 1 a.m. and he knew that Shari was in bed. They had spoken several times over the course of five days, each engaging in idle chit-chat versus discussing what was happening to them. And still, they hadn't firmed up their plans for the weekend. Enough! Hamilton stood, then stretched. He was through playing games and threw caution to the wind. He picked up the phone.

"Hello," he began pensively. "I didn't wake you, did I?"

"No, I'm in my studio doing a little sewing," Shari replied. "Now, I know why I'm burning the midnight oil, but why are you up so late?"

"Working on my book. I get lost in this thing and forget all time."

"I totally understand."

"So, are we on for later today?" Hamilton asked, saving his work before shutting off his computer. "I assure you, you will have a good time."

"Hamilton, I told you I wanted to go."

"That you did. Okay, I'll be by to get you at 11. How's that?"

"That's good. What about my soror's brunch on Sunday?"

"I haven't forgotten. What time should *I* be ready?"

Shari laughed. "Well, the brunch is at Noon."

"That's a plan. Think you can put up with me for an entire weekend?"

"Only if you think you could put up with me," she responded.

Silence fell between them. Both looked around their respective surroundings, each in their own thoughts. Shari broke the silence.

"Tell me what your book is about."

Hamilton began to tell of his work in progress, telling Shari in detail the plot and subsequent ending of the book. Shari was impressed. She had never met a man so passionate about his work. She heard it in his voice, the unmistakable lift to it, the way he breathed when telling of his life-long dream. She loved it, for it was just how she felt about designing.

"That's it. According to my editor, its going to be a runaway best seller," he chuckled, then added,"Aren't they all?"

"Well, I know I can't wait to read it. When will it be published?"

"In a year."

"And when it tops the New York Times bestsellers list, you're gonna quit your job, right?"

Hamilton was stunned. The last time he spoke of doing just that, he was laughed at. "Maybe. I'm not sure. I like working at the paper." He shifted the conversation. "Hey, what about you? Didn't you tell me that you were trying to start your own design company?"

Shari hesitated, remembering how Bruce had laughed at her for even mentioning her dream. Yet, when she had first mentioned her idea to Hamilton, he had seemed interested and supported her dream of wanting to design full time—to start her own company.

"What are you going to name your company?" Hamilton asked.

"By Design," she replied.

"That sounds good."

The pair became silent. The conversation they both had been avoiding they knew needed to be discussed. Hamilton and Shari spoke simultaneously.

"Who was that guy?" Hamilton asked, interrupting Shari as she said, "That guy at the...." They both laughed nervously.

"Ladies, first."

Shari let out a sigh, threw caution to the wind, and began telling Hamilton about Bruce, their relationship, and how she almost married him. In the end, she told Hamilton how she didn't love him and he knew it, with him breaking off the engagement. Following her admission, Shari fell silent.

"Wow! Almost married the guy, ugh? Glad you didn't."

"What'd you just say?"

"I said: I'm glad you didn't. If you had, then you wouldn't have met me. But tell me this?" Hamilton smiled. "Have you ever been in love before?"

Shari cast her eyes downward. She didn't want to respond, but she didn't want to lie to Hamilton either. She threw caution to the wind. "No, have you?"

"Thought I had, but I was wrong. Had blinders on."

Shari listened as Hamilton went on tell about his relationship with Nicky. "I see we have a lot in common. You game?" He spat out before he changed his mind, hoping that Shari would understand the hidden message.

"I am, if you are." Shari responded.

With the past finally out of the way, the pair went on to talk and laugh for nearly two hours, each telling of their dreams and hopes for the future. Each secretly willing the other to be apart of each others lives.

"Princess, its 2:45."

"My God it is!" Shari stated. "Go to bed, Hamilton. If I'm going to look like anything for this barbeque, I must get a little beauty sleep."

"Then you must only need 20 minutes."

Shari laughed. "Flattery will get you nowhere. Goodnight, Mr. Edmunds."

"Nite, Princess. See you in a few hours."

"In a few," Shari disconnected the call.

CHAPTER 13

Saturday and Sunday. Shari had to laugh at the thought of she and Hamilton spending the whole weekend together. They had both been crazy, avoiding each other, but she had promised Deb to give it a chance, to try and be open enough to let Hamilton in. And he had taken the first step—inviting her and her parents to his family's barbeque.

As Shari dressed for the barbeque, she was relieved that her parents had decided to drive themselves to the barbeque, but wasn't enthusiastic about them attending. Shari knew that her mother could be a bit snobbish when it came to the men she dated. And she didn't want her mother ruining her meeting Hamilton's family. As for her father, well he continued to surprise her, having pulled her aside and telling her that her business plan was solid. In the end, she just wanted the day to go off without a hitch.

Shari looked around her room at the scores of clothes she had tried on and discarded. She had to admit she was nervous and wanted to make a good impression. Deb had called her earlier, telling her that she, Darrin and Daneda were going to be at the barbeque. Just before she hung up, Deb had told her to be herself and to wear something "hot." Shari had laughed so loudly, that she could have swore the walls rocked from her bellow. More and more Shari's own words were coming back to haunt her.

In the end, Shari decided to wear all white, form fitting white jeans, a white tank-top and the white gym shoes that Hamilton had given her. She placed a white Negro League baseball cap over her head, her shoulder length hair peeked out from under it. She heard Hamilton's Ford Expedition pull up.

Shari looked into the hall mirror. She liked what she saw. Upon hearing the bell, she told Hamilton through the intercom that she was on her way down. Gathering her purse and keys, she balanced a bowl in her hands.

Stepping off the last step, Shari paused. She watched as Hamilton stepped up, dressed in white shorts and a white polo, with a black Chicago White Sox cap on his head, black leather sandals on his feet. He grinned as he pulled a long, large, brown paper wrapped package from behind him and motioned it toward her.

"Just a little sumptin, sumptin, I picked up."

She placed the bowl on the concrete porch rails, then took the gift from Hamilton. Tearing the paper off, she smiled. "Hamilton! It's the painting. I told you not to." She examined the painting from the gallery. "Thank you." She leaned over and kissed Hamilton lightly on the lips.

"I knew you liked it and I thought it would be great in your bedroom."

"That's a good spot, or in my studio."

"Where is your studio?" Hamilton asked.

"Follow me." She handed him the painting, grabbed the bowl from the railing, cradling it against her waist, then took him by the hand and lead him around to the side entrance.

Clicking on a light, she stepped down the back stairs, unlocked a door, and stepped aside.

Hamilton's eyes widened as he placed the picture on the floor. "This is great," he replied as he walked around the large area, pausing to examine the two mannequins. He stopped at her drafting table, then held up the sketch. "I'm gonna look good in this." They fell silent as she watched him examine the sketch of himself dressed in a double-breasted suit. He wanted to ask for it, but decided against it.

Shari's face flushed. He had found the sketch of himself she had drawn. She crossed the room. Standing by his side, she looked at the drawing.

"Girl, this is serious talent."

"Thank you," she replied.

"Don't you need my measurements to make it?" He looked at her.

"Well, yeah. I do."

"Get the tape measure," he said, then walked over the full length, tri-fold mirror near the end of the basement. He stepped up on the platform and watched as Shari appeared by his side, pad and pencil in hand. Shari began to write, alternating between taking notes and laying the measuring tape at his waist.

"Hamilton, how tall are you?"

"6'3."

"How much do you weigh?" She continued scribbling.

"Oh, about 230 pounds, give or take."

"Hold out your arms." Shari placed the tape at the tips of his fingers, then giggled when she couldn't reach the end of his other arm. "You're going to have to help. Hold this end between your fingers without bending them." Hamilton complied and watched Shari in the mirror as she pulled the tape to the end of his fingertips. "Okay, now spread your legs." Shari looked up at him and laughed at the shocked expression on his face. "I have to measure the length of your inner legs if you want the pants to hang right." Hamilton nodded, then spread his legs. Shari's hands shook as she placed the tape measure on the inside of his leg, her hands coming into contact with his large bare thighs.

Hamilton silently wished she'd hurry. She was a little to close for comfort.

"Almost done. I need to measure your thighs." Placing the tape around his thighs, Shari gasped at the solid feel of them. "Done. You can step down now."

Doing so, he faced her, his eyes traveling over her smooth skin, down her full breasts, to her hands. He removed the pad and pencil from her hands, tossed them to the floor, then pulled her into his arms. "I've missed you."

Shari nodded her head slightly as his sweet breath caressed her check, his lips brushed across her face, leaving a burning trail. Turning, she caught his lips with hers, planting pliant, light kisses on his full lips. Closing her eyes, she opened her mouth to receive him, allowing his tongue to mingle with his. A moan escaped them both, as her nipples hardened against the fabric of his shirt. He pulled her closer. She could feel the heavy hardness in his shorts. She groaned loudly. Surprised by the sound emitting from her, she broke the mounting tryst.

"Hamilton, we'd better get going." His eyes were shut. Opening them, she saw the raw need in them, the fiery intensity.

"Yeah, we better," he said, opening his eyes. He moved across the room and picked up the bowl Shari had set down. "What's this?" he asked as they exited the basement.

"A little dessert. A punch bowl cake. The Thomas' go nowhere empty handed." Though she had only gotten four hours of sleep, she rose early in order to make the special desert for the barbeque.

"You didn't have to, you know that?"

"Yeah, but I did," Shari responded, dismissing his protest.

Out on the street, Hamilton took her hand in his. "When do I get my suit?"

"When do you want it?"

"How about my birthday. August 1st."

"That's soon. I may be able to meet or beat that deadline."

"Sounds good. Are you ready to meet my clan?"

"I'm as ready as I'll ever be."

Hamilton lifted Shari into the truck. "You robbed me of this the last time I saw you." He stood, his eyes fixed upon hers. "Please don't rob me of it again."

Shari smiled and swung her shapely legs into the SUV, Hamilton closed the door. Hamilton reached across her lap, the electric charge of their kiss was still there, its energy growing rapidly. He forced himself to concentrate on anything other than the feel of Shari's body against his as he pulled the seat belt across her, and fastened her in. "Don't want anything to happen to you." He winked.

They engaged in idle chat as Hamilton headed toward the house he grew up in. He became nervous when he found out that Shari's parents were joining them later. He just wasn't sure how her mother and father would react to his entire brood, who admittedly could be overly opinionated. Ideally, Hamilton would have liked to met them on a more neutral turf.

Upon arrival, Hamilton helped Shari out of the vehicle where she was immediately greeted by a little girl.

"Hi, my name is Ella. They call me Little Ella," the little girl with two long ponytails announced. "Are you my uncle's new girlfriend?" Shari smiled warmly at the girl, taking in the skin tone and eyes so much like Hamilton's. She bent down, her eyes level to the child's.

"I'm a friend of your uncle's," Shari stated, then put out her hand. Ella followed suit. "It's nice to meet you."

The little girl tugged Shari's hand and began leading her to the rear of the house. Almost as an after thought, Ella stopped. "Hi, Uncle

Hamilton." Hamilton smiled at his niece, then watched in rapt amusement as the small child continued toward the backyard where the barbeque was being held.

"Grandma!" Ella called out in a high voice once they reached the backyard. "This is Uncle Hamilton's new girlfriend, Shari."

"Child, go play with your cousins," Hamilton's mother chided, a smile stretched across her warm brown face. She playfully swatted at her granddaughter, then came to stand in front of Shari. "Never mind her. She's just like her mother, Helena. But, she makes us believe in reincarnation, cause she's way too old. She acts like she's been here before." She took Shari's hand in her's. "As you now know, I'm Hamilton's mother, Ella. Nice to meet you."

"Same here, Mrs. Edmunds. I brought this for the barbeque." She motioned to the bowl Hamilton carried.

Ella waved her hand. "Baby, you didn't have to do that. We have more than enough." She took the punch bowl, then called over into a crowd of children. "Junie, take this and set it in the refrigerator." Ella then took Shari by the hand and led her through the backyard. Hamilton smiled at Shari as he watched her disappear into the crowd of his family, his mother stopping at everyone and introducing her.

For the whole day, Hamilton and Shari stole looks at each other. Hamilton had laughed when his oldest sister, Helena, sat at the card table, choosing Shari as her Bid Whist partner, then placed an empty coffee can on the table—its bright read label read: Can of Kick Ass. For two hours, Shari and Helena had beat every single person who dared sit across from them. As he sat watching from his perfect view from the mouth of the back yard, Haley came and sat next to him.

"I see you two talked. I like her, Hamilton."

He looked at his sister and smiled. "Yeah, we did."

"Good. She's great, Hamilton. She seems to fit right in. And you

139

know how Helena is. Don't give nobody a chance. She and Nicky were oil and water."

Hamilton laughed at his sister's observation. They both knew as the oldest, Helena took her role seriously and was hard pressed to accept anyone into the family. Hamilton looked back at Helena and Shari, just as they slapped high five and called for another pair of victims. Hamilton knew he had to put a stop to the beating his sister and Shari were dispensing among their opposition.

"How about a dance?" Hamilton held out his right hand. Shari looked up into his smiling face, nodded then excused herself from the table.

"Can you step?"

"Can I sew?" Shari stepped into Hamilton's outstretched arms. He placed his arm about her waist. They dipped slightly forward then backward. Hamilton spun Shari out then brought her close before releasing her. Her hand was in his as their feet moved in sync to the popular steppers song, "The Jones'." They were joined by Darrin and Deb, then Helena and her husband, Anthony. A small crowd gathered as each couple put on their own show, with Helena cheering Shari on.

"Go on girl, show these folks what you're made of!" Helena said loudly.

Shari smiled as she attempted to make the old two-step look effortless. She twirled her hips as her feet followed, her hands in Hamilton's as he followed suit. When he spun her, she followed his movements, not once out of step. At the end of the song, the small crowd clapped. But Hamilton wasn't finished as the next song segued in.

"Let's slow it down, show off." Hamilton teased. He looked down into Shari's face. He pulled her close and began to sway slowly side to side in unison to the sultry sounds of "Love's Holiday," by Earth Wind and Fire. "You're too much. Is there anything that you can't do?"

Shari laughed. "Well, I can't skate backward. I can't ice skate. I can't knit, nor have I mastered baking bread from scratch. See." Shari looked up into Hamilton's face. "There are some things I can't do."

Hamilton shook his head.

After several hours had passed, which included everyone sitting down to eat, Hilary announced it was time for the annual jump rope contest. "How about some double-dutch. Haley and I won the last time."

Hamilton looked at his baby sister, an expression of mock terror on his face. "That's only because *y'all* let the kids turn."

"Spoil sport," Haley hit Hamilton on his arm. "Let's give him a chance to redeem himself. He made the Edmunds family look bad."

"Oh, its on!" Hamilton rose. "Hey, Helena, its time." Helena grinned, jumped up from the table, ran into the house, then returned moments later with a white bundle. Shari looked from Hamilton to the faces of his sister. Their mother came to stand near Shari.

"Honey, you are about to witness one of the Edmunds trademarks. They love to jump double-dutch. They taught Hamilton how to jump when he was a little boy." Ella took Shari by the hand and motioned for her to stand. "At first, my husband thought it would make him soft, if you know what I mean, but all it did was make my boy more sure. He loves his sisters so much, that he didn't mind the taunts he got from the other boys in the neighborhood. When he got older, like around 12 or 13, he didn't jump for years, but once when he was home from college for the summer, he and girls had a contest. They've been doing this ever since. It' s actually funny to watch."

Shari nodded as she listened to Hamilton's mother continue, adding that she felt between all of her children, Hamilton and Haley jumped the best. Shari looked over at Deb, who only shrugged her shoulders and raised her right eyebrow, almost as if saying: This I've got to see this.

The yard emptied onto the front of the house. Throngs of voices battled among the large family. One uncle bet ten dollars that Hamilton would "beat those girls into the ground," while another stated Hamilton had "lost his touch with age." Matthew came to stand next to Shari.

"Girl, you are in." He said, winked, then walked over and joined the crowd which formed in front of the Edmunds home.

Shari turned her attention to the numbers being called out. Helena ran to Shari. "You're my partner. You *can* jump, can't you?" Helena looked at Shari accusingly. "Because if you jump like you play cards, then girl we gonna beat the pants off this rookie bunch."

Shari nodded. She and Helena were second. Hamilton and Haley were last. As Heloise and Hilary began, with Shari and Helena turning the rope, Helena sang an old jump rope tune, Shari joined in, their voices melodic:

"Fudge, Fudge, Fudge, call the judge, momma gotta new born baby..."

Hamilton came and stood next to Shari.

"I see you left your Advil and water bottle at home," he taunted. "I want you to know, baby, those shoes ain't gonna help you. You're going to need more."

"See, I saved the Advil and the water. I wanted to make sure they were there for you, 'cause *you're* gonna need 'em." Shari said, then made a silly face at Hamilton as she continued to turn the rope.

"We shall see," Hamilton smiled.

Hilary's right leg got caught in the rope, which ended she and Heloise's turn. Next it was Helena and Shari. Both stood on opposite ends of the rope, motioning their bodies to and fro, the losing team turning. Upon hearing the beginning of another jump rope tune, both jumped in, their feet beat the pavement in unison. Helena began to turn her body full counter clock wise inside the rope. Shari followed suit. Cheers and laughter could be heard over the crowd and the pair jumped, then switched places inside the twirling rope. When they got to "red hot peas," the rope turned faster. Shari and Helena doubled their actions, the soles of their shoes tapped in unison on the pavement.

"Nah!" Helena screamed out. "Now, you all beat that!" she said as she pulled Shari into a tight, warm embrace. "You alright with me."

Hamilton stepped forward and playfully pushed Helena and Shari to the side. "Now that the rank amateur's have finished, let the pros take over."

Shari was unsure of what she would see. The thought of a man, built like a brick, standing six-foot-three, jumping double-dutch was odd, to say the least. But just as Hamilton and Haley started, she laughed at Hamilton's large feet beating the pavement along with his sister's. She heard Haley tell Hamilton it was time to beat the peas, and both pairs of feet went into double time. Shari was amazed. She had never seen a grown man, much less many boys in her youth, jump the way he did. It endeared her to know that he was secure enough in who he was to share this special bond with his sisters—evidently not worried about what anyone said, or how it appeared.

Haley twirled twice. The contest was over. "There!" Haley yelled. "We are the champs." The crowd moved closer. Hamilton's uncles exchanged money. Everyone laughed as they talked about the Edmunds children and how they wished Hamilton's father was there. Shari looked at Ella, a single tear was evident on her cheek.

She could feel the warmth without looking up. Hamilton's body heat seared her back as he came to stand close behind her. "I told you," he breathed. "Now, I guess you have to make me dinner." Shari looked up into Hamilton's face, the look in his eyes unmistakable. She knew he wanted to sample the passion they both had bottled up within themselves.

Shari blushed and looked away. She noticed her mother standing off to the side, a look of disbelief in her stare. "Hamilton, my parents are here." She walked to the edge of the lawn and escorted her parents to where Hamilton stood.

"Mom. Dad. This is Hamilton. Hamilton, these are my parents, Linda and Leonard Thomas."

"Please to meet you both. Shari talks a lot about you."

Shari watched as her father took Hamilton's hand in his and pumped it earnestly, while her mother glanced around at the gathered crowd, her expression barely hid her disdain. Shari wanted to scream and tell her mother that this was no place for airs.

Hamilton spoke. "Well, I hope you're both hungry. There's a lot of food left." He led the way to the backyard and watched as Shari's mom took short steps into the yard. "Is your mom okay?" He faced Shari.

"I don't know," Shari answered. She shrugged her shoulders, then turned to look at her father. She hoped that he could see the expression of disbelief in her eyes. "But what ever it is, I'm not in the mood for it."

To Shari's surprise, her father politely took his wife by the arm and pulled her to the side. Shari watched as her mother's face went slack, a smile, which never quite reached her eyes, became plastered on her face.

"Hello, I'm Hamilton's mother, Ella. Nice of you to join us. Come on and have some food. There's plenty." Hamilton's mother stated, then took Shari's parents by the arm and led them to the large table, which still overflowed with food. Deb appeared next to Shari.

"What was that all about?"

"I don't know and like I said, 'I'm not in the mood.' "

"Sister, I'd love to stick around, but its past Daneda's bedtime." Deb hugged Shari. "And for the record, girl, Hamilton is a definite keeper." Deb winked, then headed toward the house. She appeared moments later with Daneda sound asleep in her arms, followed by Darrin. Shari waved at them and watched as Darrin stopped to embraced Hamilton and his family.

After an additional two hours, Shari was ready to leave. She walked over to the end of the backyard, where her parents sat on lawn chairs next to Hamilton.

"It's getting late." Shari stood in front of Hamilton. She looked at her mother, then her father, who stood when Hamilton stood.

"Hamilton, its been nice meeting you. I hope to see you again." He extended his hand, then looked at his wife. "Linda, please go over and thank our host." He took his wife by the hand and lightly pushed her in the direction of Hamilton's family seated near the mouth of the large yard.

Shari tried to hide the surprised expression. She had never heard her father give orders. She was accustomed to him respond to them. Hamilton joined Shari's mother and escorted her to where his mother sat.

Shari's father faced her. "This was a really great barbeque. I haven't been to one like this in years. And Hamilton seems like a nice fellow."

"That he is, daddy."

"Well, we'll see you sometime tomorrow, Princess. Your mother and I have checked into the Hilton."

"Daddy, you didn't have to. I've got enough room."

"I know, but we're going to the Taste tomorrow and the Hilton is right across the street—no traffic to fight. We'll see you tomorrow night." Shari's father kissed her on the cheek then joined his wife and Hamilton. Shari walked to them, then hugged her mother. She was surprised at her impromptu gesture, for the last time she embraced her mother was at her college graduation.

"Your father says we need to talk," Shari's mother whispered as she returned her daughter's embrace.

"Yes, we do," Shari replied as her mother slipped out of the embrace. She watched as her mother shook Hamilton's hand, thanked him for the invitation, then left the yard. She shook her head.

Moments later, Hamilton took Shari by the hand and led her around the yard as he bid goodnight to his extended family members. It took them an additional hour to pack food to go and to clear off several tables. Once completed, Shari said her individual goodbyes to Hamilton's sisters and their families before she sought out his mother.

"Baby, you are welcome here anytime," Ella hugged Shari. "I expect to see you back real soon."

Shari nodded, then left with Hamilton.

"I had a great time, Hamilton. Thank you for inviting me," Shari glanced at his proud profile as he drove down the street. She enjoyed watching him when he interacted with his ten nieces and nephews, as well as his sisters and their husbands. She even liked how he ignored her mother's initial response to him. He would be a great family man, she said to herself. Shari shook her head. *What was wrong with her?* she wondered. Their third date and already she had herself walking down the aisle with him.

"It was an honor. My mom and sisters really like you."

"How can you tell?"

"My sister Helena told Haley that you were good in her book.

Helena bases everything on how you come across. You had her when you sat down at the card table." Hamilton chuckled. "Besides, she loves to see what folks are made of. See if they take themselves too seriously, and from the looks of it, you've passed all her tests with flying colors. And I may even passed muster with your mother."

"How so?"

"Well, she stopped looking at me as if I was from another planet," he answered, chuckling. "And your dad's cool. We talked about stocks and entrepreneurship. I even told him about my book. Yeah, I'd say today was pretty good."

Shari nodded her head as she absorbed Hamilton's words. She had never really cared if her date's parents and siblings had liked her, but she had cared what Hamilton's family thought of her.

"Well, you've got a great family."

"They're not half bad." Hamilton replied. He drummed his fingers along the steering wheel. "Hey, are you tired?"

"No, not really. More stuffed than anything." Shari chuckled. "Normally, with all of that good food, I would need a nap by now, but surprisingly I'm not sleepy. I guess its the company."

Hamilton turned the corner and headed to Lake Shore Drive. After a 20 minute drive, they arrived at North Avenue Beach. Hamilton parked at the end of the beach, got out, then walked around to assist Shari from the vehicle. He took her hand in his and they began to walk toward the rocks that cradled the beach.

They walked several feet to the rocks and sat down. The darkness around them shielded them from sight.

Hamilton reached out and lightly touched the side of Shari's face, his fingers stroked the smoothness, allowing them to record the silky softness. "I'm glad you enjoy my company. I wasn't sure at first."

Shari didn't want to talk about the wall they had erected, but if not now, when would they? And if they didn't discuss situations that made them uncomfortable, would they ever be able to? "I know, and I think it had a lot to do with being unsure."

"Are you unsure about me, my Queen?" Hamilton took Shari's hand and put it to his lips. He kissed the back of her hand, then the palm, before tracing the lines of her hand with his tongue. An electric shock shot up her hand, across her chest, then down the entire length of her body. She closed her eyes. "Are you?"

The sensations of his tongue was wrecking havoc on her senses. So much so, that she could only nod in response. "Shari, I won't hurt you, ever—I promise."

"Promise?" Shari breathed as Hamilton's luscious lips made a path up her arm to the bottom of her neck. He lingered long at the base of her neck, alternating between kisses, licks and nibbles. "Promise." He crossed his finger over his left breast. He breathed against her neck, then returned to his oral assault. "I want to be with you, Shari."

He turned her face to him, his index finger made a trail across her lips before he captured them with his own. At first he played, nipping her lips with his teeth. The more he played, the further her body rested against his. "Tell me I can have you, Shari. Tell me—I need to hear it—feel it."

Just before she responded, a loud clap of thunder, followed by lightening startled Shari. The sound pulled her out of the trance Hamilton had placed her in with his unique brand of foreplay. Hamilton straightened.

"It's about to pour. Let's get out of here." Just as they rose from the rocks the sky opened and the heavens poured fourth steady but cool torrents. Shari took Hamilton's outstretched hand and began to run along side of him. He took the keys to his SUV out of his pocket. Rain slid down the side of his face. Shari watched as he fumbled with the keys. She glanced around, then stopped him, her hand steadied his. She pulled him to her, took his face in her hands, and kissed him. She allowed the long pent up passion to take over.

Hamilton returned her kiss. His lips upon hers became fierce and unrelenting as his member came to life at the feel of Shari's small hands tugging at his silk shirt. Above the sound of the rain, Hamilton heard Shari's words and he knew, no matter what, that they would never be the same. This night, as he had hoped, would signal a turning point in their relationship.

Hamilton broke the kiss, unlocked the door, then opened it. "Not here. Spend the night with me and let me take you to paradise." He breathed. Drops of rain rolled down his face and onto hers.

Shari nodded as he lifted her into the vehicle. The kiss remained on her lips.

Paradise, she repeated to herself as she closed her eyes and laid her head back on the headrest. She didn't move when she felt Hamilton place a blanket across her. She remained silent, even as she listened to him sing to her, his smooth baritone eschewing the words to the Isley's "Sensuality" playing on the radio. Her mind raced. She thought of how it would feel to lay in Hamilton's arms, feel his weight upon her, his face buried in her hair. The sheer thought of his body next to hers caused her to shiver.

"We're almost there." Shari heard Hamilton say softly.

Shari kept her eyes closed, for she didn't want to open them and it all be a dream—an aberration of her imagination. She wanted Hamilton, that she knew, but what would happen after that. What would they mean to each other? She didn't even want to imagine it. Instead, she remembered the very words she had spoken to Deb so many moons ago: you only live by loving. And for once, Shari was going to heed her own advise. She would give herself to Hamilton without reservations.

CHAPTER 14

"Baby," Hamilton touched Shari's shoulder. "We're here."

Shari opened her eyes. The rain had stopped, leaving shiny, large puddles on the black-topped street.

In an instant, Hamilton appeared at her side and helped her step out of the SUV. She looked up at the massive grey stone in front of her.

"We're home," Hamilton announced as they climbed the steps of the concrete porch. He opened the door, then stepped aside to let Shari enter. He moved around her, disarmed the alarm system, then turned to watch her. Shari stood in the dimly lit foyer, slightly shivering from the cool air she felt from what she assumed was the air conditioning.

"Are you cold?" Hamilton asked as he walked slowly toward her. "Let me warm you." He bent his head, then pulled her into his massive arms. His lips, once again, found hers and unmercifully wrecked havoc on them as he alternated between kisses and nibbles. Shari let her hands roam up and down his back, her fingers alternately kneaded and massaged. When she let her hands fall, lightly brushing across his behind, she noted its firmness. She wanted to feel him without the barrier of clothes.

As if reading her mind, Hamilton swooped her up in his arms and carried her up the large wood staircase. She watched the fire in his eyes, the wanton passion that told her she couldn't run even if she wanted to.

His room was dark, and it took several moments for Shari's eyes to adjust to the darkness. Hamilton placed Shari on the floor. "Don't move." He commanded. She saw his form move about the large room. First, she heard the music seep out of a speaker somewhere overhead. The beginning of the song caused her to smile as the soothing voice of Peabo Bryson began, the rich melody beckoned her to just let her feelings flow. Shortly, her eyes were rewarded with the lighting of two candles sitting on a night stand near Hamilton's king-sized bed. Hamilton motioned for Shari to come to him. She did as he commanded and walked slowly toward him, the flame from the candles danced in his eyes.

"You are so beautiful, Shari. Let me make love to you." He sat on the side of the bed and began to disrobe Shari. He began by removing her baseball cap from her head, followed by the scrunch which held her hair in a pony tail. Her hair fell about her shoulders. Hamilton continued as he slowly pulled the tank-top over her head, then peeled the wet jeans from her body, followed by her shoes. He gasped at the sight of Shari standing in front of him, clad only in a wicked white, lace trimmed bra and matching thong. He wanted to take her right then, wanted to forget all senses. But he also knew that what awaited him was too special to rush.

Hamilton pulled her close and let his hands explore the fullness of her breasts and lush behind. With every feel, his senses waned and warbled, sending him into a vortex of need and want. No woman had ever been this beautiful to him, this sensuous. He had to slow down or risk losing total control.

Hamilton stood, pulled back the cover, then sheet before he took Shari by the hand and led her to an adjoining room. He dimmed the lights to the bathroom. Shari smiled at the expansive room, a large Jacuzzi sat in one corner, with a shower stall next to it. Hamilton turned on the shower, adjusted the temperature, then stepped in front of Shari. He watched the dim lights dance in her eyes, then stepped back and began to slowly disrobe.

Picture perfect, Shari thought, as her eyes followed his hands as he slid his shirt over his head, took off his jeans, then finally removed his black boxer briefs. Every inch was perfectly sculptured, from his well defined pectorals to his muscular thighs.

Hamilton reached out to her and pulled her body to lay parallel against his. He kissed her face and let his hands dance across her body. He broke the embrace, opened the glass shower door, then stepped inside. He held out his hand. Shari removed her bra, then stepped out of her thong. The pleased look on his face told her all she wanted to know.

The warm spray rained across her and she shivered lightly as Hamilton began to apply a honey scented gel to her back, the soap making his hands glide effortlessly up down her entire backside. He pulled her close to him and she could feel his engorged member throb against her back as he began to apply the fragrant gel to her breasts.

He turned her to face him, then sat her on the bench in the shower stall. Hamilton knelt in front her and took her feet in his hands. He rubbed and kneaded them before moving up to her calves then thighs. He looked into her eyes as his fingers traveled slowly toward her cavern. When she closed her eyes, he smiled wickedly and continued onward as his fingers played in the folds of her labia.

"Shari," his words were low and raspy. "Look at me. Open your eyes."

Shari opened her eyes. She could see the fire dance in his eyes—the raw, unbridled mix of passion and need. And if the expression on her face was any indication, she was sure that Hamilton could see her need for him. Hamilton lightly increased the pleasurable pressure.

153

Shari arched her back. Pure ecstasy was all she could summons as he expertly circled her button—Hamilton strummed her as no other man had.

She gasped when she felt his warm mouth replace his fingers. Shari was lost, as his tongue began a symphony all its own. He played with her. Strummed her. He continued to pick and ply her with his tongue. He allowed her to come close, but not close enough for her to reach the peak she wanted, needed to ascend to.

Hamilton slowly rose. "Not here," he ordered, rinsed her off, then himself. He shut off the water and opened the door. He retrieved a large bath towel and wrapped it around her. He lifted her into his arms and carried her back to his room. He laid her on his bed, then slid next to her and covered them both. His tongue traced a searing path along her damp body, until he returned to his original exploration. This time he lingered much longer at her feminine being. He wanted to see her reach her release, wanted to watch the expression on her face as the orgasm peaked then ebbed. He started slow at first, his tongue teased and stroked. When Shari placed her hands about his head, a loud cat-like cry escaped her lips, he knew she had reached her peak. He watched as her eyes rolled backward, then fluttered shut, her face contorted in a pang of pleasure. He held his mouth on her and waited for her passion to subside.

When Shari opened her eyes, he was slightly startled, for what he saw was raw, naked passion. Suddenly he wasn't sure if he could handle the sultry siren. He had awakened her and he knew she would finish them both.

Shari pulled Hamilton by his shoulders, then motioned for them to roll over. Her lithe body rested atop his. She let her hands run across his clean shaven head, down to his face, then to the top of his chest, before coming to rest as his sides. She bowed her head and flicked her tongue across his nipples, while her hands played at the sides of his behind. "Be gentle with me. I'm fragile."

He heard Shari chuckle. "Fragile my ass," she stated between nips. Yet, his words couldn't keep her from unleashing the full power of her passion. Shari let her hands and lips take its own tour across Hamilton's body. When she came across his fully hard member, she paused. She rubbed him, filling her hands with him. He gasped as she placed wet kisses along his pelvis then his thighs. She was dangerously close, he shivered.

Shari sensuously snaked her body up his. When she reached his face, she kissed him and allowed her tongue to play with his.

"I can't stand it," Hamilton growled. He rolled her over, then groped around the night stand. Shari watched as he attempted to rip open the condom package. His hands trembled slightly.

"Let me," Shari took the package from his hands, then rolled the sheath over his engorged member. They paused—searching for any sign that would state what was about to transpire wasn't suppose to— that the feelings they were sharing weren't real. When none showed, Shari held her arms open to him, his eyes seared hers. She could plainly see the confused mixture of want and lust.

This can't be happening, she thought as he moved over her and positioned himself at her womanhood. Slowly he began to ascend, inch by inch into her. He stopped, then looked at her. The passion and fire in her eyes beckoned him onward and he could no longer control the act as he went further. He sank inside of her and groaned at the tightness of her. He didn't want to move, for he knew if he did all would be lost.

Shari sighed wantonly as she moved her hips.

"Baby," he moaned. "Please don't move. Please don't."

But Shari couldn't obey. The feel of him deep inside of her made her shamelessly rotate her hips into his. She heard him let out a long sigh as he began to fluidly move inside of her.

Their backs arched as the passion fire roared, their motions taking over, spilling out across the silence of the room. Shari began to move with him, her hips taking on a frenzied dance of their own. The fullness and length of him caressed her, and she ground her hips up into his, wanting more. And he gave her what her body called for, what her body asked of him. As the passion fire grew, he felt the release beg, attempt to escape, but he wanted to feel her reach her own peak before his and tempered his movements.

"Tell me this is real, baby. Tell me."

"This is real. I'm real. I'm here, Hamilton." Shari moved under him, her hips gyrated against his.

"Baby, you better stop that or I'm going to loose it. Literally."

She smiled, yet was remised to stop. She couldn't. The feelings had taken over and her body willed itself as her hands roamed across his taunt behind.

"Okay, baby. Talk to me—tell me what you want."

She sensed that he didn't want to hear words, instead she let her body speak for her—constricting her walls, sending torrents of pleasure throughout their bodies.

"Yess, that's it," Hamilton responded, his arms wrapped around Shari's body. "Yes, baby, that is it. Give me all of you."

With his command, Shari intensified her constrictions, allowing her walls to encase him, trap him in a sweet embrace. She sensed his need was close and she began to gyrate faster, her hips crashing into his. Their movements became frenzied, as Shari felt her own release coming strong. She snaked her legs around his waist and allowed the passion fire to erupt, calling out his name. Hamilton's strokes became more languid as he moved in and out of her love, his member throbbed as he released his passion. She muzzled her mouth against his chest as she called out his name.

A single tear rolled down her cheek as the fire in her smoldered. Hamilton kissed away the tear, rolled them over, then wrapped his arms around her.

"Woman, you'd be the death of me for sure," Hamilton whispered in Shari's ear. "The pure death of me."

Shari smiled and allowed her body to still. She listened to Hamilton's heart beating softly as it began to lull her to sleep. As she drifted off, she thought of the man whose arms she was in and knew that she had fallen in love. The thought jarred her, and she looked up into Hamilton's face. He smiled at her, his hand soothing her back.

"Stay the night," he ordered softly. "I want to see you in the morning."

"It'll be a sight," she whispered.

"Remember, I have four sisters. Trust me when I tell you that I'm prepared."

Shari chuckled, then laid her head back on his chest, her body nestled perfectly upon his. If this was a dream, she told herself, she never wanted to wake up.

Two hours later, Shari awoke to Hamilton's lips upon her nipples. They made love again, this time slowly. After their second release, they talked in hushed tones, wrapped in each others arms. Shari told him more of her plans to begin her design company.

Hamilton really liked her idea and knew that after he had seen her studio, followed by her taken his measurements, he wanted to help her make her dream become a reality.

"If you need anything, let me know. I'm here for you." He kissed the top of her head.

Shari snuggled closer. This was what she had wanted, what she had waited her entire life for. She closed her eyes and let the warmth of his support soothe and comfort her. Maybe, she thought, just maybe I can have it all. She drifted off to sleep secured in his arms.

CHAPTER 15

Shari's eyes popped open. She looked around the unfamiliar room. Her eyes rested upon the dark angel who had awakened her body and placed love within her hands. She sat up, pulling the sheet to cover her naked breasts.

"Good morning." His voice reverberated through her, his hand caressed her back. "I hope you slept well."

She turned to see his broad smile. "That I did."

"Come here," he ordered, his arms open to her. She complied, and laid in his arms, his fingers stroking her hair. "You look great in the morning."

Shari looked up at him and swatted his arm. "And you, my good man, are a bonafide liar." They both laughed. "What time is it? We have that brunch date with Deb, Darrin, Denise and Jon."

Hamilton looked at the clock on his night stand. "It's seven-fifteen. What time are we suppose to meet them?"

"Deb said yesterday that Denise doesn't feel like cooking, so we're suppose to meet at the House of Blues at twelve," she replied. "And I need to go home and change clothes."

"We've got time," he responded, a mischievous look upon his face. "Just enough time," he said, covering Shari with his body. She smiled as they began again.

"I called you this morning," Deb whispered, her eyebrows raised. "But as I see the two of you together, I guess I now know why you didn't answer. You must have told him about Bruce."

Shari nodded, then smiled as the couples waited to be seated. "I've got a lot to tell you." She looked over at Hamilton, his large frame matched Darrin's and dwarfed Jon's as the three strikingly handsome men talked. She watched them interact as Hamilton took Daneda from Darrin's arms.

"Looks natural, doesn't it? That's going to be you next year."

"Who's gonna be what next year?" Denise came to stand beside them. Shari snorted. "Says who?"

"Aww, come on Shari. That man is it. He's the one."

"I'll say," Denise looked over at the three men standing beside each other. "If I wasn't already married, I'd hit on that tall, dark, drink of water."

Shari and Deb looked to their soror, then laughed. Denise shrugged her shoulders, holding her hand out, palms up. "What? I'm married. Not dead. I know a good looking man when I see one." Denise turned to face Shari. "And that my sister, is one good looking brother and sexy too. Have yall . . . ," she let the words hang in the air.

Shari smiled, looking from Denise to Deb, then back to Denise. "Yall, know I don't kiss and tell."

"Hah!" Denise squealed. "She's tasted the fruit. And from the looks of it, it must be all that, a large bag of chips and a six pack of Pepsi."

The trio laughed. Deb was the first one to turn serious. "Now, the question is, will girlfriend here be open enough to enjoy it all?"

"Who you talking about?" Denise asked, her eyebrows raised. "Deb, I know you're not talking about Miss you've-got-to-love-to-live?"

"Yes, the one and only."

"Deb doesn't know what she's talking about," Shari breathed out.

"Oh, I don't? Anyway, he's the one, Shari. I feel it. Don't you?"

Thoughts of the morning she had spent making love to Hamilton was still fresh and caused her to tremor slightly. "Deb, you're hallucinating. We're just taking it one day at a time."

She went back to watching Hamilton. He was everything she wanted in a man. He was attentive, intelligent and was a magnificent lover. But still that didn't make for a great relationship. They hadn't disagreed. Hadn't had their feelings tested. She didn't want to wish—didn't want to hope that Hamilton would be the man she had hoped for. She was afraid and she knew it, but her heart wouldn't let her run. And she was glad for it.

The group sat and talked throughout their meal. As they prepared to go their separate ways, Deb pulled Shari to the side.

"I'm gonna come by later, okay?"

Shari nodded her head. She knew her best friend wanted to talk about Hamilton. She loved her best friend, the woman who was the sister she never had, but she wasn't up for any lengthy discussions about her heart. Besides, she had heard it all before—had preached the very sermon herself.

On the ride to her place, Shari remained quiet. From the corner of her eye, she could see Hamilton glancing at her.

"Call me later," Hamilton began as he pulled in front of Shari's building. "I'll be working on my book and will be looking for an interruption."

"I will," Shari responded, gathered her purse and then opened the door. She paused, then turned to look at Hamilton. His handsome face and warm smile wrecked havoc on her senses. "Besides, I still owe you a dinner." She laughed at the image of Hamilton and his sister jumping rope.

"That you do," he pulled her hand to his mouth and placed a kiss on it. "And I will be back to collect." Hamilton leaned over and kissed her on her lips. He lingered long. Shari moaned.

"Umm, maybe I should pay you a visit tonight." He winked.

"You know we both have to go to work tomorrow. If you do what you did last night or this morning, neither of us will get any sleep." The spot between her legs trembled.

"True that, baby—true that."

Hamilton assisted Shari out of the vehicle and walked her to her door. He stopped at the foyer and pulled her into her arms. "Did you enjoy your weekend?"

"I had a wonderful time, Hamilton."

"How about we go out Tuesday?"

"Why don't you call me and we'll talk about it."

Hamilton lifted her chin. He kissed her lightly on the lips. "Okay. I'll talk to you later."

Shari watched him walk away. She smiled when he turned and winked at her. When she heard Rocket bark, she knew the telephone was ringing. It was a habit Rocket had since she was a puppy. Shari ran up the stairs, unlocked the door, then ran to the extension in the living room.

"Hello?"

"I'll be there in a couple of hours." Deb hung up without preamble. Shari stared at the phone. She knew that Deb wasn't about to let their earlier conversation go—wasn't about to let her sort out her own feelings without some interference. Well, Shari mused, as she remembered how she had meddled in Deb and Darrin's relationship. From information on the types of activities Deb enjoyed, to booking them on the same flight to California, Shari had supplied Darrin with enough information to woo Deb. So, what did she expect? One good turn does deserve another.

Shari walked to her bedroom, sat on the side of her bed and began removing her shoes. Sure, Shari continued, Deb could say it was easy, she had found her soul mate, had found the man she truly loved and could love without hesitation.

Shari stood, removed her linen pants suit, and put on a red sweat shirt and a matching pair of sweat pants. She brushed her hair back into a pony tail and headed to her studio. She shook her head. She really didn't want to talk to Deb—didn't want to admit that she had used the business as an excuse to keep her feelings in check.

Shari sat at her drafting table and removed the picture of Hamilton. She glanced over her shoulder at the mannequin partially dressed in the suit she had begun sewing for Hamilton before she had taken his measurements. When Hamilton had come to her studio, she hadn't shown him that she had already begun on the suit. He hadn't even seen that she had already started.

For some inexplicable reason, the sketch of Hamilton, how she had captured his eyes, stayed with her to the point where she had to at least begin to put the suit together. She had created a pattern, pinned the pattern to several yards of finely woven worsted wool fabric she had purchased in Italy, then cut the fabric as outlined by the pattern.

Shari took the fabric and began to baste, by hand, the inseam of the trousers, followed by the blazer. For nearly an hour she worked before she stopped and placed the unfinished suit on the mannequin.

She turned her attention to the documents on her desk. She gathered the documents and placed them in an envelope. They were the papers she would need to incorporate her business. Shari had decided to go to the State of Illinois building first thing on Monday morning to incorporate the name of her company. Once finished with that task, Shari turned her attention to the logo she had designed for her business. She looked at the large letter 'B' drawn in script, followed by the rest of the letters, to be cast in bold. She liked what she saw.

Three hours later, she heard Mrs. Ponticello call her name, then announced Deb's arrival.

"Hey Rocket," Deb squealed. The dog jumped up and placed her front paws on Deb's shoulders, then bathed Deb's face with her tongue. "I miss you too, Rocket, but I've already washed my face. Yuck!" Deb removed Rocket's paws from her shoulders.

"Where's Daneda?" Shari asked. She avoided her best friends eyes and continued to look over various papers on her desk.

"At home with Darrin," Deb responded, then sat on a near by stool. "Wow! Is that for Hamilton." Deb pointed at the unfinished suit jacket worn by a large mannequin.

"Sure is. I had enough fabric around here to make him a suit."

Deb stood and examined the jacket. She ran her hand along the sleeve. "This is nice and this fabric feels like silk. What is it?"

"Worsted wool from Italy."

"And you are making this for Hamilton?" Deb asked. She looked at her friend. "I don't recall you making Bruce anything."

Shari didn't reply. Deb continued. "So, are you going to give me the full skinny or what?"

Shari smiled at the thought, her mind filled with images of her laying in Hamilton's arms. "I must admit that I had a wonderful weekend. Hamilton's a true gentleman."

"Would it be safe to say that you have decided to give a relationship with Hamilton a chance?"

"Maybe. We'll take it one day at a time," she responded, her voice low and barely audible. "But to be honest, Deb, it all seems like a dream. I mean, I've had dates, gone out with plenty of men, but none of them have ever made me feel the way Hamilton does."

"Sounds as if someone is falling in love," Deb responded as she returned to sit on the stool. She watched her best friend's eyes light up, then dim. She knew fear when she saw it and decided to change the subject. Deb went on to talk about the Edmunds Family barbeque and Hamilton as he jumped double-dutch with his sisters. "Girl, I didn't know what to expect." Deb snickered. "Darrin told me that they even once had him jumping double-dutch."

"Now that would havebeen something to see." Shari laughed. "Darrin jumping double dutch. But you know, in some strange way, watching Hamilton jump made him sexier. I mean, a man has to be truly sure of himself to do that in front of a crowd of people. But..." Shari's voice trailed off.

"But what?"

She sighed. "Let's not jump the gun. Like I said, we're taking it one day at a time. Besides, I'm getting close."

"Close to what, Shari?" Deb tilted her head to one side.

"Starting the company. I may be able to quit my job by the end of summer."

"Congratulations. How'd that happen?"

"I sent dad my business plan and he's going to invest. Told me that he was all in and may have a few investors. So, you see, I need to stay focused."

"So, what does that have to do with you being with Hamilton?"

"I'm just saying, you know? I don't want him to be a distraction. I've wanted to start this business for a long time."

Deb looked at her best friend. "What makes you think you can't have both of them?"

"Oh, Deb," she responded exasperated. "You don't understand. I've dreamed of this my whole life ... and to have Hamilton in the ..."

"No," Deb interrupted. "*You* don't understand. I can't believe that this is the same Shari Thomas who sat me down and told me that you only live by loving. Besides, after the company is up and running, who are you going to share it with? Certainly not our mangy dog." Rocket's ears perked up. "Sorry baby. I still love you." Deb reached out and scratched behind Rocket's ears.

Shari chuckled in spite of the serious tone in her best friends voice. She listened as Deb continued. "Shari, I'm not going to sit here and listen to you make excuse after excuse, especially after you hitched up plan after plan to get me and Darrin together. But, I am going to do you one better. I'm going to mind my own business."

She looked up. "Thank you, Deb. I appreciate it."

"*But*," Deb stood. "If you get too stupid, Darrin and I are going to be all *in* your business." She came to stand in front of Deb. She placed her hands on Shari's. "And it's going to be hard not to, because you were so right about Darrin. You seemed to have been able to see beyond the surface and that's what I love most about you. Now, I want you to look beyond the surface."

Shari pulled her hands from Deb. Admittedly, she had grown tired of wondering if the men she had met were the one for her, or was he another game player, looking to score some quick sex while he kept his home intact. No, she wasn't up for it, and in the process she believed she had lost her ability to see beyond the surface. But Hamilton made her dream—made her believe.

"Enough said. Hey, you got anything sweet around here to eat?" Deb asked.

Shari nodded her head. "How about some chocolate macadamia nut ice cream?"

"Sounds good to me."

The two friends left Shari's studio and headed up the stairs to Shari's apartment. In the kitchen, Shari retrieved the ice cream from the freezer, then grabbed two bowls from the cabinet near the refrigerator. She placed the two bowls on the counter and scooped the ice cream into them. As they ate and laughed, Shari thought of the old days when she and Deb had shared a home.

Several hours after Deb left, Shari readied herself for bed. The sound of the phone ringing stopped her as she was about to climb into bed.

"Hello," she responded.

"Hey, baby. Ready for bed?"

She smiled. "Sure am. What about you?"

"I've got the lights out. You know that's some wicked cologne you wear. It's all over the place." Hamilton laughed. "It's going to be hard to get to sleep."

They spoke for an hour. They revealed more about themselves, of their dreams and aspirations. Yet, they never got to the question of what was next for them.

As Shari replaced the receiver in its cradle, then turned off the lights, she thought of how much she cared for Hamilton. The words Deb had spoken came back in a flurry. "Don't run."

"I'll try not to." Sari rolled over and shut her eyes.

CHAPTER 16

Shari thought she was in a deep dream as the incessant sound of a door chime invaded her mind. She opened her eyes, then looked at the clock on her night stand. She began to fuss. "Who ever it is ringing my bell at 1 a.m. better be damn near dead." She pulled herself out of the bed and stalked to the intercom. "Who is it?"

"It's me, baby."

Shari depressed the button, unlocked the door, and waited at the top of the stairs. She watched as Hamilton came into view. She smiled as he walked up the stairs.

"I couldn't sleep. I told you that your cologne would keep me awake," he said. "I hope you don't mind. I know its late." He hugged her.

She looked up into his eyes. "It's alright, but next time how about you give a sister a little warning?" She raked her hand over her head covered in a black silk scarf.

His eyes trailed down her body, clad in a short plum colored chemise. If the way she looked was considered bad, then he was in for one hell of a surprise. "You're beautiful." He pulled the scarf from her head and let his fingers play in her hair. He planted a kiss on her lips. "I'll do that the next time."

He followed her into the apartment, then to her room. And though he thought about the love they had made the day before, the fierce intensity of it, in reality Hamilton just wanted to hold her in his arms—to soothe the incessant fear his emotions had awakened.

Shari climbed into bed, then pulled the quilt and sheet back for him to join her. Hamilton took off his clothes down to his boxer briefs. He slid between the sheets, rolled to his side, then pulled Shari to him, his groin nestled against her full behind. He groaned, the feel of his hard member reminded him of the night they had spent together.

They both yawned. "One of you is sleepy, the other is very much awake," Shari teased.

"I know, but if you don't move, he'll go to sleep too." They chuckled, Hamilton's arms about Shari. And though she felt herself twinge at the feel of Hamilton's member against her, she was admittedly tired herself. After a few moments, Hamilton's breathing leveled, a slight snore escaped his lips. Shari closed her eyes and let slumber catch her. In the morning, she thought.

Sunlight streamed through the vertical blinds, casting rays off of Shari's warm brown skin. She opened her eyes to the feel of Hamilton's hands as they smoothly and expertly explored every inch of her. She was surprised to notice that the chemise she went to bed in was no where to be found.

"Mr. Edmunds, I'm afraid to ask you where my night gown went." She rolled over to face him, a wicked smile stretched across his handsome face. Hamilton raised his right eye brow and motioned over his shoulder with his head. "Down there, somewhere." Shari shook her head, opting to let him continue to awaken her.

"You're quite beautiful in the morning, you know."

"Umm, hmm," she replied, his fingers now entwined into the

folds of her being. She wanted to stop him, wanted to at least brush her teeth, but the arousal he had started could only be stopped by him. And she didn't want him to let her go.

Shari sighed loudly and gave in to him. She opened her heart for the second time and let all that she felt flow freely through her veins. As his fingers circled her being, she held onto him. She felt herself become lost, entwined in the pure simplicity of it all. She felt the stirring—felt it deep while it rose from the bottom of her feet. Her body reacted, causing her hips to meet his fingers. She grabbed his hand and motioned for him to continue as the wave took over and washed her entirely.

Hamilton protected her as he rolled the latex sheath over his member, then pulled her to rest atop him, his hardened shaft sunk slowly inside of her. He couldn't hold back—couldn't stand the heat—the warmth—the constrictions of her cavern.

"Shari," he called out her name. Their hips met one another—their bodies as one. As he reached his orgasm, he held Shari to his chest and willed his heart to relay what his mouth would not—he was in love with her. In all of his adult life, he had never felt this strong about any woman.

Spent, Shari rubbed her hands across his face—her body and mind satiated. She knew that whatever happened after this, if Hamilton broke her heart, she would never be the same.

"Sweetheart, I need to shower. And we're both going to be late for work."

"Umm." Hamilton stroked her hair. His hands roamed down her back to rest on her behind. "I'm willing to be late every morning if I can wake up to you like this." He released her, then followed her into the bathroom.

After their shower, they dressed, then shared a light breakfast of toast, fruit and orange juice. Hamilton drove Shari to work. He kissed her gently upon the lips as she climbed out of the SUV. "I'll call you later, baby."

Shari smiled as she headed for the glass double doors to Macy's— she looked over her shoulder. Hamilton stood outside his vehicle and watched her as she walked toward the building. She waved at him. He waved back, but didn't move. She waved both hands in an attempt to shoo him away. He smiled as he shook his head, "no," then motioned for her to come to him. Shari returned to him.

"Aren't you going to be late?"

Hamilton pulled Shari into his arms. "That's all I wanted," he said, then kissed her on her lips. "Go to work," he ordered as he rounded his vehicle, opened the door, then climbed into the drivers seat. He waved, then sped off.

Shari stood at the curb, her face flushed. "Umph, that man."

Shari's day went by in a blur. Just about every minute of her eight hour day was absorbed by constant thoughts and images of Hamilton. At one point, as Shari sat in a Spring design meeting, she continually scribbled her first name and Hamilton's last name together in her leather bound note pad. Shari Thomas-Edmunds. She scratched the name out, then rewrote it. Shari Edmunds. There, she mused, she liked the latter one.

At the end of the meeting, Shari waltzed into her office and smiled broadly at the large bouquet of red roses sitting atop her desk. She took the card from a plastic stem and read it aloud.

Thank you for a wonderful weekend. Hoping with all my heart that we have many more. Sincerely, Hamilton.

Shari picked up the large crystal vase and brought the flowers to her nose. She inhaled the poignant fragrance, then shook her head and grinned.

"Hamilton, what am I going to do with you?" On cue, her heart responded where her lips could not: *I'm going to love you, Hamilton.*

She sat the vase down, then herself. She loved him and that was all there was to it. And she had to tell him, but she was afraid. *Maybe*, she argued with herself, *I'll wait until he says it first—I mean, most times if the man says it first, it breaks the tension and makes it okay for the woman to say it.* Shari shook her head again. She had become agitated with herself for making such a big deal out of the whole situation. It was time to grow up, she berated herself, and enjoy what Hamilton had placed at her feet. If he didn't feel the same, so what, at least she knew she could love.

Shari looked at the roses again, smiled, then turned her attention to her work. Yes, it was time. Besides, she knew the emotions, the love she felt for Hamilton, couldn't be controlled—even if she wanted to.

CHAPTER 17

For two weeks straight, Shari and Hamilton saw each other every day. Between his busy schedule as an editor and the re-writes for his first novel, and Shari's own hectic work schedule and continued movements to open her own company, the couple found time for each other. Yet, Shari was plagued by the things unsaid—the words that were never spoken between them. Sure, they spent a lot of time together, but Hamilton had never said if they were an exclusive item, and Shari never inquired. She knew what assumptions could do to a relationship.

Shari rose from her desk and looked out the window. She sighed loudly, her rampant thoughts kept her from devoting her full attention to the upcoming season's designs. Despite her continued arguments with herself, the uncertainty wouldn't leave her. And every time the uncertainty reared its ugly head, images of Hamilton seeped into her mind and attempted to crowd out the negative ones. A tingling sensation rode along her arms, goose bumps rose fast and furious. Though she had slept with a few men, she had never encountered one as passionate as Hamilton. Shari shivered. Hamilton's eyes had bore a hole in her soul and refused to free her.

"Shari," the voice of her assistant interrupted her thoughts. "You have a call on line one."

"Shari Thomas here," she spoke into the receiver.

"Hey," the voice began. "How's my baby's day going?"

She smiled. "I'm doing well, Hamilton. How is your day?"

"It will be better if my lady would agree to spending the evening with me."

Shari paused, an inexplicable fear rose from her chest. Her emotions were raw and exposed. Shari loved Hamilton—had felt it the night they first made love. But she couldn't verbalize it. She couldn't put into words what her heart wanted her mouth to say. And she knew it was time for her to lay her cards on the table and tell him how she felt.

"I'd love to, Hamilton," she said. Her need to see him, feel his body close hers, overrode her fear. "What do you have in mind?"

"How about we have dinner at your place? I'll cook."

"Really?" Shari replied. "Now that sounds like a plan. Are you going to pick me up."

"Yeah, what time will you be finished?"

"I'll be finished at around 6. How's that?"

"Six it is—see you then."

"Okay, sweetie." Shari disconnected the call and forced herself to turn her attention back to her work. For the next several hours, Shari worked feverishly at on the plans for the upcoming Fall designs.

At 6 exactly, Shari rose from her desk, grabbed her coat, and walked out to meet Hamilton.

"Hey, baby." Hamilton pulled Shari into his arms. He placed a kiss on her lips. "How did your day end?"

"I got a lot done. I finished the plans for the upcoming show, and started on the Spring Design show."

Hamilton assisted Shari into the SUV and smiled as she continued to talk about her day. He nodded, his thoughts roamed to a place he hadn't been in a long time. He loved Shari. Loved her to the point of where he knew that life without her would mean nothing to him. He knew, in that moment as he listened to her warm voice, that he wanted her to live with him, as his wife, for the rest of his life. And he had to tell her.

"Hamilton," he heard Shari call his name. "What's wrong?"

"Oh, nothing, just listening to you." He took her hand in his and kissed it. "Keep talking. I love your voice."

"You like hearing me rattle on?" Shari laughed. "Next thing you'll be telling me that you want to move in?"

"Would that be so bad? Just think, you can cook for me everyday," Hamilton replied, then glanced at her. *That was weak*, he told himself. What he wanted to tell her was how much he loved and cared for her. Instead, he intimates that they should live together.

"Yeah, right," Shari said. "I only cook on the weekends, Hamilton. You know that. I can't see cooking everyday. It's too taxing. Besides, you cook. Why can't you be the one to cook everyday?"

He tilted his head to one side. "Why couldn't we share the cooking duties?"

Shari wondered how had a conversation about her day turned into one with her cooking everyday. *Hell*, she thought, *they hadn't even discussed the status of their relationship*. As far as she knew, they could date other people, because neither had bothered to tell the other that they were an exclusive item. She guessed they just assumed.

"Okay, I'll cook Monday and Wednesday. You cook Tuesday and Thursday. Friday will be date night. Saturday will be leftover night and Sunday you get down in the kitchen!" Hamilton laughed. He turned his head slightly to see Shari's expression. A slight smile showed on her face, but never quite reached her eyes.

"For some reason, that deal still includes my doing the majority of the cooking. When do I get a chance to design?" Shari asked.

"Anytime you want."

Shari turned her head and watched the buildings pass along

Martin Luther King, Jr. Drive. For some reason she didn't believe him. All she could see was her as a domestic goddess while her dreams took a back seat to his needs. She shook her head. This isn't what she wanted.

"Oh, we need to stop by the grocery store. I've got to pick up some items for dinner," Hamilton said. He pulled into the parking lot of the grocery store.

Shari followed Hamilton around the large grocery store. She watched as he methodically chose various items. He had taken several pieces of fruit and turned them over in his hand before he made a selection.

As he pushed the cart, his mind wandered. He fantasized about Shari, thoughts of her in his kitchen with nothing on but an apron as she prepared him dinner. He felt himself stir and admonished himself to push the thought to the back of his mind.

At one point, as they stood in an aisle, Hamilton wanted to pull her into his arms and tell her exactly how he felt. He changed his mind and decided he'd do so during dinner. For once in his life, he wanted to open up and be honest about how he felt.

An hour later, in the check out lane, he noticed that Shari had been staring at him oddly. He couldn't discern the expression on her face. Was this too much like a married couple, he wondered. They were shopping together—discussed household duties and made life plans. And he liked it.

Shari felt uneasy. She noted a change in Hamilton's stare, in the way he watched her. To her, his stare foretold of a serious conversation to come. But what? She wondered as they placed several bags of groceries into the rear of the Expedition.

Seated, she listened to Hamilton's deep voice, as he talked about nothing in particular. Shari thought about the scene in the grocery store. They had acted like an old married couple.

As they entered her block, Shari watched Hamilton as he shut off the engine, then turned in his seat to face her. The lines above his forehead were visible as his light eyes stared into Shari's deep brown ones.

Hamilton was surprised to see fear in her eyes. The last thing he wanted was for her to fear him—fear the emotions he knew they had kept at bay for over a month.

Shari became uneasy. She was afraid as she looked into Hamilton's intense light eyes. She tired to ignore the inner voice which intimated something wasn't quite right. She stepped quickly out of the vehicle.

In her apartment, they put away the groceries, then Hamilton began to prepare dinner. He made cube steaks, smothered in homemade gravy, topped with onions and green peppers, accompanied by garlic mashed potatoes, corn and dinner rolls.

Shari set the table, while Hamilton retrieved two wine glasses. Rocket was close on his heels.

"Did you feed the dog?" Hamilton called out to Shari.

"Oh, no I forgot. Din-din Rocket!"

Hamilton laughed out loud as he watched the animal sprint out of the dining room. Rocket's paws made loud noises as she rushed to the kitchen to eat. "No wonder you and Deb named her rocket."

Once Rocket fed Shari, she and Hamilton sat down to dinner. Shari continued to watch Hamilton. She could see he wanted to say something, had watched his mouth open and close several times, yet never uttered anything profound.

After the meal was finished, Hamilton insisted upon washing the dishes, and upon completion, he suggested they retire to her sitting room. Hamilton turned on Shari's stereo. The sultry voice of Howard Hewett seeped out of the overhead speakers. Hamilton laid on the chaise and pulled Shari to lay atop him.

"That was some meal, man. Keep cooking like that and you'll never get rid of me."

"That's the plan. But wait," Hamilton lifted Shari's face. "Don't you still owe me a meal?"

Shari laughed. "You have eaten enough meals over here to last you a life time."

Hamilton sighed heavily. "A life time isn't long enough."

Shari noted the unsteady rise and fall of Hamilton's chest. Okay, she steeled herself, this is it.

"Shari." He took her hand in his. He decided it was time to tell her how he felt. He ignored the mounting tension that circled them. To Hamilton, it was now or never.

"Shari, I ..." He was interrupted when Rocket began to bark loudly. Someone knocked on the door. Shari looked at Hamilton.

"It must be Mrs. Ponticello." Shari stood, then headed to the door. She opened it. Her mouth fell open. "Bruce!" Shari blurted out. "What are you doing here? How did you get in?"

"The door was open. We need to talk. We need to talk about us. I hope I'm not interrupting anything?"

Shari turned her head. Hamilton came to stand by her side. Rocket sat next to Hamilton. She growled lowly. Hamilton stretched out his hand. "I'm Hamilton. And you are?" His eyebrows were raised.

"Bruce. Bruce Nelson. I didn't mean to interrupt—I can come back another time."

"No need. I was just leaving." He turned away. Hamilton returned moments later with his coat in hand. "I don't want to interrupt your important talk. You know?" He stated snidely. He paused, then looked at Shari. She could see the fire blaze in his eyes as it burned out of control. His face was a mixed mask of rage and pain.

No! Her mind screamed as she watched him brush past she and

Bruce. No, this can't be happening. She faced Bruce.

"What are you doing here?" She cried.

"I didn't mean to cause a rift. Besides, what kind of man would leave his woman with her ex-fiancé?"

"Bruce, you are out of line!" She hissed. "You need to state your business, then leave."

"Aren't you gonna invite me in?"

"No!" Shari folded her arms across her chest.

"Well, at least lets walk and talk. I've got a lot to say."

Shari shrugged. The last thing she wanted was to have Bruce in her apartment. He had already caused enough damage. Then again, she thought that maybe if Hamilton hadn't left and if he saw her escort Bruce out, he would know there's nothing going on between the two of them. She shook her head.

"Wait right here." She shut the door in Bruce's face, grabbed Rocket's leash, then returned. "Might as well walk the dog." Rocket growled again. "Easy, girl."

"You know that dog never liked me."

Shari didn't respond as she stepped outside. She looked up and down the block. She had hoped that Hamilton would still be in front of the apartment. She sighed.

"You've got 15 minutes." Shari insisted, then walked away. Bruce followed. They walked several blocks to a nearby park. Shari released Rocket from her leash, then sat on a nearby bench.

"Shari, I just wanted to tell you thank you." Bruce stood near the bench.

She looked up at Bruce. "Thank me?"

"Yes, thank you. We were all wrong for each other, but my love for you wouldn't let me see it. I'm just glad we came to our senses before it was too late. Besides, I saw the way you looked at him. Saw it the night at the gallery. You never looked at me with that kind of love in your eyes."

Shari looked away. She hadn't been fair to Bruce, yet because of him she was free to experience true love—a love with Hamilton. "No, Bruce it's me who needs to thank you as well as apologize." She took his hand in hers. "I wasn't fair to you. I was in love with the idea of being married, of having a husband and maybe even children—never mind the simple fact that I needed to be in love with the man I was to marry."

"And you really didn't love me, did you Shari?"

She shook her head. "No I didn't. And I never said it." She watched the pain cross his mocha colored face, then register in his dark brown eyes. "Bruce, I cared deeply for you, but even you said it. It wasn't enough."

"Thank you, Shari for being honest. Now I feel I can really move on. I've met someone, but I needed to know how you felt. Needed to hear how you truly felt. You know, put some closure to us."

Shari stood and hugged Bruce. She was glad to finally be granted an opportunity to tell the truth — to allow the past to be released. Now, she had to go to Hamilton.

"If it will help any, I'll call your boyfriend and tell him that my intentions were pure. I didn't mean to cause any trouble."

Shari laughed. "No, that won't be necessary. Let me handle him." She kissed his cheek. "Take care, Bruce and good luck."

"Thanks. Same to you. He's going to make you a good husband, you know."

Shari nodded, called out to Rocket, then left the park. She jogged home, Hamilton's angry face plastered in her mind. She had to go to him. Had to make him understand that she loved him, and only him. She stopped. Finally, her mind was in concert with her heart. She wanted Hamilton and was madly in love with him. She began to run. She had to let him know.

CHAPTER 18

Shari ran up the stairs when she heard her telephone ring. It had been three days since Hamilton had left her apartment after Bruce's untimely appearance. She had called him two days straight—he had yet to return her any of her calls.

As she reached the phone, she looked at the caller-id, then frowned.

"Hello mom or dad." She sat down on the pale couch in her living room. "What's up?"

"Just calling to see how you're doing. We haven't heard from you in a while."

"Mom, I've been busy." Shari looked out of the window.

"Too busy to call us? Shari, please."

"Sorry, mom. How's things in New Mexico?"

"Great. Your grandmother is still the same. And your father is doing well."

Shari had to smile. She had witnessed her father gently give her mother orders, and she was sure that her mother hadn't liked it one bit.

"Shari, are you serious about that Hamlin fellow?"

"Hamilton, mom. His name is Hamilton."

"Okay, Hamilton. Are you two serious?"

"Why?" Shari clipped.

"Baby, I don't want to get all in your business—your father has taken to telling me to mind my own business—but, you're my only child and I want you to be happy. I'm not sure Hamilton can do that for you."

"Says who?" Shari said, then stood and began to pace the length of her apartment. "Mom, you only met him one time."

"Once is enough. I listened to him, Shari. He's a dreamer. He'll forever dream. He has no solid plans for the future. And we both know there's no real money, no real security in writing." Her mother huffed. "Now, Bruce, he had a plan . . ."

Shari interrupted. "And we all know if you want to make God laugh, make plans."

"Don't get cute, Shari. I'm only concerned with your well being. Bruce has a good head on his shoulders. He's a doctor and he'll always be able to support you."

"Mother, what if I don't want to be financially supported? What if I want to be loved? To have a man believe in me?"

Shari heard her mother gaffe. "Chile', that's for fairy tales."

"Don't you love daddy?" Shari stopped. Her mother had paused too long. "Mom? Did you hear me—do you love daddy?"

"Don't be silly. Of course I love your father."

"When you married him, did you love him?" Again silence in response to her question. "You didn't did you?"

"To be honest, no. Not in the beginning I didn't. But your father has been a wonderful provider. A good and honest man. I learned to love him."

My God, Shari's mind screamed—she didn't want that kind of relationship. She didn't want to marry a man she didn't love and she had no plans on doing such. She didn't want to have a mate just for financial security and to bear children. She wanted love, and Hamilton had offered it to her. Shari was stunned by the revelation.

Shari then thought of the times her father had reached out to her mother. She couldn't recall ever seeing them in a loving embrace nor stealing glances at each other. Finally, she understood Linda Thomas. Her mother hadn't known what real love was; and neither had her daughter, up until now.

"Mom, I love Hamilton, and I'm going to be with him."

"What happened to Bruce?"

Shari returned to the living room and sat down. She patiently explained how she felt about Bruce and how she had never loved him. She ended by firmly, but gently reminding her mother that she was a grown woman quite capable of making her own decisions.

"I just want you to be happy," Linda said. Shari could tell her mother was crying. "And I believed Bruce was your happiness."

"Mother, do you understand what I'm saying to you?"

"All too well." Linda began. "I've been holding this in for a long time. Your father has known forever, but I've never told you."

Shari held her breath. She couldn't imagine what her mother had to say. Her voice became soft. "Go ahead, mom. I'm listening."

Shari sat still as her mother told of her first love, how she had given of herself only to have her love thrown in her face. "He was a dreamer like Hamilton. Always had big plans, but never followed through on any of them. Including marrying me."

"You've held that in forever?"

"Yeah. I didn't want to look crazy. But that's not all."

Shari stood and began to pace again.

"I became pregnant and my father insisted that he marry me," Shari's mother stated.

"What was his name?"

"That's not important. He left me pregnant and at the alter. I have never been so ashamed or heartbroken. Your father was the best man—he helped me pick up the pieces."

"What happened to the baby?"

"I miscarried shortly thereafter and your father has been by my side ever since."

Finally, Shari thought, *this explains it all*. Mom doesn't want me to be hurt. "Oh, mom. I am so sorry."

"And so am I. I've placed all of my faded dreams and hopes on you. I was poor and had nothing, believing that *that* man could give me something, make me somebody. But you. You have drive and determination. And I didn't get that until I realized just how much your father meant to me."

She couldn't believe what her mother had said, yet her words was the key, the very thing she need to hear. She loved Hamilton and she wanted to be with him. The fear which had paralyzed her came back to push her forward. She wasn't going to loose him.

"I know you love Hamilton. And I could see that he truly cares for you. I'm sorry about Bruce, but if you don't love him, you two did the right thing. I was just afraid that you would end up like me."

"Mom, I am you, with a twist." Shari said, hearing her mother laugh. "I feel in my heart that Hamilton's the one for me. I want him mom. I want to be with him. I want to love him."

"Like I love your father."

"Yeah, mom. Will you let me be my own woman? Make my own mistakes?"

Her mother sniffed. "You already are. Ignore me. I was just afraid, that's all. I didn't want to loose you any more than I have already."

"Mom, you haven't lost me—we just had a temporary parting of the minds, that's all."

"Well, for the record, after your father and I married, I knew that no one would ever love me like he does. I even realized that his friend would never love me like I deserved to."

"Oh, mom, thank you. I needed to hear that."

"I should have told you this a long time ago. Maybe you wouldn't have wasted your time on Bruce," Shari's mother sniffed. "Baby girl, this has been too refreshing for me. Is there anything else?"

Shari paused. She had enjoyed the open, frank conversation she had just had with her mother. She didn't want to ruin it. Yet, she felt that if they were going to have an adult relationship, she needed to come clean. Shari began with her plan to begin her own design company and ended with her knowledge of her father's prostrate surgery.

"Again, I'm sorry for not telling you about the surgery. That was simple of me—no other explanation would make any sense. As for your business plan, I saw it and your studio. I won't lie and say I'm not afraid for you, but your father said in order for you to be happy, I must allow you to be your own woman." She let out a sigh. "So, go and be your own woman. I'm here — we're here if you need us."

A single tear rolled down Shari's cheek. This was what she wanted from her mother, to let her make her own decisions and to have her mother respect them, whether she agreed with them or not. "Thank you mom."

"No, thank you. We should have done this a long time ago."

Shari chuckled through her tears. "We sure should have. Why don't you come back to Chicago? We can hang out, maybe even do a little shopping."

Shari heard her mother sniff. "You've never invited me to come visit you. Baby, I'd like that."

"So would I. How about you come down for Labor Day?"

"Sounds good," Shari's mother said, then changed the subject. "Where's Hamilton?"

Shari sighed and sat back down on the chaise. She told her mother what happened.

"I say you need to make haste and go to him."

Shari laughed. "I will. And I'll let you know how everything goes."

"Shari?"

"Yeah, mom?"

"I love you."

"I love you, too. Bye, baby."

Shari stood, grabbed her keys and rushed toward the back door to her studio. She retrieved the suit she had made for Hamilton. She looked at the calendar over her desk.

"Today's his birthday," she said.

She placed the suit in a plastic garment bag, then rushed up the stairs. Her mind raced as she thought of several items she needed to get for Hamilton's birthday—a card, maybe even some flowers from his mom's shop. She called his job and was informed that he was working from home. Good, she thought, he'll be there. She estimated it would take her at least an hour to make her stops before she got to his house. Shari stopped when she heard Mrs. Ponticello call her name.

"Are you going out?" Mrs. Ponticello asked as she stepped out of the back door of her apartment.

"Yeah. You need something?"

"No, I was just wondering. I've heard you pacing up there for the past two days. Are you okay?"

Shari stepped down the final stairs and sat on the bottom step. She looked up into the kind grey eyes. "When did you know you loved your husband?"

Mrs. Ponticello smiled, then joined Shari on the step. Shari watched as her grey eyes twinkled—her face blushed. "I loved him the moment I laid eyes on him. I knew he was the one for me."

"How did you know?"

Mrs. Ponticello pointed to her heart, then her head. "Every time I was around him I was giddy, but I was also afraid. But I didn't let that keep me from him. I loved him and I guess the love just overrode my fear."

Shari smiled. "Wow! Just like that?"

Mrs. Ponticello nodded. "Just like that."

Shari hugged her landlady and kissed her on the cheek. "I'll be back. I've got some important business to straighten out with Mr. Hamilton Edmunds, Jr."

As she climbed into her Avalon, she prayed it wasn't too late—too late to let the man she loved know how she felt. And though the fear of rejection was there, she wasn't about to let the errant emotion keep her from telling him how she felt. She headed to Edmunds House of Flowers.

Shari stepped into the flower shop. She closed her eyes and inhaled the sweet fragrance of flowers that greeted her.

"Shari," Mrs. Edmunds came to her. "It's so nice to see you again. What are you doing here?"

"I came to get some flowers for Hamilton's birthday."

"Oh, my boy loves flowers. You know, not enough women give flowers to men. Roses are his favorites," she said. "Let me make you an arrangement." She smiled at Shari. "Fill out this card while I make the arrangement. Won't be but a minute."

Shari watched as Mrs. Edmunds disappeared behind the large counter, then to a back room. She smiled when she overheard Mrs. Edmunds sing a Barbra Streisand tune about a woman in love. Her voice a warm soprano. Moments later, Mrs. Edmunds returned. "Will these do?"

Shari beamed at the large bouquet of red, long stemmed roses.

"They're beautiful."

"Thank you dear." She patted Shari's hand. "I hope you don't mind me saying this, because I try hard to stay out of my children's business, but my boy is crazy about you. And true he has the stubbornness born of a mule. But he's a good man, and I'm not just saying that because he's my son. He's more like his father with every passing day."

Shari looked into Mrs. Edmunds eyes, so like Hamilton's. She smiled. "Thank you, Mrs. Edmunds."

"No problem—glad to do it. Are you going to personally deliver them to him?"

Shari nodded.

"Well, he's at home. Haley called me earlier and said she spoke to him."

"Thank you." Shari smiled and pulled several bills from her purse.

"No, baby. This one is on me."

Shari hugged Mrs. Edmunds, then headed to Hamilton's, ready to admit how she felt about him—tell him that though she had never been in love, she knew she loved him and do so without fear— without hesitation.

Hamilton climbed out of bed, stretched, then rubbed his eyes with the backs of his hands. They stung, and he was sure that his eyes were beet red from lack of sleep. He had decided to work from home, yet he hadn't been able to rouse himself enough to do any work. He looked at the phone on the night stand near his bed—thoughts of Shari clouded his vision. It had been three days since Bruce unexpectedly showed up on Shari's doorstep. He said he needed to discuss their relationship. *Hell*, Hamilton mused, *I thought **we** were in a relationship*. He punched his pillow.

"Oh, well," he said out loud. "So be it. She wants to be with him, then that's cool with me." He had spoken the words, but his heart hadn't agreed. He was remised to lie to himself. He had fallen in love with her and there wasn't a thing he could do but go along with how he felt. All the women he had dated, even Nicky, hadn't come close to making him feel loved like Shari did.

The right side of his brain had continually tried to tell him that Shari wasn't Nicky—even his sister, Helena told him that Shari wasn't Nicky—but for some reason, he just couldn't let it go.

"I've got to get with it," he spoke aloud, then decided to do some yard work. He felt the strenuous work would provide him with the opportunity to think of something other than Shari.

Hamilton dressed quickly in a pair of faded jean shorts and a black tank. He pulled a black Chicago White Sox cap onto his bald head. He headed to the kitchen to exit through the back door, which would lead him into the back yard where he kept his lawn equipment locked in the garage. The sound of the phone stopped him. He walked over to the cordless phone situated on the kitchen wall. He picked it up on the third ring.

"Hello."

"Hey big brother. Happy Birthday. What are you doing home?" Haley sang.

"Sitting here waiting for you to call me," he replied, laughing.

"Very funny. Where's Shari?"

"At work, I guess."

"What do you mean, at work, you guess? Aren't you going out to celebrate the big 4-0?"

"No, we're not."

"Alright, Hamilton, what's going on?"

He wanted to tell his sister to leave him alone, to mind her own business, but he also knew that doing so would be futile. "Well, we've taken a break, so to speak."

"Bull, Hamilton. What happened?"

He told his sister what had transpired. "And she wants the other man. So, I'm going to let it go."

"Man, you are about to become a chuckle head." She snapped.

"Look, Haley, I'm just not up for a whole lot of crap right now. I've got this book to finish, and my job's got me humpin' to please."

"Excuses, Hamilton. Tired ones at that. Look, I'll talk to you later, because right now I can't believe that you're tripping like this. Did she say she wanted to go back to her ex-fiancé?"

"No, she didn't. But she didn't ask him to leave, either. Come on! What am I suppose to do? Sit around and wait for her to make up her mind like some chump? Naw, I don't roll like that, Haley, and you know it."

"No, you come on. It takes two, Hamilton. I bet you didn't, once again, ask her why the guy just showed up. Did he seem surprised to see you?"

Hamilton tilted his head to the right. He had to admit that he hadn't used the right side of his brain. "Look, Haley, I've got to go. I've got work to do." Hamilton wanted to kick himself, for as he thought about it, Bruce did look awfully surprised to see him. Had he stuck around, he might have found out what the guy wanted. But no, he just stormed out. Then on top of it all, he had ignored Shari's phone calls. Stupid. Just plain old stupid.

"Hamilton, don't give up on her. Don't let your bruised ego ruin your common sense," his sister chided. "That's all I'm gonna say." She hung up.

He shook his head, then continued outside. If he knew Haley as he did, she'd be on the phone with the rest of his sisters, retelling the story, albeit with a few extra words thrown in for effect. He wasn't up for any discussion on how he had overreacted. *Damn*, he cursed as he stepped into the garage, pulled out the various lawn items he needed, and began to mow the front lawn.

Hamilton shut off the lawn mower and watched intently as the cream-colored Mercedes paused in front of his house. He shut off the engine of the lawn mower and stood motionless as he watched Nicky slide out of the vehicle. For the life of him, he couldn't figure out why she was at his house. He hadn't spoken to her in years, and he had preferred it that way.

"Hi, Hamilton. I see you're looking good as always." Nicky's long, shapely legs strolled up to him. She place a diminutive hand on his chest, then placed a light kiss on his lips.

Hamilton stepped back. "What do you want, Nicky?" His voice was cold, but yet he had to admit she did look good. Too good. The white jeans shorts and white tank top, hugged her every curve. Her hair cascaded around her pear-shaped, warm caramel-colored face in soft curls. He spied the large diamond on her left hand.

"Aren't you going to at least invite me in?"

"What ever it is you have to say, you can say it here. And please hurry, I've got to finish my yard."

He watched her eyes dart around the expansive yard. He noticed that her eyes never rested upon his. Yes, it had been a long time, but not long enough.

"I have to go to the bathroom."

"You passed several to get here."

Nicky sucked in air and Hamilton knew he was making her

angry. If it was one thing he remembered about Nicky, and that was she didn't like it when she didn't get her way. "Look, Hamilton. I need to talk to you. To explain what happened."

Hamilton turned his back and began to walk up the concrete steps. He heard the sound of her sandal clad foot steps close behind. *This woman is some piece of work*, he thought as he opened the door. Yet, he was curious and decided to let her in. He left the door open as a not too subtle hint that she couldn't stay for long.

"The bathroom is up the stairs, to your right."

"I remember where it is, sweetie," she replied, her voice soft and sultry.

As she stood in the foyer, he watched her hips sway viciously up the stairs and wondered what would be next. Hamilton shrugged his shoulders, then went into the kitchen, where he retrieved a glass, filled it with Gatorade and drank it down. He was in the midst of his second glass when he heard footsteps behind him. He turned to see Nicky naked as the day she was born. He looked at her ample breasts, the brown nipples stood at full attention.

"Happy Birthday, baby. I miss you," Nicky strolled over to him and placed her body against his. Hamilton closed his eyes and inhaled deeply. He remembered the way they use to make love—hot and furious.

"Don't you miss me?" Nicky hissed in his ear as her tongue made wet circles around his ear lobe. His hands shook as they reached out to her and pulled her against his hardened manhood. Hamilton's hands roamed across her back, then down her taunt behind. His mouth came into contact with hers. Shari's warm face became firmly planted in his mind. He moaned, as Nicky ground her pelvis into his. She fumbled with the clasp which held up Hamilton jean shorts.

"That's it baby. I need you. I made a mistake. Please forgive me."

Hamilton stopped. He pulled Nicky away from him, his manhood gone slack. He looked into her cognac-brown eyes. "Nicky, go home to your husband," he barked. "Go back to the man you deserve."

A loud crash caused Hamilton to look up. He pushed Nicky aside then rushed toward the open door. He looked at the floor and saw the remnants of a broken vase, water and red roses among the shards of glass. He then noticed a black plastic garment bag, with By Design stenciled in white bold letters across the zipper lay sprawled on the floor, feet from the broken glass. A envelope, with his name on it, was attached to the hanger with grey ribbon. He knew it was from Shari.

"My God," he spat out, then rushed outside. He grimaced as he watched Shari run to her car. "Shari!" He called out as he ran down the steps, then into the street. "Shari, wait!" He called out, as Shari sped away from the curb.

"Damn!" He looked back at the open door. Slowly he descended the stairs and returned to the kitchen. Hamilton shook his head. Repulse replaced the heated fire in his eyes. "Nicky, get your clothes and get out!"

Nicky looked away and placed her hands across her breasts. She was wounded, Hamilton could see, but no more than she had wounded him. Once and for all he needed to lay it out for her, tell her the things that he should have said long ago. She didn't move.

"What do you think I am, Nicky? Do you think I'm some robot without feelings? Think you can just come over here, out of the blue, get naked and bam! We're a couple again? Damn, you think I'm that weak?"

"I just thought . . ."Nicky's voice trailed off.

Hamilton's voice softened. "Get dressed and leave, Nicky. We were over before we began." He walked away from her and went to sit in the living room. He didn't bother to look up when her heard her run up the stairs. She returned several minutes later.

"She can't give you what I can," Nicky said defiantly as she sat across from him.

"It's not about who can do what Nicky. It's about trust. And I know I could never trust you again." He stood and walked over to the fireplace.

"So, Hamilton, what are you saying?"

He spun around. "I just said it. That's the problem—folks don't say what needs to be said. If you wanted someone else, why didn't you just tell me."

Nicky jumped to her feet. "I tried, Hamilton. But you're so closed. Not once did you ever tell me that you loved me. The only way I knew was from our love making and the engagement ring. Outside of that, I never knew where I stood with you. Not once did you tell me how you truly felt."

He rubbed the growing stubble on his cheeks. It was true, he hadn't voiced what was in his heart, yet it still didn't give her just cause to sleep with another man.

"So, that makes this all right—my inability to tell you how I felt?" He sighed. "Nicky, it's true. I had a problem voicing what I feel here." He tapped the skin over his left breast. "And I acknowledge that— own it. But it still doesn't erase what happened. And I won't go back to yesterday."

Nicky grabbed him around his waist. "But it can be better. I'm in the midst of a divorce, and once its final, we can start over. We were good together, Hamilton."

He gently pushed her hands from his waist. "Were, Nicky. Were." He walked to the door and opened it. "You better leave now." He watched as the truth registered on her face, in her eyes. She paused in front of him, and he could see the fear in her eyes. "And Nicky." He inhaled deeply. "Please don't ever come back."

She nodded her head, then exited. Hamilton slowly closed the door behind him and turned the lock. His mind whirled. He looked at the garment bag. He removed the envelope and opened it.

"Hamilton, my love. Please call me. I need to talk to you. I love you. Shari. PS: Happy Birthday."

He shook his head as he unzipped the bag. He wanted to scream as he removed a double-breasted blazer, then a pair of cuffed slacks, both the color of midnight grey. He rubbed his hands across the light fabric, its smooth texture reminded him of silk. He let out a loud sigh, versus the tears he wanted to shed. *It's not what you think*, he scolded, then laughed sadly as the words sunk in. *It's not what you think*.

He placed the suit back in the garment bag, then thought how no woman had ever taken the time to create anything for him. His thoughts switched to how he had reacted to Bruce's arrival and he had not allowed her to explain.

His mind raced. How was he going to convince Shari to believe that nothing had happened between him and Nicky—that she had arrived uninvited? Whatever he felt, he knew he couldn't let Shari believe what she had seen. He picked up the phone. The quick beeps told him he had a message in his voice mail. He knew none of them would be from Shari. As he dialed the number to voice mail, then punched in his access code, he smirked as he listened to message after message from his sisters. Each one repeated the same message: *don't give up*.

He dialed Shari's number, then left a message on her answering machine. Next, he dialed Darrin at work. He explained what had transpired, how he felt, and how much he loved Shari. Hamilton listened as Darrin assured him that he'd come up with a way for Shari to hear his side of the story. When Hamilton and Darrin finished their conversation, Hamilton prayed that his cousin was right, for in his heart he couldn't let her go without a fight.

CHAPTER 19

Shari looked over to the mannequin to her left and tried to focus. She had retreated to her studio and had been there for two days straight after she had witnessed Hamilton in the arms of another woman.

For the thousand time that day, she replayed the events of that fateful day. She had thought it strange for the front door to be open as she walked up the steps. She had heard the voices and followed it to the kitchen. There she saw Hamilton and a naked woman in each others arms.

Everything had gone dark, as she ran from the house. She needed to get away from there, get away from Hamilton. She had driven home, sure she had broken every law in the Illinois drivers manual. Her eyes were clouded by tears. Once she arrived home, she had bypassed her door and went directly to her studio. She had needed a diversion—something to take away the pain of Hamilton's lies. There was no way, she mused, that he could love her one day, then be in the arms of another woman the next. The image of the naked woman seared into her memory bank.

Two days later, as she sat at her desk at Macy's, she tried to work—attempted to force her attention on the countless designs in front of her. After three hours, she gave up and announced to her assistant that she wasn't feeling well and was going home. Once there, she retreated again to the basement. She had hoped that if she worked on a few designs, then the continued image of Hamilton would quickly work its way toward a distant memory. So far, she had created a line of evening wear for both men and women and had begun a Spring casual wear for women.

She forced her attention back to the pattern for a pair of capri pants. She ignored the continued ringing of her telephone. She watched her hands, the sharp shears entwined in her fingers, slice effortlessly across the fabric, pins securing the paper image.

After she finished with the pattern, she took the pins away and walked over to her grandmother's sewing machine. Shari threaded the needle, checked the bobble, released the foot and depressed the peddle. The machine came to life, a steady hum moved her forward, as the needle glided across the fabric. Yes, she thought, this was what she needed to get Hamilton out of her mind and out of her heart. Yet, tears had began to stream down her cheeks and left rings of water on the green fabric she had begun tosew.

After nearly an hour, she gave up and removed the fabric from under the needle. She had absently completed a rayon, olive green blazer intended for Hamilton.

"This is no good." Shari tossed the blazer onto the floor, shut off the lights and climbed the stairs to her apartment. She paused, then wiped the tears from her eyes when she heard Mrs. Ponticello call her name.

"Yes, Mrs. Ponticello."

"Come here, dear."

Shari stepped into the opened door, which led to her landlady's kitchen.

"Are you okay?" Mrs. Ponticello stood in front of Shari. "Deb called. She said she's been calling you for days."

"Is something wrong with Daneda?"

"She didn't say. But she asks that you call her immediately."

"Thanks, Mrs. Ponticello." Shari turned to leave, then stopped when Mrs. Ponticello placed her hand upon Shari's shoulder.

"Whatever it is, its going to be okay." Mrs. Ponticello took Shari into her arms. "Trust. It will be okay."

Shari sniffed. "I know. Thank you."

Shari knew what Deb wanted. She knew that by now Hamilton had relayed his own version of what she saw to Darrin, who in turn relayed it to Deb. Shari didn't want to hear it. She wasn't interested in Hamilton's lies. He had what he wanted.

Shari sat on the edge of her bed. She had refused to sleep in it. Memories of she and Hamilton as they laid lazily in each other's arms, their bodies moist from their lovemaking, were too painful to ignore. She stood up, then looked around. She couldn't erase him from her mind as easily as she had erased Bruce and all the others. But the fear she had back then was different—she feared being alone, more so than being in a love-less marriage. Shari sighed, then shrugged her shoulders. This was all too much, she thought, and all too silly. She looked at herself in the mirror.

Shari had made up her mind. She was no longer going to let trepi-dation rule her—no longer going to hide what she felt out of fear. She wanted to be loved and she wanted to love. She wanted to marry and have a family. She could have it all. So what, she had missed her chance with Hamilton, but she swore she wouldn't with the next man.

The sound of the phone broke her thoughts. Somewhere in her she hoped it was Hamilton. She looked at the caller id and smirked. She picked up the phone.

"Hello."

"Shari, why have you been avoiding me?"

"I've been busy."

"Umph, that's a good one. Try again."

"Aw, come on Deb, not now. I don't want to talk about it."

"Okay, I'll let you off the hook. Darrin talked to Hamilton. That snake. I couldn't believe it. Men. Umph, I tell you."

"I don't want to talk about it," Shari stated again, her voice firm. She changed the subject. "What's up? How's Daneda?"

"Great. Hey, I've got two tickets to a spa in Jamaica. Do you want to go?"

Shari's eyes widened. That's what she needed. Some time away. "When are we leaving?"

"How about tomorrow?"

"So, soon? Why?"

Deb crossed her fingers. "One of Darrin's clients owns a time share and gave us the use of the condo. But Darrin can't get away right now. And its only good for this weekend."

"We taking Daneda?"

"Girl, no. Darrin says for me and you to use it. Besides, we can play catch up and lounge on the beach and man watch. We'll be there Friday and Saturday, and come back on Monday. You game?"

"Sounds good to me, but I don't want to man watch. I just wanna lounge on the beach, get a tan, catch up on my reading."

"Good. Then you'll go?"

"Why not? I need some time away."

Shari and Deb went on to discuss what to wear, and the time and place to meet at the airport the next day. She began to get excited. She knew that Jamaica would be the respite she desperately needed to escape from the dull ache that had claimed her heart. All she wanted was to leave that ache on the white sands of Jamaica. Shari smiled, then placed the phone on its base. She ran to the basement to retrieve her suitcase and then began to pack.

"All done." Deb hung up. "Now let's hope she falls for it." Deb took Darrin's hand in hers, then looked over at Hamilton. "And you better be right, Hamilton, or else I'll kill you myself."

Hamilton rose from the chair and walked over to Deb. "You won't regret this." He kissed her on the cheek. "I swear you won't."

Darrin spoke up. "I know we won't cousin. Now, go home and get packed. You have a flight to catch."

"Thanks again, both of you," Hamilton said as he walked out of Deb and Darrin's home. He looked up into the dark sky and saw the Eastern star. He sent up a silent prayer then headed home to pack.

After Shari had packed her last article of clothes, she called her boss and informed her that she had to go out of town on some urgent business. She felt no remorse over not admitting that she was on her way to Jamaica. Besides, getting over Hamilton was urgent business. Next, she called her parents to let them know where she was going. She sighed loudly when her mother asked if she had spoken to Hamilton. Sadly, she stated no, then rang off. Lastly, she told Mrs. Ponticello of her plans and asked her to take care of Rocket.

Her calls completed, her business in order, she felt relieved that in less than 24-hours she would be in Jamaica, thousands of miles away from Hamilton. Her heart fluttered at the thought of him. She shooed away the thoughts and began to day dream of sandy white beaches and palm trees that swayed in the warm winds of Jamaica.

Shari looked around the terminal. She glanced at the LED clock on the departure board. Their flight to Jamaica was scheduled to leave in 20 minutes.

"Last call for ATA Flight 40, non-stop to Montego Bay, Jamaica."

Shari looked down the corridor, then heard her name announced over the loud speakers above. She stepped to a blue phone near the terminal.

"This is Shari Thomas."

"Miss Thomas? A Deborah Anderson-Wilson says she will meet you later on tonight. You are to leave without her."

Shari shook her head. *Something about this it too familiar*. Shari thought. "Okay. Thank you." Shari placed the receiver on its hook, put her black Raybans over her eyes, then boarded the plane. She took her seat in first class.

Four hours later, the flight touched down. She gathered her carry on bag, then stepped out into the magnificent warm weather of Jamaica. The wind blew lightly around her and flittered her tan linen, ankle length sun-dress about her legs.

She shut her eyes and inhaled deeply. Finally, she was in Jamaica. As she pulled her bag behind her, Shari stepped out of the airport and looked up and down at the various cabs parked along the curb. She watched as brown men of all hues jockeyed for passengers. At the call of her name, she turned to see a slender man with a sign hoisted over his head. Her name was emblazoned in large black letters. She raised her hand.

"I'm Shari Thomas."

The dark-skinned man, with warm, deep set eyes, grinned at her. "Miss Thomas, welcome to Jamaica." He bowed at the waist, his accent rang in her ear. "I am Stephen and I will be taking you to your villa."

Shari nodded her head slightly, then followed the man to a sleek black Lincoln Continental. He held the door open as Shari slid inside and reveled in the cool feel of the butter soft black leather.

"You will love Springfarm. It is one of the best and most exclusive resorts in Montego Bay."

Shari didn't reply. Her eyes were too busy absorbing the visual beauty of the island. Her gaze feasted upon azure blue water and lush green palm trees, which swayed carelessly to and fro. For her, time seemed to freeze as scene after scenic scene passed her by.

Thirty minutes later, the limo pulled off onto a secluded road. Shari sat up straight. Her eyes widened when the property, nestled on a hill surrounded by lush tropical plants and flowers came into view.

Shari stepped out before Stephen could open her door. She smiled warmly as her eyes darted from one magnificent view to the next. On both sides, she could see the magnificence of the Atlantic Ocean, while in front of her stood a three story, stucco building painted a stark white.

"Welcome to Springfarm Villa. Go check in and I will bring in your bag."

Shari walked slowly, her linen sandals tapped lightly on the concrete walkway. A tall man, his skin the color of a deep plum, dressed in white slacks and a white shirt, held open one side of the large wooden double doors.

"Welcome. I'm Michael. If you need anything, Miss Thomas, please do not hesitate to call upon me. I can be reached by dialing two on the phone in your villa."

Shari nodded absently. She had not expected the resort to be so breathtakingly beautiful. She stopped at the reservations desk.

"Miss Thomas. We are glad to see you have arrived," the woman behind the tall desk said, her dark eyes sparkled as she spoke. " You are in the Villa Amour. Michael will bring your luggage shortly. Your villa is to your right at the end of the cobblestone path. Please enjoy your stay." Shari looked into the face of the attendant and noted how beautiful and flawless the desk attendant's warm cocoa complexion was.

"Thank you." Shari walked away from the desk. Her head turned from left to right as she absorbed the lobby, its white wicker chairs with lush pale pink cushions were set semi-circle. Glass topped white wicker tables separated the chairs. Large hibiscus plants sat near floor to ceiling open windows.

Shari jumped at the feel of something cross her feet. She looked down to see a small green lizard scamper away.

Following the attendants directions, Shari made her way out of the lobby, through a set of doors, and down the path to the villa. Again, her eyes were rewarded as she whistled at the interior. Stepping onto a highly polished parquet flooring, the large living room was decorated in muted tones of teal green and warm peach, the same wicker furniture in the lobby sat in the living area. A kitchenette was over toward the right, with a small dining area nearby, the table set for two with china, flatware and crystal goblets.

Shari noticed two doors—one closest to her right and one to her left. She stepped to her right.

She opened the doors. A large white poster bed, with mesh netting hung from the ceiling to the floor. It was the focal point of the master suite. Shari slipped off her shoes, then stepped inside the room. She allowed her feet to pad quietly across the wooden floor to the large veranda. She opened the french doors, then shook her head at the view of the beach and the azure water which seemed to call her name. She stepped out onto the veranda and leaned over the rail.

After she had toured the other bedroom, which was smaller, and decorated in the same muted tones as the master suite, Shari returned to find her bag placed in the middle of the foyer. She picked up her bag, headed to the master suite, then began to unpack. She glanced at her watch. It was 6 pm in Chicago. She picked up the phone near the bed.

She called her parents, then Mrs. Ponticello to let them know she had arrived safely. She dialed Deb's home and upon receiving no answer, she left a message on the voice mail, then hung up. She glanced toward the beach and decided to go for a swim.

Shari donned a stark white one piece, the front dipped dangerously low and showed more of her cleavage than maybe she should have allowed, but she only had this suit and a tankini, which fared no better. She grabbed a large beach towel, her beach bag, her portable CD player and her key card, then headed to the pristine white beach.

CHAPTER 20

Hamilton looked around the villa. At first he thought that the idea of meeting Shari in Jamaica had been a great idea. He thought that there would be no way that she wouldn't at least have to hear him out. Yet, the closer he got to the resort, the more he began to have reservations about agreeing to Deb and Darrin's plan.

He had laughed outright when Darrin and Deb told how Shari had meddled in their relationship. Especially when Shari had booked them on the same flight, followed by the same hotel room. Now, he frowned as he thought of how Shari had run from his house when she saw a naked Nicky in his kitchen.

"Mr. Edmunds, Miss Thomas is here. She is in the Villa Amour," Michael stated.

"Thank you," Hamilton replied as he tipped the concierge. He walked to the villa after he received directions.

He said a silent prayer, then placed his key card in the door. He set his suitcase on the tiled floor.

"Shari," he called out her name. She didn't respond. Hamilton walked over to his right and pushed open the partially opened door. He walked to the veranda and looked out. His eyes came upon Shari as she lay on the expansive white beach. He quickly changed into swim trunks, then headed to the beach.

A familiar scent circled around Shari. If she didn't know any better, she'd sworn that it was that hypnotic cologne that Hamilton wore. She dismissed the thought and returned to a light slumber. When the scent got stronger, she opened her eyes and sat straight up. She looked to her right, then her left—her eyes scanned the deserted beach. She saw no one. She laid back down.

"Shari."

She heard her name, but she thought it was her imagination. The deep voice sounded just like Hamilton's. *Couldn't be*, she said to herself. Hamilton's in Chicago — he couldn't be in Jamaica.

She heard her name again, then jumped up and turned around. She stood face to face with Hamilton. She began to run.

Shari turned to see him follow behind her, his massive legs pushed him closer and closer, the blur of his white trunks became clearer.

"No," she shouted. "I don't want to hear it." Shari ran down the beach.

"Shari, please stop. Talk to me. I have to explain. Nothing happened. It's not what you think."

Shari hadn't wanted to stop, but the sudden pain in her calves forced her to give up. She dropped to her knees in the sand. "What are you doing here?" She huffed as she tried to catch her breath.

"We have to talk. It's not what you think." Hamilton stood over her, his hands rested upon his waist. Shari shielded her eyes, then shook her head. Hadn't she dreamed of him coming to her on a white sandy beach?

"Not what I think?!" She stated sarcastically as she rubbed the painful knot in her calves. "You just happened to have a naked woman standing in your kitchen, your arms around her, her body pressed up against you! And its not what I think! Bull shit. You lied to me Hamilton!" Shari glared angrily at him. Her eyes followed his every move as he hunkered down and began to massage her calves. "Don't touch me."

He released her. "Shari, this is silly. *You are going to listen to me—*

hear me out. Besides, you came to my house for a reason."

Shari looked up into his face, his beautiful light eyes beckoned her, the warm blue sky hovered over him. She acquiesced. "You have one minute."

"Can you walk?" He stood and held out his hand. She ignored his offer. She stood and began to slightly hobble toward the villa. He raked his hands over his bald head.

"The woman you saw was Nicky." He began as he walked by her side.

"Your ex-fiancé. How convenient."

"Stop it Shari and let me finish." He stated, then stopped and looked down into her face. She could tell from the tone in his voice and the anger in his eyes that he meant to be heard without interruption. "Anyway, she came over to ask if we could get back together. She said she had to use the bathroom. I had no idea she was going to come back down naked. When you walked in I was in the middle of telling her that we would never get back together. That I had found someone I love."

Shari shook her head. "A woman built like that and you didn't want her. You didn't want to sleep with her?"

Hamilton let out a long sigh. He didn't want to lie to her. "Shari, I'm a man. Yes, I got aroused. And sure I could have slept with her then tossed her aside. But I'm not that type of man, Shari."

Shari shook her head. "What do you want me to say?" She looked up into his face. He placed his hands on her arms.

"Tell me how you feel. Tell me why Bruce showed up at your door."

Shari blew out a long breath. "Hamilton, he came by to thank me. He didn't come by to get me back. He came by to tell me that he was ready to move forward, with someone else. That's all."

Hamilton rubbed his hand over his bald head. "I guess I would have known that had I not over reacted."

Shari nodded, then walked away. Hamilton stopped her. "But I need to hear you say it, Shari. I need to hear you say you love me. Can you do that? "

"What about Nicky?"

"What about her?" he replied, his face taunt. "That's over. Has been for a long time. Haven't you heard a thing I've said?"

Shari bowed her head and watched her feet as they played in the sand.

"Look at me Shari and tell me that you don't love me." He placed his hands on her shoulders. "I know you're afraid, and so was I at one time, but look me in my eyes and tell me you don't love me."

She slowly raised her head, then looked into his eyes. The warm golden color of them mirrored his words.

"Talk to me, baby." He stroked her hair, his deep voice softer. "It's time we both stopped and stood still." He stepped closer. "Tell me. . " he whispered as he pulled her into his arms.

"I love you, Hamilton." She stated, her voice barely above a whisper.

"Say it again."

"I love you, Hamilton. With all my heart, I do." Tears streamed down her face.

"That's what I needed to hear." Hamilton tightened his embrace, his mouth fast upon hers. She moaned. The familiar warmth of his kiss stole over her. Her heart began to beat rapidly. She opened her lips to receive him, to drown in the passion that left her weak. She heard herself moan as her hands came to rest on his face.

"My God, Shari," Hamilton breathed against her lips. "Don't you know that you are what I want in my life. What I need." He held close to his chest. "I love you, baby," he stated, then swept her up into his arms and carried her back to the secluded beach.

He laid her gently on the large beach towel and looked down at her. Shari's eyes were close.

"Baby, open your eyes," he ordered, then proceeded to remove his trunks. Shari opened her eyes and watched as he removed his trucks slowly, her eyes feasted upon the dark chocolate angel that stood before her.

"Stop me now, if this isn't to be," he said. When she didn't protest, Hamilton sank to his knees and began to kiss her as he removed her swim suit. "You are never to wear this again without me." He ordered playfully.

When she was fully naked, he rubbed her body, thinking that if he grew to be 100-years-old, he'd never get enough of her love.

He heard her moan, as he inched his way down her neck, to suckle on her full breasts, her hardened nipples cried out to his tongue. He lavished each one, taking the darkened perk in his mouth, then savored round, nub feel of them. His fingers trailed down her slightly rounded stomach to play in the hairs that hid her button. He wanted to take his time, wanted to love her in the manner in which his heart told him he could.

"Hamilton," Shari breathed as she arched her back. His fingers plied her hair apart and found her ripe button. Slowly he rubbed, coaxed to life the very essence of her. As she stiffened, he quickened his pace. He wanted to hear her raspy voice as she neared her first climax.

"Hamilton, please." She begged. The searing heat of his fingers seem to exceed the heat of the bright sun. He slowed his motions and replaced his fingers with his lips and tongue.

Shari's body ached. She wanted him like she wanted no other.

Wanted to feel him inside of her—fitted perfectly in her tunnel. She placed her hands on his bald head and gently pushed him closer, the feel of his tongue on her caused rippled spasms to claim her body.

Hamilton evenly stroked her, commanded her, claimed her. Shari cried out at the powerful orgasm that rocked her body. "Hamilton," she cried out as the orgasm began to subside. Hamilton looked up.

"Shari, open your eyes." Slowly, Shari opened them. "Come to me." He stated, then laid on his back. Shari trembled as she slowly eased her body onto his, her tunnel quaked upon the feel of him inside of her. Her hips began to move, took over as her body demanded another release.

"Shari," she heard him call out. "I love you, baby."

Shari paused. She looked into his eyes. He'd said it again. He'd made her his, claimed her with his mind, his body and his soul. Her mind joined her heart. This was it. There would be no turning back. No more running. No more fears. Her muscles tightened as she rolled her hips upon his. She laid her body atop his, her breasts flat against his chest. Hamilton's hands gripped her hips. "Baby, don't hurt me."

"Never, Hamilton," she responded, then began the ascent, her hips rolled, her tunnel clasped around his engorged, thick shaft. With each motion, she could feel him harden, their strokes even and fluid.

With a groan, Hamilton rolled them over. "I can't last like that, baby." He began to slowly move in and out of her in an attempt to savor the electricity which hung about them. The sac which carried his seed tightened, the sensation of her proved to be his undoing. He stroked her, loved her, and when the tight cavern became too much to bear, he drove inside her and released the passion. He cried out her name, his member pulsated at the release. Satiated, he rested his body on hers.

They remained silent for moments, each lulled by the passion of their lovemaking, the sounds of the waves as it rolled upon the white shore. Hamilton lifted Shari from the towel and carried her back to the villa, where they showered and laid in bed, wrapped in each others arms.

Their moment was interrupted by a knock on the door. Hamilton rose to answer it. Shari watched his muscled back, the taunt muscles of his behind as he left the room. Criminal, she thought, her body awakened again. He returned with a note addressed to Shari. She opened it, then laughed loudly as her eyes scanned the words. She handed the note to Hamilton.

"One good turn deserves another. Make me proud. Love, Deborah and Darrin Wilson. P.S.: Daneda needs a play mate.

"Well, I guess I no longer have to wonder how you got to come to Jamaica." Shari wiped a single tear of laughter from her eye.

"We've got to finish talking," Hamilton stated as he held out his hand to her. They stepped out onto the private veranda. "There's a lot I've got to tell you."

"Me, too."

As the sun set, Shari wrapped in Hamilton's large arms, they talked for hours. Each told of their pasts, their fears and their dreams of the future. The warm breezed comforted them, as the full moon shone across their naked bodies.

Shortly thereafter, they returned to bed. Shari laid her body upon Hamilton's. She shut her eyes and allowed the feel of Hamilton's heart beat lull her into a restful sleep. They had finally come to the conclusion that neither of them wanted to go on without the other, and had promised to love for as long as life would allow them to.

CHAPTER 21

"Hamilton!" the managing editor's voice boomed across the news-room. "There's a breaking story over on Roosevelt Road. Some folks are protesting the demolition of the SRO. All of our the beat reporters are out on assignments. Can you cover it?"

"Not a problem." Hamilton replied, then spoke into the phone nestled between his shoulder and chin. "Sorry about that. You heard?"

"Yeah, looks like someone's gonna be a beat reporter again." Shari teased.

"Never. But you'll still love me, won't you?"

"Ummm, I don't know." Shari sang. "I want a man who can take care of me."

"I'll take care of you alright, woman. Just be at home and in bed when I get there."

"Okay, Hamilton. Your wish is my command." Shari whispered into the phone, her deep voice sultry and playful.

Hamilton smiled as thoughts of Shari filled his head. "Woman, you're going to be the death of me. Get off my phone."

"Anything you say, honey." Her voice deeper.

"I love you, baby."

"I love you, too. Be careful out there. I'll see you later."

Hamilton hung up, then rose quickly. He felt like he was on top of the world. After returning from Jamaica several weeks prior, he and Shari had spent as much time together as their schedules would allow. Every night they had been inseparable. When he was at her home, he would sit and watch her design or sketch. He was impressed by her talent and had planned to surprise her with a check to open her business, as well as ask her to be his wife. He loved her, there was no doubt about it.

And when she was at his home, she would go over his re-writes with him. She would make suggestions, which he invited, encouraged her to do. He wanted her as much a part of his life as he wanted to be a part of hers.

Yes, things had definitely improved, Hamilton thought, then grinned as he grabbed the blazer to the suit Shari had made for him. He slipped into the blazer, then picked up his reporters notepad and cassette recorder. He ran out the door.

Hamilton hadn't covered a live story in years, he mused to himself. He remembered the adrenalin rush, how it coursed through him each and every time he covered a breaking story. To him, nothing could beat the electric charge and excitement of being on the scene of a story as it unfolded. As he jumped in his truck, he knew that as an editor, he had been out of touch with a lot of his old contacts. Hamilton silently hoped he would see a few faces from his days as a beat reporter. Getting the inside scoop always helped with deadline. Hamilton smirked at his last thought. Beat reporters came and went, and he knew the possibility of running into his former comrades would be slim. Still, he was excited at the possibilities.

As he drove to the scene of the story, he thought of the conversation he had with his mother and sisters. He laughed as he thought of the serious expressions on their faces after his mother had called a family meeting to discuss Hamilton's plans to marry Shari. In the end, each of his sisters had given their approval and their blessings. His mother had ended the meeting with a kiss to his cheek and admonished him to never let Shari forget how much he loved her.

"Your father told me everyday we were together." His mother had added as she walked him to the door. "And so should you."

Back to the present, Hamilton patted the ring box in his pocket, pulled his cell phone from his pocket, and dialed Shari's home number. Even though he knew she wasn't home, he wanted to leave her message, which stated how much he loved her. He disconnected the call. It was time to focus.

At the scene of the protest, he gasped when he rounded the corner and saw the large crowd gathered. The Chicago police had formed a solid line behind wooden barricades. He estimated that there were at least 200 protesters squeezed onto the sidewalk. Many of them carried placards that read, *No Home Here? No Home No Where!* spelled out in big, bold letters.

"What the?!" he exclaimed, then stepped out of his vehicle. He ran toward the crowd, his tape recorder in hand. He slipped quickly between the police and the protesters, looking for anyone who may have looked to be the leader of the protest.

He saw a man speak into several microphones which were shoved toward his face. He figured the man must be the spokesperson of the protest. Hamilton pushed his way through the crowd. His height gave him an advantage. Hamilton thrust his tape recorder forward and balanced his reporters pad along side it. He scribbled down notes which would jog his memory when he sat down later to write the story. The man spoke of the plight of affordable housing and how the city had made it nearly impossible for many of the citizens of middle—to low income to afford.

Hamilton scribble furiously, his mind made mental notes of words. He was caught up, the rush of adrenalin filled his body. When the sound of shots rang out, the crowd moved, and he was shoved backward, his tape recorder flew out of his hand. Whirls of blue uniforms passed in front of him as people began to run. Hamilton moved quickly, foregoing the search for his recorder, and ran toward where he had parked. Suddenly stunned, Hamilton felt a sharp pain across the side of his head. Dazed, Hamilton stumbled, his hand reached out and grabbed a nearby light pole as his eyes rolled upward, then shut. An image of Shari's face floated in his mind just before all went dark.

CHAPTER 22

Shari glanced at her watch. It wasn't like Hamilton not to call if he would be late. The skin on her neck and arms bristled as if a cold breeze blew over her. She looked to the open windows—the curtains didn't move. Her head began to hurt.

"Something's wrong," she told herself and ran to the telephone. She dialed information, requested the residential listing for Ella Edmunds. She rang off, then dialed the number provided. After several rings, an answering machine pick-up. Shari wrestled with whether or not to leave a message. She didn't want to upset Hamilton's mother. She hung up. She looked around her room. Hadn't Helena given her her phone number? Shari ran to her bedroom closet, pulling clothes from their hangers. She searched for the white jeans she had worn to the barbeque. When the phone rang, she ran to it. She picked it up before it could ring a second time.

"Hello. Hamilton?!"

"Girl, turn on your television to CLTV," Deb ordered.

"What's wrong?" Shari shouted into the telephone.

"I'm on may way." The phone went dead. Shari rushed to her den, picked up the remote, turned on the television, then selected the local cable news station. Her mind stilled as she watched the pictures flash across the screen as a fight between the protesters and the police broke out. She gasped as the newscaster went on to explain how shots had been fired and a mad stampede ensued. One person was dead, with dozens of others taken to area hospitals, injuries ranging from critical to severe.

Stunned, the words spoken by the newscaster droned as she pictured Hamilton lying alone, possibly dead. Her head snapped up when the reporter gave names of the critically injured. He ended the list with Hamilton's.

"No!" Shari whispered as tears began to stream down her face. "Please, God. No. Don't take him from me. Not now." She ran to retrieve her purse and keys, then left her apartment.

As she rushed to her car, she looked up to see Deb's Range Rover turn the corner.

"Get in," Deb ordered as Shari opened the passenger door, then jumped in. "It's going to be okay. He's just critical. He'll make it."

"He has to, Deb."

Memories flooded Shari as she stepped into the same emergency room she had been taken to when she had been in the car accident. She smiled at the memory of Hamilton's strong arms. She prayed to God that he would be okay, that when she saw him he would have that sexy, sensuous smile that she had come to love.

"I'm here for Hamilton Edmunds, Junior." Shari said to the desk attendant. She watched as he typed the name into a computer. He looked up at her. *Oh no*, Shari's inside screamed, *no!*

"Follow me. The family is in this room here," the attendant pointed to a room to the side, its door closed.

Shari placed her hand on the knob and turned it slowly. "Deb," she called out as she reached for her friends hand.

"I'm here."

"I can't do this. I can't loose him. I love him." Shari removed her hand from the knob.

"I know you do. Come on." Deb held her hand, then turned the knob. All heads turned in their direction. Helena came to meet them.

"Tell me, Helena, please."

"Shari, he's still with us. He's in surgery now. They're relieving some pressure at the base of his head. We don't know if he'll . . ," her words were choked off as she began to sob. Hamilton's mother stood and walked over to them. "Haley," she called out. "Take Helena outside."

Shari watched the turbulent storm wrestle in her light eyes, so much like Hamilton's. She took his mother's offered hand in hers and was led to an empty seat. The faces around them all blurred into one, Ella's, as they held each others hands.

"My baby is strong. He's going to be okay," Ella said. She searched Shari's eyes. What more could she say? She didn't know the full extent the impact his injuries would have on him, much less be able to say with any authority that he'd make it. "Yes, my baby boy is strong." Shari felt Ella's hands tighten in hers. "Shari, do you love my baby?"

Shari nodded.

"Then pray he comes back to us. He's in a coma, and unless they can relieve that pressure, he'll be lost to us forever. Pray, Shari. Pray."

She prayed harder than she'd prayed her entire life. She called on God to see them through, to bring Hamilton back to those who loved him. Shari had been too afraid to admit how she felt about him. As she prayed, she told herself that if Hamilton returned to her, she would never let him forget how much she loved him.

"Mrs. Edmunds," a doctor appeared in the doorway. "I'm Doctor Elston, your son's neurosurgeon. Hamilton is out of surgery and he'll be under close observation for the next 24-hours. This is the critical stage and we've placed him in ICU. There was a lot of swelling at the base of his skull. We drained the fluid which had built up, but he's still critical. But we have high hopes for a complete recovery—his eyes were rapidly moving behind his lids and that's a good sign."

Ella stood, her hand still in Shari's. "Can we see him?"

The doctor smiled at the twenty plus faces gathered. His brown face, and kind eyes twinkled. "Sure you can. But one at a time and no more than 10 minutes each. One of you can spend the night if you wish."

"Thank you doctor," Ella released Shari's hand then hugged the doctor.

Ella picked up Shari's hand again, then reached out to her daughters and their respective families. Enclosed in a circle, Ella began a prayer of thanks. She ended the prayer by asking God "to continue watching over my baby. Amen"

Shari wiped the tears from her eyes.

"Baby, you stay the night with him. Hear? You belong with him when he wakes up." Ella hugged, then kissed the side of Shari's face. Shari hugged each of Hamilton's sisters as they filed out of the room and headed to the intensive care unit. Shari looked at Deb, then ran into her arms and cried. The sobs heaved from her body.

"That's it, sister. Get it out," Deb whispered. "You can't show those tears to Hamilton when he wakes up. He'll want to see you smiling."

Shari continued to cry, her thoughts tumbled around how close she came to losing the one man she had ever loved.

Shari looked up to see Helena walk into the room. "He's still asleep, but we're leaving him in your hands. Take care of him. We'll see you in the morning." Helena wiped Shari's tears with the tips of her fingers, embraced her, then walked out the room. Shari looked at Deb.

"You can leave me here. I'll be alright," Shari said.

Deb looked pensive. "You sure?"

Shari nodded, hugged Deb, then walked her to the emergency

room exit. Shari returned, then asked for directions to the ICU.

Shari gasped when she saw the various tubes hooked up to Hamilton. She looked at the large bandage secured around his head, then took small steps toward him. She wanted to touch him—know that he was there.

"You must be Shari," a nurse asked as she stepped into the unit. "I'm Jessica. I'll be his nurse tonight. His mother told me that you'll be spending the night with him. How long have you two been married?"

Shari blinked. Married? They weren't married. But at this moment, it was the least of her concerns. "A short while."

"Well, that's sweet," the nurse replied as she monitored his blood pressure. "Talk to him. That will help him come around. It's important after sustaining head trauma."

Shari nodded.

"If you need anything, just ring and I'll be here. I'll get you a pillow and a blanket."

Shari nodded her head. Moments later, she took the items from the nurse, then placed them on the leather lounge chair across the room. She stroked the side of Hamilton's face, kissed him on his cheek, then dragged the lounger next to his bed and stretched out in it. Exhausted, Shari fell into a fitful sleep.

CHAPTER 23

One day turned into a week, as Hamilton's condition remained unchanged. Shari and the rest of Hamilton's family was certain that he would be awake at this point, yet they didn't give up and had gathered everyday to pray over him. And Shari hadn't left his side. Deb and Denise brought her a change of clothes and Hamilton's family brought in food. Even Darrin came to sit with Hamilton when Shari was ordered to take a break by one of Hamilton's sisters. Shari was shocked when her father walked into the private room Hamilton had been moved to two days earlier.

"Daddy?!" Shari ran into her father's arms.

"Hey, Princess," he stroked her hair as he held her.

"When did you get here?"

He released her. "Your mother and I arrived about an hour ago. She's outside talking to Hamilton's family. They're quite a family."

"I know, Dad. But aren't they great?"

"Yeah." he smiled.

"How did you know about Hamilton?"

"Lucia called us."

Shari had called Mrs. Ponticello to let her know her whereabouts. She told her about Hamilton's accident.

Shari's father pulled up a chair. "So, this is your husband? Why didn't you tell us you were getting married?" Shari's father smiled.

Shari smiled for the first time since Hamilton's accident. "Oh, daddy, Hamilton's mom told them that so I could be here when he woke up." She leaned closer. "We're not really married."

"Not yet," a raspy voice replied.

"Hamilton!" Shari gasped excitedly, then ran to his bed. She clasped his outstretched hand in hers.

"Baby, I'm reaching out to shake your father's hand."

Shari laughed as tears streamed down her face.

"But you can give me a hug and a kiss," Hamilton said.

Shari leaned over the bed, her upper body rested lightly on his, and kissed him upon his lips.

"That was dry," he chuckled slightly. "But it'll do for now. You can make it up to me later."

"Well, Hamilton. Glad to see you awake." Mr. Thomas came to the bedside, and took Hamilton's outstretched hand in his. "How are you feeling?"

"Like I've been asleep for weeks."

"You have," Shari replied, then clarified her statement. "Well, almost. You've been out for five, going on six days now."

"How long have you been here?"

Shari looked to her father. "She's been here since they bought you in."

Hamilton looked at Shari, the love in her eyes completed him— told him that his decision to ask her to marry him was the right one.

"Baby," Hamilton looked at Shari. "I need to talk to your mother and father. Can you get your mom in here and give us a few minutes. Then tell my clan to come in after that."

Shari nodded and stepped out of the room. She found her mother among Hamilton's family. Shari was happy to see her mother with them, a genuine smile on her face. She stepped to her mother, who held her arms out to her. Shari ran into them and told her that Hamilton was awake and wanted to speak with her and dad. Her mother nodded, then stepped into the room. She then spoke to Hamilton's family. After 15 minutes, her parents walked out of Hamilton's room into the hallway. Shari's mother had tears in her eyes as she smiled at Shari. Her parents approached her. Shari's father spoke.

"Princess, we'll be at the apartment." He kissed her atop her head, then embraced her. "He's a good man, Shari. I know he'll make my Princess very happy." He released her.

"He's the one, Daddy. He's the one."

"I know, Princess." He kissed her on the cheek. "We'll see you later?"

"Yeah, now that he's awake, I'll be home later."

Shari nodded, then stepped back into Hamilton's hospital room.

"You scared us there for a minute. We didn't think you'd ever wake up." Hamilton tried to stretch, his arms constricted by intravenous lines. "And miss seeing your smiling face? Never. Come here." Shari walked to stand at his bedside. She looked his eyes and remained quite. "Thank you for being here, baby."

"How could I not? I love you, Hamilton."

He motioned for her to come closer. He stroked her face and brushed away a lone tear as it slid down her face. "You are my heart, my whole world."

Shari blushed, then turned at the sound of Hamilton's family coming through the door. She smiled at the laughs and squeals of joy which came from his family. Shari hugged them each, kissed Hamilton once again, then moved toward the door.

"Where are you going?" Hamilton asked her.

"I'll be back," she smiled at him, left the hospital room and headed home.

CHAPTER 24

Shari yawned loudly. She had to laugh at the sound she made when her mother's voice came through the door.

"How un-lady like," her mother smiled. "It's time. Get up."

Shari jumped out of bed. Instantly, her eyes rested on the chiffon white wedding gown, its sweetheart neckline dipped slightly toward the decolletage and was decorated with small crystal-like beads. The train, at least three feet long, was adorned with the same beads as the bodice. The dress complimented her every curve. She smiled at her selection, sure that the gown showed off the right amount of skin while appropriate for a church wedding.

This was their day—the day she would become Mrs. Shari Edmunds. She thought back to Hamilton when he was hospitalized. When she had returned home from the hospital, Shari and her father talked about her relationship with Hamilton. And though her father refused to detail the conversation he had with Hamilton in the hospital, he had firmly stated that Hamilton was the man for her. She asked about her mother.

"Go talk to her. She's in your studio," her father had stated.

Shari found her mother in the studio.

"Your grandmother taught you well," her mother said, then faced her. "I had no idea, Shari. You are so talented."

"Mom, you've never really been interested." She had watched her mother as her hands felt the fabric of the dress she had designed for Deb. "This is my passion, Mom. This and Hamilton."

Her mother faced her. "I know." She came to stand in front of her only daughter. "This is your dream. And I now believe that you should chase *your* dreams. You know, all I ever wanted was the best for you. But it took Hamilton's accident—the deep love I saw in his eyes for you—for me to see that chasing your dreams, and being with the man who truly loves you is what's best for you."

Shari sniffed. She held back tears. "Thank you, Mom. That's all I ever wanted from you." She had stood and hugged her mother. For two hours, Shari showed her mother the designs she had sketched followed by the ones she had sewn.

Their time together was interrupted by a phone call. It was Hamilton's sister, Helena.

"Can you come back to the hospital?"

"Is Hamilton okay?" Shari asked.

"He's fine, but he's being incorrigible—giving the nurses a hard time. He's acting so childish. We thought that maybe you can get him to cooperate."

Shari found Helena's story hard to believe, yet she agreed to return to the hospital.

When she arrived at his room, the door was slightly ajar. Hamilton's sisters stood at the door, one behind the other. Helena spoke first.

"We want to thank you for taking care of him. He's very special to us, but mostly to me. When he was little, he never let me forget how much he loved me. And as he grew to be a man, especially after our father died, he stepped into place and became the man you now know." Helena ended her speech with a hug. Hamilton's other sisters hugged her, then pushed opened the hospital door and lightly shoved her in.

Shari gasped at the sight of the small table that sat near the hospital window, draped in a long white cloth. It was set for two. Two candles burned in silver candle holders. A cart sat nearby, with covered dishes on top.

Hamilton walked out of the bathroom. Dressed in tan slacks and a black silk shirt, the only remnants of his hospital stay was a bandage visible at the back of his cleanly shaven bald head.

"Have a seat." He walked over to the table, pulled out the chair, and slid it in place once Shari was seated. "Care for some champagne?"

"Should you be drinking?"

He smiled. "Be quiet woman, it's sparkling grape juice."

Sounds of Teena Marie's "Now That I Have You," seeped from a small CD player situated on ledge of the window. Hamilton sat across from her and took her hand in his.

"Shari. How do I thank you? How do I repay your love?" She tried to interrupt him. "No, let me finish." She watched as his hands stole into his pants pocket. "If I searched this world over, I'll never find a love like that of which you've given me." He stood, then got on one knee. "I know we haven't dated that long." He pulled a velvet box from his box. "Yet, I can't imagine spending another day without you by my side. Marry me, Shari." He opened the box, then removed the sparkling gold band with a pear shaped diamond, rubies surrounded the diamond. He placed it on her ring finger. "I can't promise you that there won't be ups and downs, but I can promise that I'll never let you forget how much I love you."

Shari hugged him close. "Never?"

"Never." He kissed her. "Will you, Shari? Will you become my wife?"

Shari nodded as tears streamed down her face.

Back to the present, Shari smiled at the thought of the day he proposed, then grinned at the way they had made love on the small hospital bed while his sisters stood guard outside the door.

Finally dressed, Shari accepted her father's hand as they stepped into the white, horse-drawn carriage for the short ride to the church. Her heart beat quickly in her chest as the steeple of the church rose in the horizon. She wasn't apprehensive, the fear long gone. A feeling inside of her told her that this was right, that Hamilton was her life partner.

As the church bells tolled the hour of five, the wedding march began. Shari gasped at the scores of faces that stared at her as she walked down the aisle. At the alter, she winked at Deb, her maid of honor, and laughed at the sound of her goddaughter, Daneda, when she heard her squeal loudly from the second pew.

She looked at each of her soon to be sisters-in-law as they stood atop the altar, dressed in deep plum, floor length evening gowns with modest v-necks. Shari had designed and sewn each one. She nodded at each of them.

When she reached the altar, her father kissed her, then placed her hand in Hamilton's. "I'm giving my baby, my princess, to you. Take good care of her. If not, bring her back to me."

Hamilton shook his hand, then took Shari's hand in his. "She won't be going anywhere but here, by my side, Mr. Thomas."

Shari's eyes never left Hamilton's as they exchanged their wedding vows. Upon the announcement that they were husband and wife, Hamilton slowly raised the mesh veil, pulled her to him and kissed her full on the lips.

"There's more where that came from," he whispered in her ear as Father John presented them to the crowd as Mr. & Mrs. Hamilton Edmunds, Jr.

At the wedding reception, after Matthew, Hamilton's best man, finished the toast, Hamilton rose. He looked at Shari.

"Today, I've made a great step, but I also know that had it not been for the grace of God, my family *and* Shari, I wouldn't be standing here today." He took her hand in his. "A bride and groom are supposed to exchange gifts, and I thought long and hard. Shari had already given me my gift by agreeing to marry me." Shari looked at the gold filigree bracelet secured at his wrist. She had it made especially for him, with letters inscribed on each link, which spelled out their names. "So, outside of my love." He pulled her to her feet. "I'm going to give her this."

Hamilton pulled an envelope from the breast pocket of his black tux. "Read it."

Shari's hand shook as she opened the envelope. What looked like a check floated to rest atop the table. She smiled broadly and tried to will her tears not to fall. She picked up the check and looked at the sum. "My God, Hamilton!" She looked at several zero's behind one number.

"My wife here." He paused, then grinned. "That sounds nice." He continued. "My wife is the proud owner of her own clothing design business—By Design—and I expect each and everyone of you here to help me keep her in business."

Shari threw her arms around his neck. She rose on the tips of her toes and kissed him. "Thank you. Thank you for believing."

He looked at Deb as she sat in the seat next to Shari. He winked at her. "By design, baby. All, by design."

EPILOGUE

"Ha! Get up," Helena cried out. "Next!"

Deb shook her head. "Darrin, I didn't know there was another soul who loves bid whist as much as I do."

They laughed as they recalled that fateful night when they had first met at Denise's annual backyard party. They joined hands. "Yeah, neither did I. Hey, where's Shari?"

The pair looked around the yard. Their eyes searched for Shari. Deb stood and walked over to Denise. "Have you seen Shari?"

"Yeah," Denise said as she cradled her son in her arms. "I saw her run into the house."

Deb walked to the side door and stepped inside. She loved the old Victorian house Shari shared with Hamilton. She called out Shari's name, then heard a muffled sound. Deb opened the powder room door and saw Shari lean over the commode.

"What's wrong?" Deb asked, then called out Hamilton's name at the pale expression on Shari's face. Hamilton rushed to them. "She's sick, Hamilton."

Shari stood, her arms outstretched. Hamilton grabbed her around the waist and guided her to the couch in the nearby living room. "Baby, do you want to go to the hospital?" His eyebrows knitted together, concern stretched across his handsome face.

"No, sweetheart. I'll be okay." Shari looked up. Half of her guests stood around her. Hamilton's mother parted the crowd and sat next to Shari. She placed the back of her hand over Shari's forehead, then looked into her eyes.

"Yes!" Ella laughed. "I knew it. I knew it when I first laid eyes on her. She's pregnant."

Shari thought back. She and Hamilton hadn't used any form of birth control since they married. After a year and a half, and Shari hadn't gotten pregnant, they figured maybe it wasn't meant for them to have children the natural way and began to consider adoption.

Hamilton knelt in front of her.

"I'm going to be a father?" He looked at Shari. She shrugged her shoulders. He straightened. "Hey! I'm going to be a father." He picked Shari up and hugged her close.

"Hamilton, if you don't want to be covered, I suggest you put her back down." Helena chastised.

He placed her back on the couch. Suddenly, Shari jumped up, bolted past him and slammed the powder room door behind her. Hamilton excused himself and joined Shari. They came out nearly half an hour later.

"Well, I guess we're going to be parents." Shari smiled weakly. "All the signs are there. Tomorrow, I'll make an appointment to see my doctor."

Deb appeared before them. "Sounds good, but in the meantime." Deb handed Shari a brown paper bag. "Why don't you humor us all?"

Shari opened the bag and pulled out a home pregnancy test. She looked at Deb. "Carrying around kits?"

"Hey, you never know," Deb laughed. "No, I don't carry kits around. I ran out and got it. I have got know—now!"

Shari shrugged, then retreated upstairs with Hamilton behind her. After 10 minutes, Shari and Hamilton reappeared. Hamilton grinned proudly.

"The pink bars says yes," Hamilton responded to all gathered. He placed his arm protectively around Shari, then kissed her on her forehead. "And all this time we thought something was wrong."

Nine months later, Shari gave Hamilton another gift of her love, an eight pound baby boy, whom they named Joshua Hamilton Edmunds. The child, who's dark curly hair and smooth cinnamon complexion, bore the same beautiful light-brown eyes as his father. She looked at her son as he suckled greedily at her breast and thought of how her wishes had come true. She had it all: a husband who loved her, a healthy son and her own design company. All by design.

AUTHOR BIOGRAPHY

Barbara Keaton

My mother, who is the light of my life, says I always wrote stories. She often relays how my stories were about characters with strange names who fought amongst each other, mostly vying for power. I have been writing since I coup put pencil to paper! I was born in Chicago, in 1964, and as a native, I loved my city and could not imagine living anywhere else. I attended Catholic schools up until the twelfth grade, but it was in grammar school at the hands of the Oblate Sisters of Providence where I solidified my love and respect for written word. My maternal grandfather, the late Thomas Hill, instilled in me my passion. As the Oblate's, this little known order of black nuns taught with an iron hand and truly believed in the future and success of black children. Outside of my mother, I owe much of who I am to my Grandfather and those incredible nuns! In 1987, I received a BA in Communications from Columbia College. After graduation, I worked as a bus operator for the Chicago Transit Authority for nearly 3 years.

EXCERPT FROM
BODYGUARD
BY
ANDREA JACKSON

CHAPTER 2

She was something else, all right. She had apologized for doubting his abilities, but not for kicking him, he noted. The lady had some guts underneath the 'Miss Thang, all-that-and-a-bag-of-chips' veneer.

She sat across from his desk, looking like a magazine picture with her long, flowing gypsy dress and perfect hair and makeup, her legs crossed at the knee and leaning in a long elegant line. Her hair was a cap of glossy black tresses, parted on the side and falling in one long elegant sweep down her cheek to caress her chin. Straight black brows suited her, drawing attention to the vibrant sparkle of her heavily-lashed eyes, which regarded him steadily. She was exactly the kind of woman that poor Natalie was probably pretending to be when she actually knew nothing of the world.

Natalie would have died to have a tenth of this woman's poise and unconscious sensuality. There was nothing in the least flirtatious about the way she sat across from him. But somehow, she managed to stir his blood to a pleasant simmer.

Reluctantly she drew an envelope from her purse and handed it to him.

"I got this yesterday."

He opened it and glanced over the neatly-typed hate letter: "You claim to make people better than they were. But you don't have the ability. You've made a lot of enemies, Brandon bitch, and it's time you paid. Then everyone will know that you're a PHONY!"

"I've gotten several of those in the last few weeks. It was upsetting but I thought it was just a prank. But there were also phone calls." She shuddered. "First he just breathed. Then he began to spew obscenities."

"You didn't recognize the voice?"

"No. It's kind of distorted, as if it was being filtered through some device."

Harris nodded. "What else?"

She took a deep breath. "Then he started spray painting filthy words where I would see them. On my car, on my front door, on the walls outside my office. But I still thought it was just a sick prank until…"

"The dead animals?" he prompted quietly.

She shuddered. "Yes. I called the police. They said it was a cat, left on my doorstep. And the next day there was a rat."

"Take it easy," Harris said in a soothing voice. "I understand there was an incident when bricks were thrown through the windows of your home."

She nodded miserably. "Now my car looks like it was smashed with a sledge hammer and smeared with chicken blood, inside and out. And the reporters showed up--

"Because of the message to the news show," Harris supplied.

The anonymous faxed message to one of the local television stations declared that Dominique Brandon should be checked out because she was obviously in trouble.

Dominique nodded shakily. "After that, everything was a mess. "

"I would imagine so," Harris said dryly.

"I thought I could ignore this--person. Let the police handle it. But Tony thinks we need to take a more active path. I just want this to be over."

"I'll do what I can," he said softly. "You have my word on it."

Their gazes met for a moment and uncertainty flitted across her expression briefly. As if she weren't sure what his word meant. And he found himself willing her to trust him. But the next instant, she was all professional again, discussing hours and fees. Half an hour later, they had come to an agreement and drawn up a contract.

Harris stood up to shake her hand in farewell. "I'll see you tomorrow, Ms. Brandon."

"Please, call me Dominique," she said with a smile. A car salesman's smile. A politician's smile. Polished. Dazzling.

He tried not to gulp. "Sure. I'm Harris."

"Harris." She repeated his name and slid her fingers free of his. Then she was gone.

Harris cursed himself silently. He was acting like a damn idiot. Putting a potential client in a choke-hold wasn't standard procedure by any means. But she had asked for it, with her condescending air. He despised people who flaunted their presumed superiority.

Nothing had prepared him for his reaction, though, when he held her in his arms, so close and helpless. He could feel her heart beating under his restraining arm and her pulse in his hand. Her skin was so incredibly soft to the touch. He couldn't remember ever feeling anything so soft and smooth. And she smelled like...sin.

Blissfully sensual indulgence. Imagine someone who looked so business-like wearing a scent so come-hither. Hers was a subtle scent, not easy to detect unless you were as close as he had been. Yet he had thought he caught a hint of it occasionally during the rest of their interview. It had driven him crazy. He could still almost smell it on the hand she had taken…

"Hey, Harris." Tanisha opened his door without warning, the way she usually did.

"Yo," he said, quickly dropping his hand from his face, trying to sound normal.

"We got a new case, Harris? Who do you want to assign to it?"

He wrenched his thoughts back to business as he shot instructions at Tanisha. This was just another case, that was all. He'd better remember that. He wasn't about to get involved with a woman like that.

When Tanisha left him alone, he strode to his desk and began to organize a file for Dominique's case.

* * *

There were no reporters in sight when Dominique went to her office next morning. She was glad of that. Maybe this thing would just die down and go away. It had to be some kind of prankster. She couldn't believe that anyone could hate her so much.

But she had hired Harris Knight. His agency, she amended. The memory of him holding her in his office yesterday kept intruding into her consciousness too often for her peace of mind. She was no innocent. But she couldn't deny that Harris's touch had aroused her in a way that was wholly new to her.

She'd have to watch her step around Harris Knight. And if there were no more threats in the next week, she'd fire him. She couldn't afford to waste money and she had a feeling that he could disturb her peace of mind.

When she walked into her office, the first thing she saw was Harris Knight. He was in a huddle in the middle of the room with Tony and a woman she didn't know.

The woman looked like a movie star. She stood about six feet tall, had a perfect hourglass figure, and wore skin-tight black leggings and leather ankle boots. Her very short white-blonde hair contrasted vividly with her flawless milk chocolate skin. She wore a wireless telephone headset. Mattie and Karen, the other office clerk, was trying to look busy, but all three of them kept sneaking peeks at the eye-catching trio standing in the middle of the floor.

They didn't turn as Dominique walked up to them. "Good morning."

Harris's tawny-green gaze swung to her. She felt her breath catch. She had a feeling that he didn't miss much with those eyes. "Good morning...Dominique."

Only a slight pause before he used her name.

"Two, two, nine. That's a roger, K.C.," said the blonde woman. "Contact A-1 when you're done."

Dominique cocked a skeptical eyebrow at her. The woman looked back with calm disinterest, her fingers touching the headset. Then Dominique realized she was talking into the mouthpiece of the headset. She smoothly hit a switch on a waist pack as Harris touched her arm, an arm that was bronzed and well muscled; not bulky muscle-- sexy muscle. Dominique didn't need Tony's goofy look to tell her that men would find this woman attractive.

"This is my associate, Shayla," Harris introduced her. Shayla nodded, her face expressionless. "She'll be working closely with me on your case. She'll also be your primary bodyguard. I try to assign same sex operatives to avoid awkward situations."

"Like what?" Dominique couldn't resist asking. She was thinking of how he had held her yesterday in his office.

Harris's generous mouth curved in a humorless smile that made the corners of his eyes crinkle. "Like if you have to use a public bathroom."

"Oh." She clamped her mouth shut, determined not to give Harris Knight another opportunity to laugh at her.

"If I'm not around, you can discuss any concerns or problems with her." He seemed perfectly remote and business-like this morning. Which was as it should be, she reminded herself.

"Thank you."

"Your brother and I were going over the security plan. I'd like to discuss it with you at your convenience."

"Fine, give me a minute to sort myself out and then we can talk."

She crossed the room, walked through the door of her private office, and promptly tripped over a metal box on the floor. Something snaky slithered down over her head, trapping her arms, tightening as she fell. And a man she had never seen before, a man with a rugged, menacing face appeared right in front of her and grabbed her.

Dominique screamed.

"Damn!" growled the man in a furious voice.

Instantly, Harris and Shayla were at her door, Tony right on their heels, looking worried. Harris was the first to reach her, and she instinctively flung herself against him to get away from the man.

"What the--?" Harris grunted.

She saw now that the snaky thing was a coil of heavy cable which had apparently fallen from somewhere over her door. And by the look of relief on Harris and Shayla's faces, the man was no threat.

"What are you doing in here?" Dominique demanded, pushing out of Harris's arms and struggling to regain her composure.

"This is K.C., another associate of mine," Harris explained.

Now she felt foolish. "Why is he in my office? And what is this stuff?" She flung the last of the cable to the floor.

"It will be an alarm system once K.C. gets it installed."

Dominique still thought K.C. looked more like a prize fighter than an electrician. She wondered what else he did for the Knight Agency. "Listen, I'd appreciate it if you instructed your people to be as unobtrusive as possible."

Harris gave her a sardonic smile as he left the office. "Whatever you say, ma'am."

Checking her calendar on her computer, she learned that most of her appointments for the day had been cancelled. No doubt the fear had already begun to spread among her clients as they followed her story on TV.

She instructed Mattie to call and cancel the rest with the information that she was putting business on hold until she could ensure security. That was the move she would have advised one of her clients. She wouldn't let her business suffer. She could just imagine what the Brandon relatives would have to say if that happened.

Next she called Tony into her office.

"I talked to Mom last night," she said. "Uncle Paul called her from Washington and gave her a lecture. Now she's practically hysterical."

"Damn!" said Tony in sympathy. "What does Uncle Paul expect you to do about this?"

"I don't know, but Mom wants me to close the business and move in with her until they catch this guy."

"Is that what you're going to do?" he demanded.

"No," she said. She was sure of that much at least. She rubbed her eyes. "Tony, I've worked too hard to build this business. It's all I have. I know the family doesn't think much of it, but I'm not going to let it go down the drain without a whimper."

"Don't worry. I'll keep Mom off your back as much as I can. Why don't I go over there today and talk up this bodyguard business?"

"That would be great. Tony, I...I want to thank you. I didn't mean to drag you into more trouble when I brought you down here."

"Hey. I'm getting to be good at it. Damsels in distress? Just call old Tony." He grinned, but his dark brown eyes were still worried.

Impulsively, Dominique reached out to grasp his hand.

He looked at it and went on in a tight voice. "I owe you big time, Neeka. You've always gotten me out of my scrapes. I guess it's payback time."

She was touched. Tony's brush with the law in New York seemed to have matured him. She was seeing a new strength in him. The feeling was disquieting as well as touching.

"You can count on me anytime, little bro'," she said.

"Maybe it's about time somebody looked out for you."

The sudden stinging behind her eyeballs was a surprise. How many times had she thought the same thing? Then Tony switched the mood with a blink and a sly grin. "And if that means I have to spend a lot of time hanging out with you and your, ah, Amazon bodyguard--" He wiggled his brows to make sure she got the point. "Well, hey, that's just the sacrifice I have to make."

Dominique laughed. "Poor baby."

"You want to see Harris now?" he asked.

She was immediately sober. "I suppose so."

"What's wrong? Don't you like him?"

"He seems to know what he's doing," she said cautiously. "He's quite a character, isn't he?"

Tony shrugged. "As long as he does his job. I'll get him."

But Harris was nowhere to be found around her office now.

It took twenty minutes to locate him in the parking garage of her building. Then he spent another fifteen minutes talking to the attendants and the building security personnel.

Finally he came sauntering into her office. Dominique was furious by now, suspecting that he was taking his time in order to pay her back for not seeing him immediately.

"I'm glad you found time to see me," she greeted him. She still thought he looked like a bum. He had shaved, but his jeans were torn in both knees. She had to admit the shabby look worked well on him. She found herself gazing at his broad chest in the tight-fitting T-shirt and wondering if it was smooth or covered with curly, thick black hair. He plopped into her visitor chair and put one ankle on the opposite knee, drawing her attention to his long legs. He opened a leather notebook on his lap.

"No problem. I just have a few questions. Tell me about any business rivals. Have you made a gain recently at the expense of a competitor?"

"No, of course not."

"Think about it. It may not seem like much but perhaps it was the final thing that sent someone over the edge. And of course, we have to consider that this might be a personal attack. There are indications that that could be the case."

"Like what?"

"Your person, not your business, seems to be the primary target. The tone of the letter is personal in nature, too."

"I don't know anyone who talks like that!"

"You know someone."

She sighed as there was no denying that.

"I'd like you to give it some thought and let me know by tomorrow if you come up with any names. In the meantime, I need to go through your client files."

"Absolutely not. Those are confidential."

"Listen, babe. I'm not here to out your clients. I'll keep your information confidential and I'll only access as much information as I need. But your stalker could be a disgruntled client."

"My clients won't like being considered suspects."

"Don't worry. We can be discreet."

She hesitated. "Could I ask you a favor? I'd like the client records to be for your eyes only."

"Certainly, if that's the way you want it." He stood up, snapping shut the notebook. "That's about it for now. Will you be in the office all day?"

"I have some shopping to do for a client and a speaking engagement at lunch time."

"Fine. Shayla will go with you. And I'd like a copy of your schedule. I need to know exactly where you plan to be every moment of the day and night."

Her gaze met his. Dominique swallowed the instinctive protest that rose to her lips. "Fine," she said stiffly. "I'll have Mattie take care of it."

2003 Publication Schedule

January	Twist of Fate	Ebony Butterfly II
	Beverly Clark	Delilah Dawson
	1-58571-084-9	1-58571-086-5
February	Fragment in the Sand	Fate
	Annetta P. Lee	Pamela Leigh Starr
	1-58571-097-0	1-58571-115-2
March	One Day at a Time	Unbreak My Heart
	Bella McFarland	Dar Tomlinson
	1-58571-099-7	1-58571-101-2
April	At Last	Brown Sugar Diaries & Other Sexy Tales
	Lisa G. Riley	Delores Bundy & Cole Riley
	1-58571-093-8	1-58571-091-1
May	Three Wishes	Acquisitions
	Seressia Glass	Kimberley White
	1-58571-092-X	1-58571-095-4
June	When Dreams A Float	Revelations
	Dorothy Elizabeth Love	Cheris F. Hodges
	1-58571-104-7	1-58571-085-7
July	The Color of Trouble	Someone to Love
	Dyanne Davis	Alicia Wiggins
	1-58571-096-2	1-58571-098-9
August	Object of His Desire	Hart & Soul
	A. C. Arthur	Angie Daniels
	1-58571-094-6	1-58571-087-3
September	Erotic Anthology	A Lark on the Wing
	Assorted	Phyliss Hamilton
	1-58571-113-6	1-58571-105-5

Other Genesis Press, Inc. Titles

A Dangerous Deception	J.M. Jeffries	$8.95
A Dangerous Love	J.M. Jeffries	$8.95
After the Vows	Leslie Esdaile	$10.95
(Summer Anthology)	T.T. Henderson	
	Jacqueline Thomas	
Again My Love	Kayla Perrin	$10.95
Against the Wind	Gwynne Forster	$8.95
A Lighter Shade of Brown	Vicki Andrews	$8.95
All I Ask	Barbara Keaton	$8.95
A Love to Cherish	Beverly Clark	$8.95
Ambrosia	T.T. Henderson	$8.95
And Then Came You	Dorothy Elizabeth Love	$8.95
A Risk of Rain	Dar Tomlinson	$8.95
Best of Friends	Natalie Dunbar	$8.95
Bound by Love	Beverly Clark	$8.95
Breeze	Robin Hampton Allen	$10.95
Cajun Heat	Charlene Berry	$8.95
Careless Whispers	Rochelle Alers	$8.95
Caught in a Trap	Andre Michelle	$8.95
Chances	Pamela Leigh Starr	$8.95
Dark Embrace	Crystal Wilson Harris	$8.95
Dark Storm Rising	Chinelu Moore	$10.95
Designer Passion	Dar Tomlinson	$8.95
Eve's Prescription	Edwina Martin Arnold	$8.95
Everlastin' Love	Gay G. Gunn	$8.95
Fate	Pamela Leigh Starr	$8.95
Forbidden Quest	Dar Tomlinson	$10.95
From the Ashes	Kathleen Suzanne	$8.95
	Jeanne Sumerix	

Gentle Yearning	Rochelle Alers	$10.95
Glory of Love	Sinclair LeBeau	$10.95
Heartbeat	Stephanie Bedwell-Grime	$8.95
Illusions	Pamela Leigh Starr	$8.95
Indiscretions	Donna Hill	$8.95
Interlude	Donna Hill	$8.95
Intimate Intentions	Angie Daniels	$8.95
Kiss or Keep	Debra Phillips	$8.95
Love Always	Mildred E. Riley	$10.95
Love Unveiled	Gloria Greene	$10.95
Love's Deception	Charlene Berry	$10.95
Mae's Promise	Melody Walcott	$8.95
Meant to Be	Jeanne Sumerix	$8.95
Midnight Clear (Anthology)	Leslie Esdaile	$10.95
	Gwynne Forster	
	Carmen Green	
	Monica Jackson	
Midnight Magic	Gwynne Forster	$8.95
Midnight Peril	Vicki Andrews	$10.95
My Buffalo Soldier	Barbara B. K. Reeves	$8.95
Naked Soul	Gwynne Forster	$8.95
No Regrets	Mildred E. Riley	$8.95
Nowhere to Run	Gay G. Gunn	$10.95
Passion	T.T. Henderson	$10.95
Past Promises	Jahmel West	$8.95
Path of Fire	T.T. Henderson	$8.95
Picture Perfect	Reon Carter	$8.95
Pride & Joi	Gay G. Gunn	$8.95
Quiet Storm	Donna Hill	$8.95
Reckless Surrender	Rochelle Alers	$8.95

Rendezvous with Fate	Jeanne Sumerix	$8.95
Rivers of the Soul	Leslie Esdaile	$8.95
Rooms of the Heart	Donna Hill	$8.95
Shades of Desire	Monica White	$8.95
Sin	Crystal Rhodes	$8.95
So Amazing	Sinclair LeBeau	$8.95
Somebody's Someone	Sinclair LeBeau	$8.95
Soul to Soul	Donna Hill	$8.95
Still Waters Run Deep	Leslie Esdaile	$8.95
Subtle Secrets	Wanda Y. Thomas	$8.95
Sweet Tomorrows	Kimberly White	$8.95
The Price of Love	Sinclair LeBeau	$8.95
The Reluctant Captive	Joyce Jackson	$8.95
The Missing Link	Charlyne Dickerson	$8.95
Tomorrow's Promise	Leslie Esdaile	$8.95
Truly Inseperable	Wanda Y. Thomas	$8.95
Unconditional Love	Alicia Wiggins	$8.95
Whispers in the Night	Dorothy Elizabeth Love	$8.95
Whispers in the Sand	LaFlorya Gauthier	$10.95
Yesterday is Gone	Beverly Clark	$8.95
Yesterday's Dreams, Tomorrow's Promises	Reon Laudat	$8.95
Your Precious Love	Sinclair LeBeau	$8.95

Order Form

Mail to: Genesis Press, Inc.

1213 Hwy 45 N
Columbus, MS 39705

Name _____

Address _____

City/State _____ Zip _____

Telephone _____

Ship to (if different from above)

Name _____

Address _____

City/State _____ Zip _____

Telephone _____

Credit Card Information

Credit Card # _____ ☐Visa ☐Mastercard

Expiration Date (mm/yy) _____ ☐AmEx ☐Discover

Qty.	Author	Title	Price	Total

Use this order form, or call
1-888-INDIGO-1

Total for books _____

Shipping and handling:
 $5 first two books,
 $1 each additional book _____

Total S & H _____

Total amount enclosed _____

Mississippi residents add 7% sales tax

Order Form

Mail to: Genesis Press, Inc.

1213 Hwy 45 N
Columbus, MS 39705

Name _____
Address _____
City/State _____ Zip _____
Telephone _____

Ship to (if different from above)
Name _____
Address _____
City/State _____ Zip _____
Telephone _____

Credit Card Information

Credit Card # _____ ☐Visa ☐Mastercard
Expiration Date (mm/yy) _____ ☐AmEx ☐Discover

Qty.	Author	Title	Price	Total

Use this order form, or call 1-888-INDIGO-1

Total for books	_____
Shipping and handling: $5 first two books, $1 each additional book	
Total S & H	_____
Total amount enclosed	_____

Mississippi residents add 7% sales tax

Visit www.genesis-press.com for latest releases and excerpts.

Order Form

Mail to: Genesis Press, Inc.

1213 Hwy 45 N
Columbus, MS 39705

Name _____

Address _____

City/State _____ Zip _____

Telephone _____

Ship to (if different from above)

Name _____

Address _____

City/State _____ Zip _____

Telephone _____

Credit Card Information

Credit Card # _____ ☐ Visa ☐ Mastercard

Expiration Date (mm/yy) _____ ☐ AmEx ☐ Discover

Qty.	Author	Title	Price	Total

Use this order form, or call 1-888-INDIGO-1

Total for books	_____
Shipping and handling: $5 first two books, $1 each additional book	
Total S & H	_____
Total amount enclosed	_____

Mississippi residents add 7% sales tax